I Scream,
You Scream,
We All Scream for Ice Cream!!

CLOSET TREATS

Paul E. Cooley

Also by Paul E. Cooley

AVAILABLE FROM SEVERED PRESS

The Black
The Black: Arrival
The Black: Outbreak

AVAILABLE FROM SHADOW PUBLICATIONS

Garaaga Collection *(series)*
Legends of Garaaga — 4 Tales of the Children of Garaaga
Daemons of Garaaga — 3 Tales of the Children of Garaaga

Tony Downs *(series)*
The Hunt
After Image

The Dark Recesses Collection *(short stories)*
Mimes
Lamashtu

Others
Closet Treats
Tattoo
Fiends: Volume 1
Fiendlettes — 4 Stories from the Fiends Collection
The Street

CLOSET TREATS

Paul E. Cooley

A **Shadow Publications** Novel

Published in the United States of America
by Shadow Publications www.shadowpublications.com

Copyright © 2011, 2015 by Paul Elard Cooley
www.shadowpublications.com

Cover design, cover art, interior illustrations,
and book design by Scott Pond
Scott E. Pond Designs, LLC (www.scottpond.com)

Edited by Jennifer Melzer and Sue Baiman

Library of Congress Cataloging-in-Publication Data
Cooley, Paul Elard
Closet Treats//Paul E Cooley. —1st ed.
p. cm.
1. Horror—Fiction

ISBN: 978-1-942137-04-7

PRINTED IN THE UNITED STATES OF AMERICA
10 9 8 7 6 5 4 3 2 1

FIRST EDITION: May 2016

This book is dedicated to Tia L Brink, her belief in my work, her endless support, and her beautiful soul. Rest well.

Acknowledgments

I have been fortunate to fall in with a great group of people and supporters who have made this book possible. There are far too many to thank by name.

To those of you in The Graveyard:
    Your financial assistance made this work possible.

To the podcasting community at large:
    I owe you a debt of thanks that can never properly be repaid.

To my family:
    You never gave up on my talents, even after I had. Thank you for pushing me, encouraging me, and giving me the faith in myself to succeed.

- Paul E. Cooley

CLOSET TREATS

Chapter One

The brilliant crisp sunlight was dying. A light breeze caused the pines and oaks to wave their limbs in some incomprehensible rhythm, the occasional oak leaf separating from a branch to flail and spiral in the wind. Trey stood at the edge of the schoolyard, patiently waiting. The bell would buzz in a few moments and a tidal wave of children would burst through the school's doors.

Trey smiled to himself. Picking up Alan from school was his favorite part of the day.

He always left the house a little early. It was one of the many rituals that allowed him to retain a sense of normalcy.

Other parents had shown up. Mostly in their cars, but a few women stood at the edge of the grass. He didn't know their names. They never spoke to him, or returned his "hellos". In this day and age, ignoring your neighbors seemed to be the rule rather than the exception. He didn't move his head to look at them. He'd learned from past experience that trying to make eye contact was asking for a rebuke. What the hell ever happened to neighbor solidarity for Christ's sake?

How long until the school bell buzzed and the children came out? Trey fought the urge to pull out his phone and check the time. He normally didn't notice the minutes pass while waiting for the buzzer; only after the bell did his mental clock start keeping track of the seconds. Once, a few months ago, the buzzer had sounded and Alan didn't appear within the first couple of minutes.

The anxiety that took him that time nearly knocked him out. A steady horror film of his son, his fucking son being molested by some teacher in a back room, kept playing in his mind. He had tried to shake it off and make it go away, to end the horror loop, but it kept playing. And the longer it played in his mind, the more textured it became, sound effects of crying and chuffing, a loose belt jingling on a tile floor. Just as Trey began running for the school's backdoors, Alan appeared, turning and laughing when he saw his father. Alan had to pee before the walk home.

A cacophonous blaring of bells split the silence of the fall afternoon. Trey shook with a start. His gaze swiveled left, and his jaw dropped. Just visible through the copse of pines, a decal covered, white van sat at the road facing the playground. Two speakers jutted from the top of its roof ushering forth the brash, crisp bells.

The driver's side window was tinted black. Trey blinked and felt a stab of fear as the large van trembled slightly and a side panel door opened.

From where he stood Trey couldn't quite make out the figure inside, just a glimpse of a white uniform and pointed hat.

The school bell buzzed. As if on cue, a cheer rose from the school doors and Trey turned to watch as a mob of children poured out, book-stuffed backpacks swaying and thumping on their backs. Trey couldn't help but smile, remembering what it was like at that age to finally leave the school day behind. Looking forward to play. To dinner. To being children.

The ice cream van's bells pounded louder, silencing the children in one fell swoop. The mob stopped for a moment, as if unsure of what to do. Trey watched one of the older children, a little round across the middle, point to the van before he started running toward it. Dozens of children followed.

The mob moved off toward the van, leaving several stragglers behind. Trey was glad to see Alan was among the stragglers. His boy turned from the ice cream truck and toward his father. Alan's smile melted the tension in Trey's stomach. His boy. His son. Trey nodded to him and then Alan was in motion, his little legs pumping.

Alan jumped into Trey's waiting arms. "Hi, Dad!"

"Missed you, kiddo," Trey breathed into his ear. "You ready to walk home?"

"Yes, sir."

Trey patted him on the back and put him down. Alan raised his arm, offering his hand to Trey. Trey wrapped his son's small hand inside his own.

"Daddy?" Alan asked, "what is that?"

Trey followed Alan's outstretched free hand. He was pointing at the throng of children in front of the white van. They giggled and laughed as they shouted orders at the white clad figure.

Trey watched children digging into their pockets for change, passing coins and dollar bills into a white gloved hand.

"That," Trey said, "is the Ice Cream Man."

Alan turned to him. "But, it's getting cold for ice cream, isn't it?"

Trey laughed. "He sells candy too."

"Oh," Alan said. "But why is the music so loud?"

Trey took a deep breath and let it out slowly. "Because he wants to make sure the children know he's there." Trey paused and then muttered "Them and the rest of the world."

Alan shrugged. "Candy? Ice cream?" He looked up at Trey, a half- smile on his face. "Can we get some one of these days?"

"I think we might could do that, kiddo." Trey tousled the boy's hair. "Come on," Trey said. "We've got some kart to play."

Alan giggled. "Yes, sir, I'm ready to run you over!"

"Good deal."

They began walking down the sidewalk. With each step, they moved closer to the parked van. They would be perpendicular to it when they finally crossed the street. Trey looked down at his son, happy to see the boy wasn't even looking at it. Instead, Alan was recounting his day, telling his Dad every detail.

Trey barely heard him. He couldn't stop staring at the van. Trey looked into the darkness behind the open panels. A pair of yellow eyes gleamed back at him.

Yellow eyes. They cast a baleful glow that lit a face of scales with sharp, blood-dripping fangs. The thing was smiling at him as its misshapen, gloved hands took money from the children and passed out sweets in return. Trey froze, his mind vapor-locked.

"DADDY!" Alan's yell broke through the mental scream rising up within him. "Daddy? Are you okay?" Alan asked, his face filled with concern.

Trey cleared his throat. He wasn't sure he could speak. "I'm—" he started and then stopped. He shook his head and refocused his eyes on his son. "I'm okay." With his free hand, he rubbed Alan's coarse, short- cropped hair. "How long?"

Alan shrugged. "Just a little while this time," Alan said. "Home?"

"Yeah," Trey agreed. He smiled at his son. "Yeah, sorry about that." He lightly squeezed the boy's hand. "You take good care of your old man."

"It's a full time job," the boy said.

Laughing, the two of them made their way past the street. Alan told Trey more about his day, occasionally asking questions about history that his teacher had glossed over. Trey did his best to keep up, although he couldn't shake the image of the thing inside the ice cream van, but he managed not to ice up again on the way home.

Two

The walk home always gave him the chance to talk to Alan without interruption or distraction. The boy rattled on about his day, asking questions, laughing at Trey's answers. It was the part of the day that made Trey smile no matter how bad the rest of it had been.

"Get out your key," Trey said . The boy stared up at him and blinked. "It's your turn to unlock the door." Alan smiled at him.

He plucked off his pack and rummaged through the front pocket. Trey grinned. "You got toys in there too?"

Alan smirked. "No, Daddy. No toys. Just," he said as he lifted the key ring out of the pocket, "lots of pens and things."

Trey cocked an eyebrow. "Things?" he asked. "And what would those be?"

The key fit into the dead-bolt with a little resistance. He looked back at his father. Trey shrugged. With a sigh, Alan managed to turn the key until the lock clicked. "I have some change in there," Alan said as he struggled to release the key from the lock. "A little pencil sharpener." Alan grunted as the key popped out from the lock. He turned back to his father and smiled. "And the charms Mommy gave me."

"Ah," Trey said.

Alan opened the door and walked through, holding it open for his father. "Always the little gentleman." Trey grinned and followed his son inside. Alan smiled back and headed toward the living room. "Shoes, kiddo."

Alan sighed. "Yes, Daddy." With his back to Trey, he pressed down on the left shoe's heel and followed with the right.

The boy was always pushing off his shoes, ruining the heels. Alan placed his shoes on the shoe tree near the door. Trey shook his head, bending at the waist to untie his laces and removed each shoe with care. He placed them on the shoe tree next to Alan's. "Okay, kiddo. You have any homework to do?" Alan shook his head. "Go spark up some kart and I'll be there in a few."

The boy giggled. "I like playing, but you're going to lose to me again."

Trey laughed. "Give me Koopa this time. Maybe then I'll stand a chance."

Alan shook his head. "Riiiiiiiight."

Trey watched him scurry into the living room and then headed into his study. The computer screens were dark, no LEDs flashing, the room silent. Trey slowly lowered himself into the chair, and pressed the power buttons on the monitors. The dual 24" widescreen monitors flashed into life, bathing the room with an electric glow.

Trey checked his email, laughing at the responses from Bangalore. "Those guys really hate me," he said to the screen. There was an email from Dick and he opened it. The email contained a picture of Trey, wildly off-balance, his long hair flowing in the wind, as he threw a frisbee down a hill. Dick's email read "Want to get your ass kicked again tomorrow?"

Dick. Jesus. He hadn't spoken to Dick all day, and that was a rare day. He'd been so wrapped up in the code, his iPhone alarm was the only thing that had kept him from being late to meet Alan for the walk home.

Dick, the retired neighbor across the street, always kept his messenger client going, but Trey hadn't bothered to start his today. The chatter from India had gotten to the point where he just didn't want the damned thing on anymore.

He wrote back a response to Dick, promising to be ready at 10 am, but didn't respond to the smack. He knew it infuriated Dick when he didn't acknowledge the trash-talk . But every once in a while, Dick would send an email with no rude words or arrogant statements. That's when Trey would pounce, sending back all the smack he could muster.

"Daddy?" Alan called from the living room.

Trey put the computer back to sleep before turning off the monitors. The study immediately went dark. Trey turned in the chair to leave and stopped.

The closet. The closet door was partially open. A sudden chill left him goose fleshed and freezing. His heart rate rose, the sound pounding in his ears.

"Daddy?" Alan called again.

Trey froze. A green light burned in the sliver of absolute darkness. A smooth oval of emerald malevolence. It would come out of the closet. It would grab him, drag him screaming into its lair. It would—

"Daddy?" Alan appeared in the doorway.

Trey looked away from the closet to his son. The boy's face was cloaked in shadow, but Trey could see the worry lines on his forehead.

"Are you all right?"

"I—" Trey looked toward the closet. The green light was gone. "Can you turn on the light, son?" Trey's voice shook.

Alan reached out and flipped the switch. The black halogen torch in the corner of the room blazed to life and chased away the darkness.

Trey took a deep breath and then walked toward the closet door. He grasped the doorknob, let out the breath, and then opened it.

Plastic drawers with computer parts stared back at him. Cables and cords wound neatly together, hung from the door's back. There was nothing in there. No monster. Nothing.

Trey chuckled, but it sounded more like a sob. He pushed the door closed, making sure the bolt slid firm. "Okay," he breathed, "you can turn off the light now."

"Okay, Daddy." The torch went dark, driving the room back into gloom.

Trey stared at the door. The fear had left him.

"You still want to play kart?" Alan asked.

Trey turned back to look at the boy. He smiled at him. "Give me Koopa?"

Alan sighed. "Okay, Daddy. But I'm still going to kick your butt."

"Just try it," he growled and zombie-loped toward his son. Alan squealed and ran from the room, Trey's laughter following close behind.

Thirty minutes of "kart," as Alan liked to call it, was enough to leave Trey feeling nauseous. Trey knew they called his generation the "video game" generation, but he was one of the few that suffered from QuIMS. 2D graphics games were fine, the kind where the world stayed relatively static. But the lifelike 3D games, where the world bounced and spun, always managed to get to him.

Alan had called him chicken for leaving the game after the third bout of races. Trey had clucked and pumped his arms up and down, laughing, as he made his way into the kitchen. It was time to cook dinner anyway.

He pulled out the pasta, placing it on the kitchen island. With an ease borne of repetition, he opened the freezer and scooped out the white container of sauce. Another turn, another grab, and a frozen sausage sat atop the cutting board. Pasta. Sausage. Trey's famous sauce. Oh, yeah, it was going to be a good dinner.

The sauce thawed on the island, leaving him time to cut up the sausage. He reached for the CUTCO cleaver from the butcher's block and sliced neatly through the plastic package. The sausage unfolded from the wrapper with effort. Once naked and on the board, he picked up the knife and began cutting it into pieces with quick, sharp, diagonal strokes. The sausage quickly turned from coils of brown and gray meat into neat, oblong pieces.

He smiled at the sound of Alan's yell in the other room. He'd either won or lost. It didn't matter. It was Friday night, and that meant Alan was free to play.

It also meant Trey and Carolyn would be free to play.

As he prepared the water for the pasta, he looked up at the microwave screen. The soft, green display told him it was 5. Trey blinked at the numbers and frowned. The green. The Closet Man. He'd been seeing the Closet Man as long as he could remember. Its eyes were always the bright, verdant color of a burning emerald.

He couldn't believe he'd forgotten to close the closet. He'd managed to open it and rummage through it, but only after he'd turned on all the lights in the study and adjusted the lamp so that it lit the door and interior. God, he hated closets. But forgetting to close the door all the way... He shook his head.

One thing the meds never seemed to do was dispel the Closet Man.

Trey waited for the water to boil and walked to the pantry. Carolyn had insisted on removing the pantry door shortly after they moved in. She quickly tired of Trey jumping every time he walked into the dark kitchen and found it open.

He opened the bread-box and removed a loaf of french bread. Garlic bread. He looked back at the clock to check the time. *Yeah*, he thought, *I have time.*

Parmesan cheese. The real stuff, not the crap from the can. Roasted garlic cloves left over from preparing his last batch of sauce. Another knife from the butchers block. He minced the garlic, enjoying the smell as the water started to boil behind him. He prepared the bread, covering each side of the split loaf with cheese and then shaking the garlic over it.

Into the oven. Pasta into the kettle. Sausage into the pan. Add sauce.

"Daddy?" Alan called. "You're making me hungry!" "Good. We'll eat as soon as Mommy gets home."

"Okay," Alan said. "But I'm going to tell her how badly I beat you."

"I'm sure you will," Trey yelled back.

Besides picking up Alan from school, the hour or so before Carolyn got home was his favorite part of every weekday. Cooking. Playing with the boy. Unwinding.

He looked back at the microwave display, watching the timer tick down. Green.

The eyes in the ice cream van. They weren't green. They had been cat's eye yellow, glowing with crimson centers. Trey frowned as he stirred the sausage, listening to it crackle in its own grease. He'd have to tell Kinkaid about that next month.

The sauce bubbled. Trey inspected the sausage, nodded to himself, and drained the pan. He combined the sausage and the sauce, stirred in some fresh oregano, and turned down the heat. Simmer. The pasta and garlic bread would be done in a few minutes.

The sound of the garage door opening made him smile. "Guess who's home?" Trey called to the living room. The electronic chatter from the game stopped with a beep. He listened to the sound of Alan's feet on the wood panel floor as he ran into the kitchen. "Hey," Trey said, "slow down before you slip and bust your butt."

Alan laughed and scrambled into the laundry room. When the door to the garage opened, Alan yelled "BOO!" Carolyn screamed in mock terror and then laughed.

Trey just nodded to himself, continuing to stir the sauce.

"Where is my dinner?" Carolyn said as she placed her arms around his neck.

"Almost ready," he said. She stood on her toes and kissed his cheek. He chuckled. Then she bit his ear. "You better stop that," he said. "The cook is on the clock."

"Well, hurry up. You have more cooking to do later." Her hand squeezed his ass.

"Work, work, work," Trey said.

Chapter
FOUR

The words on the page had started to blur. Alan knew he should close the book and turn off the light, but he fought against sleep. Harry Potter and his friends were getting ready to battle the basilisk, but that's not why Alan wanted to stay awake. He loved the book, but he'd already read it twice. He needed Daddy or Mommy to kiss him goodnight. Just having them walk in the door and touch his cheek, smile at him, was enough to protect him for the night.

Alan shook his head, trying to clear it, and then rubbed at his eyes. He glanced at the digital clock on the nightstand. 9:30 glowed on its display. Any minute. *Please*.

He looked across the room to his closet. The door was closed. Alan smiled. The Closet Man. Alan didn't worry about the Closet Man. Alan had other things to worry about.

Daddy's seizures were happening more often now. The one on the way home from school had been bad. Mommy and Daddy had told Alan that he needed to try and keep track of the time when Daddy had one of them. It was important. If Daddy's "blank-time" was longer than a couple of minutes, he needed to find an adult, and fast.

When he was five, Daddy had blanked at the playground. Alan was sitting on a swing, learning how to pull on the metal chains to give himself momentum, learning how to pull forward on the chains to stop. Daddy was watching him from a bench. Alan was giggling, rising higher and higher into the air. When he called to his father, there was no response.

Alan turned to the left to look at his father and saw the vacant stare. Daddy was sitting on the bench, elbows on his knees, head cradled on spread hands. His eyes were staring straight at Alan, but unmoving.

"Daddy?" Alan called to him.

Other kids on the playground, moving through the wooden jungle gym, or crawling through the metal web, had been oblivious. Alan had slowed the swing enough to jump off. Daddy didn't move.

"Daddy?"

But Daddy didn't respond. Alan made his way over to the bench and stood directly in front of his father. He tapped Daddy's shoulder. Daddy didn't move. "Daddy?" Alan started counting. When he reached ten, he held up a finger on his right hand. The next ten, he put out another finger. He was to his thumb when Daddy lifted his head. "Daddy?"

"You're not—" Daddy raised his eyes to Alan's. "Um," he said. He shook his head, wiped a line of drool from his face and then smiled at Alan. "Hi," he whispered.

"You blanked," Alan said.

"Yes, I guess I did," Daddy said. Daddy was smiling, but Alan, even at that age, could tell it was forced. "How long, kiddo?"

Alan held up his hand. "5 fingers. 10 each."

Daddy nodded. "Okay," he said. He shook his head once more. "I want to see you swing some more."

"Are you okay, Daddy?"

His father nodded, the smile wide, but strained. "Yes, Alan. I'm okay."

Daddy stared at the swing-set. Another child was already sitting on the swing Alan had been using.

"Guess you lost your spot, kiddo," he said. "Sorry about that."

Alan shrugged. He really wanted to get back on the swing. It wasn't fair another kid had taken it. He wouldn't say it, though—he knew it would make Daddy feel bad.

"It's okay, Daddy. I was tired of it anyway."

They'd walked home after that, both of them sweating in the too hot sun.

The seizures, or "blanks" as Daddy called them, were happening more often. Alan would never tell Daddy that he worried about that. Some days, when in school, he imagined his father walking to the school or back home, standing on the sidewalk, unmoving. Would Daddy fall to the pavement? Would he fall in front of a car? Alan shivered at the thought.

A creak from the stairs interrupted his thoughts. Alan cocked his head to one side, listening to the sound. Light steps, almost inaudible over the churning of the heater. Alan smiled. "You coming to tuck me in, Daddy?"

His father's head peeked into the room, a wide grin on his face. "I. Have. Come," he said as he stepped through the doorway, arms outstretched, legs stiff as he marched toward the bed. "To tickle!"

Alan squealed as his father descended upon him, fingers lightly pressing against Alan's sides.

"Gotcha!" Daddy yelled in triumph as Alan collapsed into giggles. Daddy stepped back, smiling. Alan's laughter slowed. "You ready to go to sleep?"

"Yes, Daddy," Alan said.

"Good, because I have more tickling to do." Alan flinched and Daddy laughed. "Not you, kiddo." He put a finger to his lips. "Shh," he whispered, looking around as if someone might hear him, "I'm going to go tickle Mommy!" Alan giggled again. Daddy reached out a hand and rubbed the boy's head. "Now," he said, "go to sleep." Daddy bent down and kissed Alan on the forehead.

"Yes, Daddy," Alan said.

His father stood back up and shook his head. He mouthed "I love you," turned, and walked out of the bedroom, closing the door behind him.

Alan let out a sigh and snapped off the lamp. The room descended into darkness. Daddy's kiss would keep him safe from the whispers. It always did.

Chapter
Five

Carolyn lay against Trey in the dark. Her head curled against his shoulder, her body pressed close against his hip. His right hand absently stroked her hair, playing with the strands. "So," she said, "did you have a good day?"

Trey's fingers stopped in mid-caress. He felt her stiffen against him. "Um," he said, "um, yeah." He forced his fingers to start the job again, but he knew it was too late.

"What's wrong, baby?"

He shook his head in the dark. "I— Well, I had a seizure today."

"Blank?" she asked, her voice flat.

"Yeah. Blanked."

"How long?"

Trey shrugged in the dark. "Alan said it was only a little while. Less than a minute, I guess."

"What set it off, honey?" she asked, holding him tight.

"I—" He stopped. The ice cream man, those yellow eyes staring at him from the van's shadowy interior. "It's, um, it's stupid."

She pulled herself up and rested her head on an elbow. She bit her lip, her brown eyes staring into his. "You don't get to do that, Trey," she whispered.

"Fuck," he said. "I know. It's just—"

"Just tell me, baby." She reached out with her free hand and brushed her fingers against his cheek. "Just tell me."

"Okay," he breathed. He closed his eyes. "There's an— There was an ice cream van at the school today." He swallowed. "I saw glowing, yellow eyes inside the van."

"Inside the van?" she asked.

He opened his eyes and looked at her, feeling embarrassed. "Yeah. Stupid, I know."

"You mean all you saw were eyes driving the van?"

Trey sighed. "No, baby. The side door slides and the guy hands the treats out over a little counter."

"So you saw him in the shadows of the van?"

"Yeah," Trey agreed. "Only I saw those eyes."

Carolyn nodded. "Do you know what it was?"

"Me being a fucking psychotic?"

Carolyn laughed and then shook her head. "That's not what I meant." She twirled a finger in his chest hair. "Do you know why you saw that?" He opened his mouth and then closed it. "You don't get to do that, Trey," she whispered. She bent and kissed his lips. "Just say it."

"It was like the Closet Man." His face flushed with warmth. "Only, it wasn't."

"Did it scare you?"

He nodded. "Yeah, it did. But not the same way."

"Okay," she said, kissing him again. "Can you talk about it yet?"

"No. Need to think about it."

"Oh, that's going to be a problem," she said. "Because you're going to be busy." Her hand brushed against his inner thigh. He moaned. "Very very busy," she chuckled and kissed him again.

Chapter Six

She listened to the wind buffeting the house, her body pressed close to Trey's. As he slept, his breathing was barely audible above the ebb and flow of the skeletal tree branches clacking together. Sleep may have taken him, but she had been awake for the last hour.

Another seizure. Trey was having more and more of them lately. It was why he didn't drive. Although he knew how to drive a car, he never had in their ten year marriage. She didn't expect she'd ever see that happen either, especially now they had a child.

But the seizure didn't bother her as much as the "Closet Man."

She shuddered in the darkness. Trey had always been afraid of closets. When they first moved into the house, she had wanted to put all their clothes in the closet in order to save space in the bedroom. Instead, they ended up compromising: all his clothes were kept in a chest of drawers in the bedroom while all her clothes hung in the closet.

She'd never understood his fear of closets. A childhood fear that had managed to seep into adulthood. It was silly, of course. A grown man afraid of dark, enclosed spaces. He'd even removed the door of the master closet and moved it to the garage. She knew if he had his way, none of the closets in the house would have doors at all.

She readjusted herself against his body. He let out a little moan and pressed back against her, as if making sure she was still there.

Carolyn grinned in the darkness. Trey. Her lover, the father of her child—her husband. She loved him, but didn't understand his phobias. She guessed she never would.

But seeing the "Closet Man" in the real world? That was...new.

She shivered. Had that precipitated the seizure, or the other way around? More questions for Kinkaid. Maybe next time Trey went to see the doctor, she'd go with him. She could call Kinkaid, of course, and let her know, but didn't like the idea of going behind Trey's back. Trey was self-conscious enough about his mental illness as it was.

"The Closet Man." A pair of eyes that stared back at Trey from dark, enclosed spaces. Green eyes. Always green eyes. Except for the eyes in the ice cream van. She frowned. Something was changing. Whenever Trey saw "the Closet Man," he ended up freezing in place, but remained conscious. He'd call for help, or he'd just stand there too afraid to speak.

Their son knew all of this. They'd taught him about Trey's... idiosyncrasies at an early age. He knew what to do when Daddy blanked, or when Daddy froze in front of a closet or other dark place. At eight years old, Alan knew as much about Trey's condition as she did.

Alan. She placed an arm around Trey, hugging him closer to her. Would her son start having the same mental problems? How long before he too wouldn't go near a closet? How long before he started seeing things, or freezing up during stressful situations?

She hugged Trey tighter. In the darkness, he sighed.

Carolyn closed her eyes again and floated. She listened to the rhythm of Trey's breathing and felt her own match it. Within a few minutes, she was finally asleep.

Chapter
Seven

The room was still dark when Trey awoke. Carolyn lay on her back on the other side of the bed, snoring softly. As usual, she had kicked off the blanket and her breasts formed two small mounds below the sheet. Trey sighed.

He swung his legs out from beneath the blue sheets and black comforter in an attempt to keep from disturbing her. She needed the sleep.

Tip-toeing to the chest on the far wall, he slid open the bottom drawer, pulled out a pair of sweat pants, a sweat shirt, and a T. His disc golf garb in hand, he stepped into the dark bathroom. He closed the door, once again thankful he'd oiled the hinges to keep them from squeaking.

Trey's skin had already puckered with goose flesh from the morning's cold. Since they kept the thermostat at a cool 68 during the winter, stepping naked from the warm bed inevitably left him chilled. He slipped on the sweat pants, not bothering with underwear. The T and the sweat shirt followed. He reached into the hamper and pulled out a pair of athletic socks, giving them a quick sniff. He recoiled at the stench.

He sat on the window seat and pulled on the socks. With any luck, the smell would drive Dick crazy. Disgusting, yes. Funny? Absolutely. He knew it was juvenile, but hell, so was Dick.

Trey stepped out of the bathroom and made his way to the bedroom door. He gave Carolyn a last look. Her light snores were still audible above the sound of the heater. He opened the door and stepped into the cool hallway.

Alan's bedroom door stood open. Trey sighed. The boy was already awake. Trey cocked his head, listening. Sure enough, he heard the sounds of the Wii. He had to get that kid some exercise today. In another year or two, Trey hoped Alan would be throwing discs with him and Dick. Of course, that would require Dick to give up one of his nastier habits.

He stepped down the wood panel stairs, lifting each foot and placing it down as gently as possible. A stair squeaked beneath his feet, sounding much too loud in the quiet hallway. He gritted his teeth as the electronic beeps and boops from downstairs ended with a chime. He continued stepping until his feet hit the floor. He stopped. "Alan?" Trey called. "If you try and spook me around the corner, I'm going to ground you for a week."

"Ah, Dad," Alan giggled. He stepped forward into Trey's sight. "You're no fun at all."

"That's right," Trey agreed. He walked to the boy and patted his head. "Have you had your cereal?" Alan nodded. "Good. I'm going to be leaving soon. Do not," he waggled a finger, "wake up your Mommy. Understood?"

"Yes, Daddy," Alan said. "You going to play discs with Dick?"

"Yeah, kiddo. Time to throw some plastic."

Alan smirked. "Is he going to win again?"

"No," Trey growled. "I'm gonna take him today."

Alan nodded, his smile wide. "Uh-huh. I'll ask him about that."

Trey chuckled. He placed a finger to his lips. "Shh, kiddo. You're not supposed to call your Daddy a loser."

"I didn't," Alan said. "You're just not as good as Dick at discs."

"Right," Trey said with a sigh. "Your old man stinks at disc golf."

"But he doesn't at Mario Kart."

"Yeah, right," Trey said. "I need coffee, kiddo. Get back to your game."

"Yes, Daddy," Alan said. He padded back to the sunken living room and stood in front of the television. Trey watched as he unpaused the game and started swinging at digital baseballs. He shook his head and made his way to the kitchen.

Chapter Eight

After filling his travel mug with coffee, Trey walked through the laundry room to the garage door. He took a deep breath.

"The Closet Man is waiting inside," a child's voice sang in his mind.

Trey shook his head. "No," he whispered to it, "there is no Closet Man." Trey opened the door.

Cold air seeped out to chill his face. A pair of green eyes blinked at him from the darkness. Trey closed his eyes and stood still. Nothing happened. He reached his hand out and fumbled for the light switch.

A barely audible click and he could see light through his closed eyelids. Exhaling, he opened his eyes. The garage was lit by two brilliant lights. He walked through the open door and to the side wall. His disc golf bag hung from a hook. He grabbed it and then turned to face the rest of the garage. The lawn mower, weed whacker, and other garden implements stared back at him. His bicycle, waiting for spring weather, hung atop a pair of hooks from the ceiling. But no eyes. No Closet Man.

Trey turned back to the door, flicking off the light switch as he stepped through. He closed it without looking back. The tightness in his chest released. He took another deep breath and then blew it out through his nose. Every trip to the garage was like that, seeing those green, fluorescent eyes until light pushed away the darkness.

He sipped at the coffee and headed toward the front door. His phone sat atop the bookcase in the hallway. There was a single text message. "Ready, bitch?" It was Dick, of course. They weren't even supposed to leave until 10:00, but, as usual, Dick was chomping at the bit.

He headed back into the living room, watching as Alan pounded another digital baseball toward the cartoon fences. "Leaving, kiddo."

"Okay, Daddy," Alan said without turning around. "Go bust him up"

Trey chuckled. "I'll do my best."

"No," Alan said, turning around with a smirk. "Do better than that."

"Smart-ass," Trey growled as he walked outside and into the cold.

Dick's garage was already open. The big man stood next to his old car, munching on an apple. Dick was well over six-feet tall and weighed about 290. The man was muscled, but a huge pot belly stuck out from beneath his shirt. He grinned as Trey walked down the driveway and across the street.

"About goddamned time," Dick said and took another bite from the apple.

"Bite me," Trey said with a grin. "I'm thirty minutes early."

"Big whoop," Dick said through a mouthful of apple. "You ready?" Trey nodded. Holding the apple in his mouth, Dick pulled his keys from his pocket and opened the door. It swung open with a groan of protest.

The Regretta, an old VW Jetta Dick had bought some years back, still ran, but Trey was certain it was headed for the shop in another month or two. Ever since Dick had broken the 100k mark on the odometer, he'd christened it "the Regretta."

Trey opened the passenger side and placed the disc golf bag on the floor. He bent down and fell into the seat, travel mug still in his hands. Dick groaned as he bent and managed to slide himself in.

"One of these days," Trey said with a grin, "you're going to lose enough weight to actually fit in this thing."

"Fuck that," Dick snarled as he put the keys in the ignition and placed the apple in his lap. "I'm just going to get a big-ass SUV made for fat people."

Trey laughed. "That's called a Winnebago, Dick."

Dick turned to him, his face set in a scowl. "Fuck you, Leger. Goddamned cajun."

Trey just smiled at him and took another sip of coffee.

Dick shook his head. "That's it. I'm kicking your ass so bad, you won't even admit the score to your son."

"Are you kidding? He believes my lies. It's the nature of fatherhood."

Dick harrumphed and started the car. After several chuffing sounds and squeals from the starter, the engine fired. The radio sparked to life, Pink Floyd smashing through the speakers.

"Christ, turn that hippie shit down!" Trey yelled above the din.

With a grin, Dick turned the volume up, put on his seat belt, and pulled out of the driveway.

Chapter
Nine

The disc golf course was mostly empty. A few cars sat in the parking lot, but most of those were from the tennis players. Trey watched as Dick scanned the hills, looking for discs flying through the air. Nothing. He turned and smiled at Trey. "Looks like we're loners today."

Trey scowled. "I guess you're going to imbibe, then."

"Well, fuck yeah," Dick said. He headed toward the practice tee beneath the blanket of pines and brush. Trey followed, his bag hanging from his shoulder. When they reached the edge, Dick pulled out a dirty white disc. He dropped his bag to the concrete and held the frisbee between his fingers.

"Watch and weep," Dick whispered and flung it. The disc flew between the branches, heading toward the metal basket. It hit the dirt just before the basket and spun around in a small circle before stopping. He turned to Trey. "All right, whipper-snapper, try and top that."

Trey lowered his bag to the concrete and pulled out a blue disc. "Move aside, old man," he said and pushed Dick out of the way. Dick laughed, raised his hands, and moved to give Trey enough room. Trey stood parallel to the basket and flung the disc forehand. The disc took off with an awkward wobble, made a slight left turn, and then struck a tree limb. The frisbee bounced and landed in the brush.

"Fuck."

"Not a good start, young'n," Dick said in a flat tone. "Maybe you should try again with a little less suck?"

Trey turned toward Dick. The man was smiling at him. "Maybe you should drink a big cup of shut-the-fuck-up." He smiled at Dick and then slapped him on the back. "It'll get better."

"I fucking hope so," Dick laughed. "I don't want to be here all day." The two men grabbed their bags and headed between the trees.

Dick waited on the path while Trey crawled into the brush and stood where his disc landed. Mindful of the brambles, Trey picked up the blue frisbee, lined himself up, and flung the disc again. It stayed low, barely flying above the branches of an oak, slipped through a pine tree's nest, and landed next to the basket.

"Told you," Trey said as he walked back to the path.

Dick harrumphed and then walked to the basket. He didn't even bother dropping his disc in the chains. It was just practice, after all. Dick turned toward the concrete walkway and Trey followed his gaze.

Dick turned to him. "Yup, it's time." He pulled a small glass pipe from his bag and a Bic lighter. Trey opened his mouth to say something, but Dick already had the pipe to his lips, flaring the flame into the small bowl and inhaling. The smell of marijuana crept through the winter morning. Dick exhaled a large cloud, coughed and then turned back to the walkway. Still no one there. He smiled at Trey and took another hit.

"Fucking hate it when you do this," Trey whispered.

Dick shrugged, tapping out the coals while he held in the last of the smoke. He blew a cloud toward Trey, watching it whisk and break apart in the wind. "Well," he said in a gravelly voice, "tough shit." Once the pipe was back in his bag, he bent down, picked up his disc, and headed toward the first tee.

Trey sighed and followed. "One of these days," he said, "you're going to get busted again."

Dick rolled his eyes. "Sheriff McCausland ain't gonna throw me in jail," he said. "I don't deal. I don't buy. I just, um, have a medical problem."

"Right. A medical problem that started in the 70s."

The older man laughed. "After the old bitch Dawson complained, and he came by, I haven't had any more problems with her. He told her I have chronic arthritis. Old bitch bought it too." He winked at Trey. "One of these days this shit will be legal. Until then, I'll just keep seeing McCausland at the cigar store."

"Uh-huh," Trey said. "Why don't you throw a goddamned disc."

"Man," Dick said and looked up at the first basket in the distance, "I need some Floyd."

Trey laughed.

Chapter
Ten

Trey let himself into the house. Alan and Carolyn were gone. He smiled as he walked up the stairs and to the bathroom. They would bring food. After walking around the 18-hole course for an hour and a half and searching through mud and brambles for his discs, he was damned hungry.

He stripped off his dirty sweatpants and damp sweatshirt. Dick hadn't even noticed the socks. Dammit, Trey thought. He'd forgotten to find an opportunity to stick them in his face. Maybe next time.

Naked, he turned on the hot water and stepped into the shower.

The water cascaded through his long hair, wiping away bits of bark and moss. Although it had been cold, they hadn't yet had a freeze, and everything in the forest was still alive. The oak trees were mostly naked, but the pines still had needles, ferns still had fronds, and brambles were still everywhere. Shit, he counted himself lucky he had managed to skirt the patch of poison oak on hole five.

He opened his eyes and watched water patter out onto the bathroom floor. He cursed and then pulled the shower curtain shut. The world immediately darkened and his stomach knotted. A wave of claustrophobia hit him and he had to close his eyes and take a deep breath before the feeling passed.

Every damned time he got into the shower it was like that. When he'd met Carolyn, he'd only been showering for a few years. Before that, it was the tub or nothing. Two baths, really. One to get the crap off him, drain the dirty water, and then a bubble bath to clean the skin. His hair had been shorter then and he'd used the water from the tub to wash his hair.

In his twenties, he finally decided to break the habit and take showers. But damn, it was difficult. The claustrophobia was hard to break. And twelve years later, he was still fighting it. Trey longed for the day when he could stand in an elevator and not have his heart trip-hammer in his ears.

He picked up the bottle of shampoo and slowly lathered his long hair.

Dick had kicked his ass at disc golf, as promised. Dick had said they should rename the game to "Trey's 18 holes of suck." Trey chuckled as he remembered Dick's laughter. The guy was an asshole. A funny asshole. A good friend.

Trey washed the shampoo out of his hair and quickly rubbed soap over his skin. Another final rinse of everything and he shut off the water. He reached for the shower curtain and stopped.

"He's out there, Trey," a voice whispered in his mind. "He's out there and waiting for you."

Trey shivered, but not from the cold air against his wet skin. He took another deep breath, closed his eyes, and pulled the shower curtain open. He stood there for a moment, naked in the cold, while the voice continued its chant.

He opened his eyes. The bathroom was empty. No bad man waiting for him. No pair of green eyes staring back at him, or the shadow of a man standing tall against the wall. Just the clothes hamper, the sinks, the toilet.

The voice went silent.

He stepped out, water pattering against the tile floor. He grabbed a towel from the rack and wrung out his hair. The water streamed off onto the bath-mat. It was damned cold now. Trey rubbed the water from his chest, back and legs. Once finished, he put the towel back on the rack and walked toward the door.

In his peripheral vision, he saw the yawning, gaping darkness of the closet. Something was grinning in there. Watching him. Trey ignored the fear that shook his spine and walked into the bedroom. The moment he crossed the threshold and could no longer see the yawning closet, the fear abated. He took a deep breath.

The Closet Man hadn't been this visible to him in quite some time. It had been at least a year since he'd been so visible.

Trey strode to the chest of drawers, pulled out a pair of briefs, slipped them on, and followed them with a pair of old jeans. After putting on a clean T-shirt, he headed downstairs.

Carolyn and Alan still weren't back yet. Trey headed to the coffee machine and started another cup. The small cupboard caught his eye and he heaved a sigh. He opened it up and pulled his large pillbox out. He popped the lid on the first "S" compartment and dropped five pills into his palm.

White. Cream. Green. Yellow. Blue.

After retrieving a glass of water, he threw all five into his mouth and drained the glass. The pills were a miasma of different flavors and textures. The chalky taste of one hit the back of his palate on its way down and he ignored the urge to retch.

He'd been on the damned things so long he wasn't sure he could remember a time when he hadn't taken them.

He placed the box back in the cupboard. The coffee maker finished burping out the last of its dark liquid. Cup in hand, he sat at the breakfast table and stared out onto the back deck through the glass door. The water oak he'd planted three years ago had already grown a couple of feet and reached for the sky, desperately trying to climb past the canopy of pines.

The sun was already high, bathing the deck boards with light. If it wasn't so cold, he'd pull his laptop outside, set up shop on the deck, and maybe get some work done.

Rattle of keys. Trey looked around toward the living room. The jingling sounded again. Trey stood from the table and walked past the living room and into the foyer. Carolyn's tall form stood next to Alan's. Alan was trying out his new key again. Through the smoked and bent glass, he could barely make out Alan's frustrated expression.

"Won't turn," the boy said.

"Try again," Carolyn said with a sigh. "Hurry up, kiddo. These bags are killing me."

Trey fought the urge to go and unlock the door. He and Carolyn had talked about this. Alan needed to get used to letting himself in and out. That, of course, also meant he had to finally break in the damned key they'd given him. Another rattle echoed in the foyer and then Trey heard the click.

"Got it, Mommy," Alan triumphed as he opened the door. He held it open for his mother. Trey walked past Alan and took the bags from Carolyn. "See, Daddy? I can open the door all by myself."

"Yeah," Trey said with a laugh as he headed into the kitchen with the groceries, "I see that." Trey smelled quiche. His stomach growled with delight. He placed the bags on the island, and turned into Carolyn's waiting kiss. "Whoa," he whispered, "what was that for?"

She smiled. "I'll show you later." She winked and kissed him again.

Just as on Friday, and most other days, the school parking lot was already filled with cars getting ready to pick up kids. Trey stared at the mostly empty bike racks, wondering once again why more of the kids didn't ride to school and back. If it wasn't for the fact Trey enjoyed walking Alan to and from school, he would have suggested they get the boy a bike.

But that could wait. Middle school was only a couple of years away. By then, Alan would probably be ready to move on from this routine.

Trey knew it was inevitable, but it didn't make it any less painful to think about.

He looked past the playground and through the copse of trees. The cream colored ice cream van sat parked at the curb, its sliding door was still closed. From this distance, he couldn't make out any movement behind the tinted windows. The ice cream man was surely getting ready, making sure he had coins and bills for change and whatever else it was Ice Cream men did before serving the children.

"Scooby-dooby-doo, where are you?" a phantom voice sang in his mind.

Trey shivered. In his peripheral vision, he watched the woman a few feet away from him turn her head to look at him. He ignored her.

"Scooby?" he thought.

He fought away the jitters and stared at the school exit. The school bell's buzz would fill the world in a moment and children would start streaming through the glass doors. Alan would run out with them, but not quite be part of them. The thought of Alan's excited face made him smile. But the boy's lack of friends, and the way he always stood apart from the other children, made Trey feel a little sad too.

The teachers had said not to worry, that one day he'd find his place among the throng. Whenever he and Carolyn asked Alan about it, he just stared at them as if they were speaking Greek.

The kid was too smart. "Gets that from his mother," Trey thought to himself. "The aloofness? That's all me." Trey sighed.

His eyes wandered once again to the parked van. It bounced a little, as though someone inside was moving about.

Trey smirked. "Maybe Mr. Ice Cream is porking Mrs. Ice Cream," he thought to himself.

The school buzzer sounded, giving Trey a start. The two women waiting to walk their children home both sighed in relief, as though the wait had been excruciating. Trey tried not to glance toward them. He was certain they already thought him a closet pedophile, rapist, or something worse.

Jesus, didn't anyone talk to one another anymore?

The glass doors opened and as if on cue, the ice cream van's music began.

Trey snapped his fingers. "Do Your Ears Hang Low?" That was the song. He had tried so damned hard to remember its name and there it was, just like that.

The river of children swept through the doors, most heading toward the white van. Trey watched them, their packs slapping their backs in time with their frantic footsteps.

Trey turned back toward the school.

Alan walked out the door, his eyes finding Trey almost immediately. The boy smiled at him and quickened his pace. Trey wanted to wave at him, but he knew that wouldn't be the "cool" thing to do. He stood at the curb, the quiet, unobtrusive old fart.

"Well? You ready to go home?" he said as Alan approached.

The boy sighed. "I guess so. I mean I'd much rather stay here than play on the Wii—"

Trey shook his head and growled. "No Wii until homework is done."

"Ah, Dad," Alan said in his best "poor me" voice. "Sooner we get home, sooner I can get it done and play, right?"

Trey nodded. "You got it, kiddo." He reached out and touched the boy's shoulder. "Let's do it."

"Yes, sir," Alan said.

They made their way to the sidewalk in silence. Trey felt the jitters again. He didn't want to look at the ice cream van, but something glowed in his peripheral vision.

Alan turned to look at the van. "He sure has a lot of kids today," Alan said.

Trey kept his eyes straight ahead. "There is no Closet Man," he muttered.

"What, Daddy?"

Trey turned toward him and then stopped. His eyes locked on the long arms that jutted from the van, taking money and handing back wrapped treats. Talons. Not fingers. Talons attached to wretched, scaly flesh. He opened his mouth and then closed it.

"Daddy?" Alan's voice said.

He looked down at his son. "Yes?"

Alan shook his head and grabbed Trey's right hand. "Come on, Daddy. The van doesn't like you."

Trey nodded to him. "Guess you're right. Another one?"

"Just a little one," Alan said.

They walked in silence down the sidewalk, Trey fighting the urge to look back over his shoulder. The thing, no, he scolded himself, the man in the ice cream truck was not the Closet Man.

"Scooby-dooby-doo" the childish voice sang in his mind.

"Shut up," Trey muttered. Alan said nothing, just squeezed his father's hand a little tighter.

Chapter Twelve

From the study, Trey listened to the sound of Alan reading his homework aloud in the living room.

During days when Carolyn wasn't home and his son was in school, every minute was spent listening to music. While he coded, while he debugged, while he posted on forums and tracked down issues, every second was filled with the sounds of electronic beats mixed with guitars. It kept the left side of his brain asleep enough for the right side to work without interruption.

But when Alan was home, Trey never listened to music. He knew it should have cut his productivity down, but it usually didn't. Just knowing the boy was in the other room was enough to put a smile on his face and keep him focused. Perhaps the music was merely there to reduce the loneliness. Trey didn't know and didn't want to know.

As he went through the lines of code, his left brain woke up enough to let him know that Alan had stopped reading to himself. There was a new sound. Music. Bells. Trey shivered. He cocked his head to one side. The sound was growing louder. He and Alan had only been home for forty minutes or so, but he'd already forgotten about the ice cream man. Until now.

The bells. They were the same fucking bells.

That voice, the phantom child voice, started to sing, "Do your ears hang low? Do they wobble to and fro?"

The bells grew closer, their steady shriek silencing the birds tweeting in the trees and blotting out the sound of moving traffic.

Trey stood, his body wracked with ice cold goose pimples.

"Daddy?" Alan asked.

Trey jumped and turned to face the boy.

Alan's expression wasn't worried, so much as confused. "Did the Ice Cream Man follow us home?"

Trey gulped. Alan's expression turned fearful. "You're spooking him," Trey thought to himself. With effort, he managed a false smile. "No," Trey said, walking forward to the boy. He ran his hands through Alan's sandy blonde hair. "He's just making the rounds."

"Trying to sell to all the kids in the neighborhood?"

"Yes," Trey agreed. "And some adults, I'm sure."

Alan giggled. "Good business sense," the boy said.

Trey laughed, a real laugh, and his smile felt less wooden. "Yes, it is. What made you say that?"

The boy bit his lip, a habit born of watching his mother for many years. "We learned a little bit in class. Mrs. Smith said that if you run a business, you want to get as many customers as possible."

"Yes," Trey said, bending down to give the boy a hug, "that's true." He realized the bells had grown loud enough he had to raise his voice so Alan could hear him. "Why don't you go back to reading? I'm going to go outside for a minute."

Alan wrinkled his nose. "To smoke?"

Trey felt a flush of embarrassment. "Yes. And yes, I know it's bad for me."

Alan shrugged and then hugged him. The boy walked back into the living room.

Trey patted his front shirt pocket, making sure his smokes were still there. The pack's reassuring rectangular contours set his mind a little at ease. He had cut back significantly on his nicotine habit, rarely having more than a few cigarettes a week. Sometimes, when he was jonesing or felt nervous, he could just touch a pack of cigarettes and it would settle him. But he knew he needed the real thing to stem the anxiety.

The taloned hands handing out treats flitted into his imagination. The yellow eyes, the burning, crimson pupils.

"Was just an illusion," he said to himself. "Just another psychotic delusion my brain played on me." He walked with trepidation to the front door. He paused for a moment, hand on the knob. "I'll go outside," he thought, "and watch it. Prove it. No boogeyman in the neighborhood. Just another working class guy trying to make some cash." He swiveled the door knob and opened the door.

The cacophonous bells were positively brain-numbing in volume. They were so loud, Trey wasn't sure he'd ever be able to hear again. The white van was at the street's entrance. He watched it travel down the other side of the block. It would hit the cul-de-sac, round it, and then travel back. He was sure of it. Trey deftly plucked the pack of cigarettes from his shirt pocket, opening it by feel, and pulled one of the white cylinders out. Without looking at the shirt pocket, he replaced the pack and retrieved the lighter in much the same way.

It was a ritual for him, something he'd practiced in high school and in college. Before the— Well, before the first incident. The routine had always provided that bit of focus. When he first started doing it, spending so much time practicing it, he didn't realize it was one of the first signs of his condition. He often imagined many other people did the same thing, that he wanted to be normal, just like them.

Eyes still focused on the back of the white van as it made its way through the cul-de-sac, he lit the cigarette on the first try. He inhaled deeply as the van turned to face him. He stopped part-way through his exhale. The van. The fucking van. The windshield was...tinted? A shuddering hiss of air through his teeth brought the smoke out in a continuous, if jerky, stream.

He shook his head as the white van traveled closer. The bells had receded during its travel down the block, but the sound was now a rushing storm coming straight at him. His mind was barely aware that his neighbors were doing the same as him, stepping out onto their front porches to watch, to figure out what was going on.

The windshield, a black cyclopean eye contrasting starkly against the van's white hood and face, seemed to stare at him. The metal grill's steel grinned like a predator.

Trey felt another wave of cold rise up his spine. "That can't be legal," he muttered aloud. "Tinted fucking windshield?"

The van was no more than fifty or so feet away, its body visible. The first decal Trey saw stopped his heart in his chest. It was of a ghoul holding a bloody human heart in a taloned hand. The ghoul grinned with ferocious yellowed teeth.

Trey's scream locked in his throat.

The second decal was an ice cream cone made of intestines and offal. A child's screaming severed head sat atop it, wild eyes just visible over the cone's lip. A single word was carved in blood just below the graphic "YUMMY". Next to it was what looked like a misshapen ice cream bar. Trey dropped the cigarette as he realized the ice cream treat was the blackened, burned body of a screaming child, impaled through its backside by a long stake. As he watched, the screaming mouth began to move, the body wriggling.

Trey stepped backwards, nearly tripping over the lip of the patio deck. The van passed by, heading toward the other cul-de-sac, the music still cheery and inviting. Trey took another step backwards, finally catching the deck's edge. He fell onto the deck, his ass hitting the wood with a thunk. The world spun around him, his vision unfocused and blurred.

He heard a distant voice yelling, but he couldn't make out the words.

When a hand touched his arm, he nearly loosed the scream he'd been holding back.

"Trey!"

His vision snapped back into focus.

Dick sat on his knees in front of him. "Hey, man, you okay?"

Trey looked up into the man's grizzled, bearded face. He marveled at the many white hairs tangled within the otherwise black beard. "I—" Trey struggled to speak and coughed instead. Dick grabbed his arm and pulled him up. Trey stood on rubbery legs, feeling as though he might fall down again at any second. Dick put his arm around his waist and took part of Trey's weight. "I fell down," Trey managed.

"Yeah," Dick said. "You did." The blasting music had receded but now it was rising again. "That shit is killing my ears," Dick said. He walked Trey toward the front door. "Is Alan home?" Dick asked over the din.

Trey said nothing, nodding instead.

"Goddammit, I'm going to kill that asshole," Dick said as he looked over his shoulder.

Trey turned with him, once again facing the street. The van was passing them now. Trey took in a shuddering breath and stared at the dark passenger window.

A pair of glowing yellow eyes stared back at him. Long white teeth glowed in the van's cabin. Trey's legs gave out again, but Dick was ready for him, taking his weight with a small grunt.

"Easy," Dick said, unaware of Trey's silent scream.

Chapter
Thirteen

The bedroom was dark. Trey flexed his fingers beneath the covers, playing the chromatic scale on an invisible trumpet. It was a relaxation technique from his teenage years. He couldn't possibly blow a decent tone on a horn anymore, but his fingers remembered the notes perfectly.

He ignored the twinge of pain in his hand—he'd been tapping out the patterns for an hour.

Through the bedroom door, he heard soft voices from the foyer. Dick and Carolyn were talking. He couldn't make out their conversation except for a few words. He concentrated on slowing his fingers, turning the chromatic scale in his head into a slow winding progression of tones. Up from the low G all the way to high. He imagined the notes as ovals climbing the staff ladder. The front door squealed open and then closed.

He listened to the light footfalls on the stairs. He smiled. It was Carolyn. Alan climbed stairs like they were an enemy to be defeated, his feet slam dancing on each step. But Carolyn's steps were always quiet, slow, methodical, especially at the end of the workday.

Trey kept his eyes closed as the bedroom door opened and then closed softly.

Her footfalls stopped at the bed's edge. He imagined her standing there, staring at him, wondering if he was sleeping. After a moment, she walked into the bathroom and closed the door. She'd change out of her work clothes, neatly hang her skirt and suit jacket up. Then she'd roll off her stockings, and hang them as well.

Sweat pants, a sweat shirt, and slippers. That's what she'd be wearing when she stepped out of the bathroom. He waited.

The bathroom door opened. Trey felt the bed's surface dip as she climbed in with him. He opened his eyes, feeling her naked skin against his own. A cool arm reached beneath his pillow as she snuggled up against him. Her breath tickled against his neck.

"Hi, baby," he whispered.

She said nothing, making a purring noise in her throat instead. They lay like that for some time until she rolled him onto his side, spooning against him beneath the warm comforter.

"Nothing like coming home to a warm, naked man beneath the sheets," she whispered.

He grunted.

Her free hand stroked his hair. "I'm here when you want to talk, baby."

Trey said nothing and closed his eyes. The warmth of her against his back soothed him. He didn't want to talk about it. He didn't want to think about it. The anti-convulsant he'd taken was already making him feel sleepy and disconnected. In that state, there was very little that could bother him, but it was difficult to talk, much less string coherent thoughts together.

They stayed like that for a while, her breath slowing, fingers tangled in his long hair. He knew she was dozing and it made him smile. Alan would be downstairs, working on his math problems until he became hungry enough to knock on the door.

Trey's son knew the routine. When Daddy had an episode, he was to be left alone, but Alan was to stay aware for any odd behavior, and check on him occasionally until Mommy came home.

The kid was remarkable. Trey smiled in the darkness.

He felt his thoughts slowing, turning into an even flatline. Then he was asleep.

W hen he awoke, he felt cold. Carolyn's body was still pressed up against him in the darkness, but her skin was...wrong. Her breathing was ragged, broken by soft grunts.

"Carolyn?"

There was no response other than a slight shift from beneath the pillow. Her fingers scratched against his scalp, the pain immediate and bright. Trey yelped and sidled away from her. He threw his head sideways to yell at her and then began to scream.

An elongated face grinned at him, glistening canines yawning toward him in the room's darkness. Red rings danced in the center of its glowing yellow eyes. Its hand moved toward him, sharp talons ripping through the fabric of the bed.

Trey screamed again and fell off the edge. He landed on his ass, his head smashing into the wall. The thing was slithering, moving toward him. He could hear its talons slashing through the bed sheets, the protest of threads as they parted in rips and shreds. Its breathing grew louder, a quick series of grunts and growls.

Trey held his head in his hands and slammed sideways into the wall. "Not real," he whispered. The grunts came closer and he felt its hot, sewer breath puff into his face. "You're not real!" he screamed.

The lights in the room flicked on. "Trey?" Carolyn asked. She knelt beside him on the floor. "Trey?" she whispered. He slowly pried his fingers open and looked through them at her face. Her blonde hair was tied in a ponytail leaving a single, long bang dangling down her forehead. He dropped his hands from his face and stared at the bed. Whatever had been there was gone.

He looked up at her. "I—" Trey croaked.

She put her arms around him and he shivered for a long time, tears streaming down his face.

Chapter
Fifteen

The cup of tea sat steaming on the edge of the kitchen table. Carolyn had heated up dinner for him. He normally plowed through her chipotle meatloaf, but he ate it more out of obligation than hunger.

"You're going to call Kinkaid in the morning?"

Trey looked up from the dinner plate. He felt like making a sarcastic remark, but decided against it.

"Yes. I, um, already sent an email."

Carolyn smiled. "You think the meds are off?"

He shrugged in response. "I— I don't know."

"Dick's worried about you."

With a grim chuckle, Trey lifted another fork full of the meal into his mouth. He chewed with mechanical determination and swallowed. "That's because he knows there's a madman across the street."

"Stop that," Carolyn whispered. "That's not it, and you know it."

Trey dropped the fork and opened his mouth to talk.

"Trey? Dick said something about an ice cream van?"

Trey nodded and began to speak.

"Just listen, okay?" Trey shrugged and reached for the cup of Chai. "Dick said its windows are tinted."

Trey nodded.

"You saw something."

Trey nodded again.

She leaned forward and placed a hand on top of his. She squeezed as she looked in his eyes. "Dick said the van made him feel...uneasy."

Trey's eyes widened. "He felt it too?" he asked in a whisper.

Carolyn smiled. "Yes, Trey. He did."

"I know I'm crazy. Brain chemistry all fucked up and all that." He dropped his eyes to her hand. "But I never had a delusion like that. Never."

"What did you see?"

The image of the ghoul, the thing's elongated face, its fierce glowing eyes, the long sharp teeth glistening with blood and half chewed flesh, rose into his mind. He shuddered.

"Don't want to talk about it, baby."

She nodded. "Okay.."

"Is Alan—" his voice dropped the sentence as soon as he'd begun to speak the words. Alan. He'd completely come unhinged in front of his son. He knew his screams had scared the boy. How could they not?

"Alan's okay, Trey. He knows that Daddy had a daymare and then a really bad nightmare."

Trey continued staring at her hand. The hand rose, the fingers spreading beneath his chin. She lifted until his eyes met hers.

"Alan's okay. He's okay."

A single tear appeared in the corner of Trey's eye. He wiped at it. "He's such a bright kid. And I'm fucking him up one day at a time."

She rose from her seat and stood behind him. Her fingers worked into the knots in his shoulders, gently brushing at first and then digging into the muscles. Pain ripped through his back. He tried to relax, flexing his fingers in the chromatic scale. The knots in his shoulders slowly dissolved, the pain dissipating into pleasure. Her arms wrapped loosely about his neck and she kissed his cheek.

"You're not fucking him up, Trey. You're not." She kissed him again. "He loves his father, and he understands." Another kiss. "Just like I do," she whispered.

Trey tried not to weep. "Take me upstairs," he said softly. "I think I can sleep."

"No you can't," she said softly into his ear. She gently bit at his earlobe.

He moaned.

"You have some work to do first." She kissed the hollow of his neck. "Then I'll let you sleep."

Chapter
Sixteen

Kinkaid's office was a testament to the modernity of psychiatry. Whereas the doctors' offices Trey remembered from childhood sported white, cinder block walls, this one had muted wood paneling and the occasional abstract painting hanging on the wall.

The good doctor was the only one in her practice. A nice, private, comfortable practice with only a single administrative assistant to handle appointments and patients.

Trey sat in one of the leather chairs across from her counter, staring at the floor. The lights in the room were muted much like the wood paneling. He'd always wondered if Kinkaid eschewed bright lights to induce calm in her patients, or if she was secretly a vampire.

"Shit, better not say that to Kinkaid," he thought, "or god only knows how much Thorazine she'll shoot me with."

The assistant's computer let out a low gong noise, barely audible from across the room. She turned from whatever she was working on, and read the computer screen. Trey stared at her in anticipation. She nodded to herself and then raised her eyes to his. "She's ready for you," she said.

Trey stood and walked from the chair to the door. "Thank you, Vivian." He opened the door and entered Kinkaid's office.

Kinkaid sat at her workstation, typing into the computer. "Have a seat, Trey," she said without looking up.

Trey shrugged and sat on the expensive and comfortable leather couch. Not for the first time, Trey marveled at her sense of taste and wondered if she had a fetish for Corinthian cowhide.

"There," she whispered to herself and struck the return key. She turned in her computer chair to look at him. "You look like shit," she said with a grin.

"I'm sure I do," Trey said with a chuckle. "Carolyn dropped me off. I'm—" He swallowed hard. "I, um, wanted to be alone with you."

She nodded at him and grabbed her leather portfolio. "I understand." She wrote something down on one of the pages. "So talk to me. What happened?"

Trey sighed. "You already think I'm crazy, right?"

"Trey," she said, her smile growing reproachful. "I hate that word." Trey blinked at her. "I prefer bat-shit insane," she said, her smile reappearing.

He laughed. "Okay, okay." He paused. "I'm seeing things."

He told her about the ice cream van. About how he'd vapor-locked on the way home from Alan's school. He told her about the decals. The thing inside the van. And the thing in his bed.

"Nothing else last night?" Trey shook his head. "Or this morning?"

"No, nothing else." He and Carolyn had made love for an hour before bed. After her tender ministrations, he'd fallen asleep easily and without dreams. He'd awakened that morning with a start, wondering if he'd find the thing next to him again. Instead, he found himself spooning against her, his free hand draped across her belly.

"Woke up without a problem. Walked Alan to school. Came back home. Now I'm here."

She nodded and wrote something else down on her pad. "You had a psychotic episode four years ago."

Trey paused for a moment, looking up at the ceiling. He tried to count months and then nodded. "Yeah, something like that, I guess."

"Was this like that?" she asked.

He shook his head. "I saw someone then. Someone who wasn't there. Carolyn found me on the deck having an impassioned conversation with them."

"You don't remember whom?"

"Not really," Trey said.

Kinkaid flipped through the notebook. Trey knew she'd had to make a special notebook just for him. Over the years, that little portfolio had had dozens of pads in it. He wondered if every patient of hers went through them like Pez, or if it was just his case.

"I, um, reacquainted myself this morning," she said softly. She found the page she wanted and looked down at it. "You don't remember who?"

"Did I say who?"

She blinked at him. "No, Trey. You didn't." She tapped the end of the pen against the leather portfolio. "You don't remember at all?"

"I can't—" He paused and took a deep breath. "When I try and remember back that far, it's like, well, like thinking through glue. I used to know this."

"But you still remember your first episode? The one in college?"

"Oh, yeah," Trey whispered. "Yeah, I remember that one all too clearly."

His first psychotic break. First real one. He'd walked into the dorm cafeteria and found himself in a circus. The people around him juggled their food, their faces painted with makeup. Rabbits danced on the trays behind the sneeze guards. He had laughed and laughed right up until they called the health center to come pick him up.

Her pen scratched against the notebook. "So your long-term memory is still okay," she said to herself. "Was this delusion like that one?"

Trey shrugged. He shifted his legs, his jeans rubbing together. "I. Don't. Know. I, well, I didn't enjoy this one, that's for sure."

Kinkaid pushed her glasses up on her nose. Her fiery red hair was still in its tight bun. It was early enough that it hadn't begun to free itself. Trey knew from experience that as the day wound on, more and more hair would struggle loose from the bobby pins.

"Trey? I'm talking about the feeling surrounding the delusion. Was this as real or more real than the first one."

"Much more. I actually felt breath. I smelled. I—" His voice trailed off. He struggled to find the words. "I felt it. Cold. Stone. Bone. It was real," he said.

She frowned. "Do you still think it was real?"

Trey shook his head. "The bed wasn't torn to ribbons. I didn't have any marks on my skin." Other than the ones Carolyn put there last night, he thought to himself. "So it couldn't have been real."

"What about the ice cream van?"

"If I accept," he said after a moment, "that last night was a delusion, then I guess I have to convince myself the ice cream van was too. One can't be real without the other."

"Well," Kinkaid replied, "I wouldn't go that far. In this case, however, I agree with you."

A tingle of fear crawled up his spine. "What do you mean 'in this case?'" he asked.

She tapped the pen against the notebook again. "Minds like yours are very susceptible to suggestion. Yes?" He nodded. "So if you see something on television or in a movie, especially if it really fires up that right brain of yours, then your brain may try and recreate it later. Do you watch horror movies?"

Trey shook his head.

"Why not?"

"They feel too real to me. I just— I don't enjoy being frightened."

Kinkaid chuckled. "Okay, what about science fiction?"

"I don't watch many movies or much television," Trey admitted.

"Right. But you do read?" He nodded. "And you read non-fiction and technical books, right?" He nodded again. "Why?"

Trey shrugged. "I don't know. Something about the logic in them calms me, I guess."

"Sure. This is sort of what I mean. You drown your right brain in facts, figures, and history. Scientific concepts and even philosophy take the right brain to visualize, but the left brain to analyze. You always talk about your brain being loosely wired."

"Yeah, I think of it as a malfunctioning motherboard. It's got some blown capacitors."

She waved a hand. "Whatever. The wires that hold the right brain from overtaking the left are a bit frayed in places. Every once in a while, something fires in your right brain that your left can't make sense of, or stop. You experience hallucinations. You suffer from delusions that things are real that aren't even there." She paused, watching the realization on his face.

"So my brain is taking in the real world, but putting...visitors in it?"

"Yes, and no. What I'm saying is that your brain processes information out of sequence sometimes. So when you see something you don't necessarily understand, your right brain captures the information and then will reprocess it later. Sometimes they come out as waking dreams."

Trey nodded to himself and stared down at the floor. "So what do we do about it?"

"We change your meds, Trey."

He shook his head.

"I know you hate the drugs. And it took us a long time to find something that didn't make you impotent or sick. But we're just going to have to hunt down something else."

"Fuck," he muttered. "The last time we did this, I could barely function for three months."

"I know," Kinkaid said softly. "This is not an exact science, Trey. Never was." She looked at her watch. "What time is your wife coming back?"

"About twenty minutes or so."

"Good. I want to spend a little time researching something. Then I'll come give you your scrip, okay?"

Trey nodded and stood. "I should—"

"You should call me immediately if you have another...episode. And I mean immediately. You're going to have to wean yourself from your current medication while you switch over to the new stuff."

"So take less of the former and more of the newer?"

"Right," she said with a smile. "Until you get to a low enough dosage to just stop the old stuff." She rose from her seat and offered her hand. He shook it. "We'll figure it out, Trey. Go wait for me and I'll be there in a few minutes."

"Thanks, Doc." He returned her smile and walked into the waiting room.

Chapter
Seventeen

Trey sat in front of the computer. The monitor was filled with lines of code. His Pidgin IM icon blinked to let him know he had new messages. He ignored it. The code on the screen, the email client with its 15 new messages, and the IM notifications barely crossed his consciousness.

The house was empty again.

Kinkaid had called the pharmacy for him, placing the prescription order. By the time Carolyn drove him to it, the scrip was ready. He and Carolyn had barely spoken until they reached the pick-up window.

Once the pharmacist handed over the small bag with the new meds and Carolyn had closed the window, she turned to him. "We'll find it again, you know. We'll find something that works"

Trey looked at her. "I don't want to go back to the hospital." He swallowed hard. "But I will. If I can't— If I can't get over this."

She reached over, placed her hand atop his. "We're not going to let that happen."

He smiled at her. "You must be as crazy as I am," he said softly.

"I—" A car behind them leaned on its horn, causing them both to jump. Carolyn flushed crimson, turned around and waved at the driver behind them. The driver responded with the middle finger salute and Carolyn laughed. "Okay, let's get you home."

Trey re-adjusted himself in his seat. New meds. Empty house. Alan was at school. He couldn't focus. He took a deep breath and drank from his warm can of soda.

Kinkaid had tried to put his mind at ease. Carolyn tried to do the same.

Trey stared at the pharmacy bag on the desk. He ripped it open, read the side effect clauses with some disinterest, and then popped the child-proof cap. Ninety small, yellow hexagons stared back at him.

He took his normal meds three times a day. In an hour or so, he'd skip his normal med, and swallow a hexagon. "It'll be a few days before the meds really start doing their job," Kinkaid had said. Yeah, Trey was well aware of that. Psych meds always took a while to hit the system. Up to thirty days in many cases. But Kinkaid seemed to think he'd start to feel the effects sooner. Trey doubted it.

The ghoul. That thing in his bed. Trey shuddered. "Christ, how the fuck am I supposed to sleep again?" Carolyn's naked body flashed in his mind. He smiled. "Oh yeah," he thought, "that worked." Trey tittered to himself and opened the IM window.

There were at least a dozen messages from Bangalore. They were pissed about his code refactor. Trey sighed. He wasn't going to respond to them. He'd increased the performance and already written more test cases than they'd dreamed of. In short, he was kicking their ass. He wondered how long it would be before Isometrics Inc. just dumped the Indian outsourcing firm altogether and hired him full time.

He closed the chat windows, changed his status to "away from desk," and opened his email client. A couple of spam messages had managed to get past the filter. Sighing, he selected them and sent them to data heaven. Then he found an email from Dick. The subject line said "Ice Cream Van."

He frowned. Dick normally sent him jokes and images from

4chan. In fact, Trey couldn't remember ever having received a serious email from his neighbor.

Trey opened it. The email had only a single line of text in it. "Want to have lunch?" He stared at the email for a moment, considering. Dick would want to talk about the incident. He'd want to know how Trey was doing. But Trey knew what Dick would really be asking: are you crazy?

Trey clicked the reply button. "Not today. Maybe later in the week." He clicked send.

Five hours until he'd meet Alan at school. Five hours. Trey yawned. The new meds. They were already throwing off his schedule. Trey cursed and stood from his chair. He put the linux box to sleep and raised his hands toward the ceiling, feeling the tension in his back release as his spine popped.

A nap. He'd need that. He was already well ahead on his work assignment— he could afford a little time for himself. Besides, the meds would more than likely keep him up all night anyway. Trey yawned again and walked to the couch. He lay down, closed his eyes, and was asleep a moment later.

Chapter Eighteen

"*Scooby-dooby-doo, where are you?*" *a phantom voice growls into song. "We got some work to do now." There is no light here, only the damp, the cold, the stench of shit and piss and fear. "Scooby-dooby-doo—"*

A whimper in the dark. A child's last reserve of sound from a strained and broken throat. Syllables mouthed, but not heard. There is nothing left to give voice to them. The constant cries for Mommy still echo in the child's mind, but they are so far away.

There is no sleep here—only the continual nightmare of the dark, the scratching sounds outside the door, and the fear that when the door once again opens and fills the space with light, the bad man will be there again. Green eyes staring down with malice and confusion.

"Scooby-dooby-doo—" The constant droning growl cuts off and the child's breath catches in his throat. Scratch. Scritch, scratch. The child shuffles back in the dark until he hits the wall. He can feel the slick texture of his own shit as it slides against his skin.

He has to get away from the door, because the bad man—

Scritch. Click. The boy tries to scream, but nothing comes out but a hiss of air.

Creak. Metal sliding. Click. A vertical sliver of light that stings his eyes. The scream finally finds vocal cords and the world explodes as the sliver detonates into light.

Chapter

Nineteen

The daylight coming through the windows had softened. Afternoon was giving way to the winter darkness as the sun descended toward the horizon. Trey opened his eyes and stared at the ceiling. His phone alarm bonged three times. He glanced at it. It was 1630.

"Oh, fuck," he said in a sleep choked whimper.

He jumped up from the couch, grabbing the phone as he headed to the stairs.

"Alan?" he called up the staircase.

No response.

His heart skipped a beat and then became a thrash metal rhythm. He was late. An hour late to walk Alan home.

"ALAN!" he yelled.

No response save for the house heater.

Trey scooped up his keys from the credenza and ran to the front door. His hand struggled with the dead-bolt and he cursed. His fingers finally managed to unclench enough to swivel it open. He opened the front door, stepped out, and locked it behind him.

A mile. A mile to make it to the school. Trey didn't bother looking at the small children playing in their yards. He didn't see Dick sitting in a chair on his patio reading a book. He didn't notice the concerned look on other adults' faces as his legs pumped him forward through the block and to the T leading to the main road. He didn't realize he was talking to himself either.

"Alan," he said with each chuffing breath. "Alan."

In the distance, he heard the ice cream van's music. A pang of fear rippled up his spine, leaving him shaking despite the burning in his lungs and legs. Sweat poured off him, staining his sweatshirt and further chilling him in the cold air. He pumped harder, each step pounding into the concrete.

He reached the cross-roads. He could either run through the vacant lots and take the back way to the school, or run through the path he and Alan always took.

"Have to get there," he mumbled through ragged breaths.

He headed for the lots, running as fast as he possibly could.

Alan. Alan would be standing in the playground, leaning against a tree with his backpack on the ground. He'd be kicking at a pinecone, or maybe playing with a stick. Alan would have his pack open, running through his homework, and wondering where Daddy was.

Or maybe the ice cream man had been there. Maybe the ice cream man had seen him, alone and waiting. Vulnerable. The adults and other children would be long gone, heading home for dinner, homework, and evening activities.

Alan would have no more of that. Alan would be in the ice cream van, his broken, eviscerated body stuffed into one of the refrigerator cases. Huge hunks of meat would already be missing from his bloodless body. The thing in the driver seat would laugh, chewing on a piece of fat from his baby boy. Or maybe picking gristles of flesh from between its teeth with a severed finger.

Trey ran through the vacant lot, his shoes sinking into the dirt with each step, brambles ripping at his jeans. He was completely oblivious to the scratches and tears and the trickles of blood seeping through the denim. He could see the side of the school now. He knew he should slow down. His heart hammered in his chest so hard, he heard nothing else.

The school. He could see the school. Another 50 yards and the playground would be in view.

Without thinking he turned and ran a diagonal path past the last house near the school. He nearly tripped over a four-year old playing in the yard, but kept going; he hadn't even seen the small child.

The playground was just ahead. He could just make out the wooden jungle gym. Another 25 yards and he'd be able to see the entire playground. He ran across the street, not noticing the squeal of tires or the high pitched honk of a car. His feet stumbled over the curb, but he managed to keep his balance. Suddenly, the entire playground came into view.

"No," Trey said as he slowed his pace and finally stopped. "No," he said again, tears appearing at the corners of his eyes.

The shrieking bells of the ice cream van in the distance, were a constant soundtrack to the triphammer of his heart and ragged breathing. Every part of his body burned, but he only felt the deep black starting to take him over.

"ALAN!" he screamed across the vacant playground.

Nothing.

Bells. He turned his head. Bells. Already the truck would be heading toward his house. Trey pumped his aching legs, heading for the main street leading to his block. Another car horn; a frustrated driver rolled down a window to scream at him.

Trey kept moving, his long dark hair bouncing in a tangled mess. Sweat drenched his shirt in the cold air. He wanted to scream Alan's name again, but couldn't find his voice.

He imagined the thing in the van munching on a wet, muscled femur as it drove with one sticky, blood soaked claw. The thing. The ghoul. It was humming to itself in the gore streaked van cabin, its gravelly voice turning a child's rhyme into something obscene and odious.

Trey could see the back of the van now. It rambled down the street.

"STOP!" Trey managed to scream. The sound was as broken and ragged as his breathing. Each footstep brought him closer to the van, and the darkness in his soul threatened to collapse him.

Alan was in there. Alan was dead. Alan was nothing more than a gutted human husk hanging from a hook, bloody juices dripping into a puddle on the floor. Alan's face would be frozen in a scream of confusion and terror.

Trey was getting closer, but his steps were slowing. He had pushed himself close to collapse and his vision was fading in and out. He stumbled, but managed to keep upright. With each footstep, his body screamed in pain.

The van was so close now. He saw a face in its side mirror. Blood streaked across the hollow cheekbone of a half grinning face. Eyes glowed yellow, those crimson swirls glaring at him. It laughed.

The van stopped. Trey slowed his pace as its door opened and the thing climbed out.

Its once white uniform was streaked with gore and gray matter. It opened its mouth in greeting.

"Your son was exquisite," it growled.

Trey screamed again, lost his balance and fell to the concrete.

Chapter
Twenty

The hospital smelled of Pinesol. Trey sat in the bed, a blanket wrapped around him. He'd gone into shock in the ER, and they'd admitted him immediately. Carolyn had given the doctor Trey's somewhat formidable list of medications and it had taken a while for them to come to the conclusion there was very little pain medication they could give him other than Advil.

He'd nearly passed out while they took x-rays of his broken arm and dug the gravel from his face. They set and cast his arm and he had blacked out.

Trey woke in the hospital bed, Carolyn at his side in a plastic chair, Alan fast asleep in her lap.

"You should go," he whispered.

She looked up at him and smiled. "How do you feel?"

Trey blinked and then winced. His arm still hurt like hell, but at least the bones no longer clicked together. "Like I'm broken."

She nodded. "I didn't want to leave until you woke up. I—" She swallowed. "I left you alone last time, and I'm not going to do that again."

He smiled, wishing he could hold out his hand to her, feel her fingers entwined in his. But the thought of moving the arm brought fresh stabs of pain.

"I know I'm not alone, Carolyn," he whispered. "Why don't you take Alan home?"

A tear welled up in her eye and she nodded. "You're going to be okay here?"

"I'm going to be okay. I'm sure Kinkaid will be here soon."

Carolyn sniffed back a sob. Alan twitched in her arms. "I'll come by tomorrow?"

"Call me," Trey said. "You have Kinkaid's number too?"

"Yes," she whispered.

Alan murmured something and his arms tightened around her neck.

She patted his shoulder. "Alan?" she said. "It's time to go home."

"Where's Daddy?" the boy said.

"I'm right here, kiddo," Trey said.

Alan turned to him, a sad smile on his face. "You look hurt. But you look better than you did." Alan's smile turned into a frown. "I'm sorry I didn't wait for you, Daddy. I didn't mean—"

"No," Trey said, "you did what you were supposed to do—you went home." Trey grimaced as a bolt of pain lashed up his broken arm. "If I had come the other way, I'd have seen you. It's my fault, kiddo, not yours."

"I'm sorry—"

"Hey," Trey said, "it's not your fault, okay?"

Alan nodded, sniffling. "Okay, Daddy." Alan loosened his arms from around Carolyn's shoulder and went around to the left side of Trey's bed. His blue eyes locked with Trey's. "Come home soon, Daddy. Get better." The boy hugged him.

Trey squeezed Alan, managing to hold his emotions in check. "I will." The boy let go of him, smiling. "Now go home and sleep."

Alan nodded to him. "You sleep too." Alan tousled Trey's hair. Trey chuckled. Alan squeezed his father's shoulder and then made his way to the door.

Carolyn kissed Trey on the forehead. "You call me. I'll keep my mobile on. You call," she whispered and kissed him again, "if you need me. I'll be here." Trey smiled at her but said nothing. She wiped a tear from her eye and turned toward Alan. "Let's go, kiddo." Alan looked back at Trey from the doorway, a tired smile on his face. He waved to Trey and Trey waved back with his left hand.

Then they were gone.

Closing his eyes, Trey shifted to try and find a comfortable position. His arm itched and ached. When Kinkaid arrived, maybe they'd finally get him some meds that worked.

Kinkaid.

As Carolyn had driven him to the ER, he'd called Kinkaid through gritted teeth. He told her he'd hurt himself and Carolyn was taking him to the hospital. "I want to come in," he'd told her.

After a moment of silence, she'd asked if Trey was committing himself.

Eyes scrunched together through the pain, Trey had told her "Yes."

He wanted to sleep, wanted to wake up and find himself back on the couch. The alarm would wake him from his nap, and he'd walk to meet Alan as always. No ice cream man; no bells shattering the silence of the winter afternoon. Just he and his son walking the path back home, and Carolyn joining them for dinner; everything as it should be.

He let out a hiss through his teeth. The arm hurt, dammit. His face burned from where they removed bits of gravel and glass.

"Scooby-dooby-doo" a voice sang.

Trey opened his eyes and scanned the room. No one was there. "Fuck you, Scooby," he whispered.

As he closed his eyes once more, he realized he was afraid to fall asleep.

Chapter
Twenty-One

Alan slept on the ride home. Carolyn cast nervous glances at him as she drove through the evening rain. The boy had been frantic on the way to pick up Trey, asking a million questions about his father. She'd calmed him as best she could, but he was still a nervous wreck when they finally put Trey in the car and headed to the hospital.

But, she marveled, Alan was always a different boy in Trey's presence. Whenever he saw his father, no matter how weak or muddled he was, Alan became less prone to panic. She smiled at him in the rearview mirror, all buckled up in the seat belt and snoring. Alan became an adult when Trey had his "bad times."

They had spent a long time explaining to Alan his father's condition. Alan didn't seem to understand it all—he only knew that sometimes Daddy needed help. That had brought something very protective out of the boy.

She made her way into the neighborhood, cursing the rain in silence. The pit pat of the drops against the windshield was the only sound in the car, apart from Alan's soft snores. She'd have to put him into bed and she had no doubt he'd fall asleep again immediately. She hoped he wouldn't wake up until morning.

The questions would come, and then worry, and concern. She wasn't sure she had the strength to deal with that.

Carolyn wiped a single tear from her cheek. She wound through the streets and turned onto Moss. The cold, light rain had barely puddled against the old concrete curb. She parked the car beneath the stripped oak canopies and the overgrown green pines and turned off the ignition.

"Mom?" Alan's sleep addled voice said from the back seat.

"Yes, Alan?" She glanced back at him in the rearview mirror.

He frowned at her. "Daddy's going to be gone for a little while?"

She nodded. The pain in Alan's voice was enough to force her to choke back a sob. "Yes, Daddy's going to be gone for a little while. But I'll take you to see him tomorrow if he's well enough, okay?"

"You mean today?" he asked with a sideways smile.

The sigh that escaped her was frustrated and relieved at the same time. Alan always knew when to be a smart-ass to make her smile. "Yes, hon. Today. We'll go see Daddy today. After I get home from work."

Alan nodded. "I walk home from school by myself?"

"No, I think I'll be able to pick you up. I'll drop you off at school and come get you if I can."

"Okay, Mommy."

"Is that okay?"

"Yes, Mommy," he said, his smile widening. "I'm a big boy. I'm not afraid to walk home if I have to. But," he said, his face stern, "don't tell Daddy I said that. I like that he walks me to and from school."

She nodded, a genuine smile on her face. "He loves you, Alan. He's very protective of you."

"I know." Alan's smile faltered. "Mommy?" he asked, unbuckling his seat belt.

"Yes?"

Alan reached for the door handle, his hand clasping it, but not pulling. "Daddy's going to come back to us, right?"

The sinking feeling in the pit of her stomach returned, as did the sob threatening to choke off her air. "Yes. Daddy'll be back."

"Good," Alan said. "I like my Daddy."

"I know you do," she said, casting her face downward to hide another tear.

"Mommy?" Alan asked.

"Yes?"

"Can you unlock the door? I'm very sleepy."

She looked up at him in the rearview mirror, wiping away another tear. "Yes, baby," she said. She opened the door and climbed out into the rain. The canopy of pines and skeletal oaks blocked most of the drops, but she still felt the cold sting of water against her bare skin. She walked to Alan's door and opened it. Alan climbed out from the car and shivered.

"Let's go inside, Mommy."

She was glad for the rain as they walked to the front door. She didn't want Alan to see her tears.

Chapter
Twenty-Two

"Trey?" a female voice asked from the doorway. "Trey, you awake?"

He opened his eyes. The room was dark. At some point, he'd fallen asleep. He guessed one of the nurses had clicked off the lights. The figure at his open door was backlit by the bright hallway fluorescents. "Who are you?" he croaked.

"It's Kinkaid, you idiot."

"Oh," Trey said. "Should have known by your bedside manner," he chuckled. "Come on in, the lithium's fine."

She clucked her tongue, walking into the darkened room. He could barely make out her features, but saw she was wearing a leather jacket and blue jeans. The jacket was still zipped up. With night in full swing, he'd no doubt it had become very cold outside. "There's no lithium here," she said. "Nothing but cuckoo juice."

"Yeah," he whispered. "I can tell."

Folding her hands, Kinkaid leaned forward. "How's your arm?"

"Hurts like fucking hell," he said. "But I guess that's to be expected."

She nodded. "I'm trying to figure out some pain meds for you, but right now, I think it's best if we keep your system clean. Can you deal?"

"I can deal," he responded and yawned. "What fucking time is it anyway?"

"It's two a.m., slugger. Afraid I couldn't get here any sooner."

He harrumphed. "Again with the beside manner."

She shrugged. "Had to sober up."

"I'll bet," Trey said. "Us crazy people driving you to drink?"

"Something like that," she laughed. "Now. You want to talk about it?"

He told her everything, about waking up and finding Alan gone. The panic, the visions of the fiend in the van, running to catch it, and then falling to the concrete. As the words poured from his mouth, he realized she looked strange without a notebook in front of her and a pen scratching marks into the sheets of paper.

When Trey finished, they sat in silence. He looked down at the bedsheets, and then drew the covers around himself. He'd begun to shiver during the retelling, goose pimples prickling his skin.

The silence was broken only by soft footsteps in the hall, the occasional monotone of some words over the hospital intercom, and muffled voices from the nurses' station.

Kinkaid clucked her tongue. "Why'd you nap?" she asked in flat, toneless voice.

Trey blinked at her. The dim light cast from the hallway barely illuminated one side of her face. He saw the frown on her face and smiled in the dark. "I don't know," he said. "Felt tired. Thought I'd just lay down."

"But you slept through the alarm?"

"Yeah, it was still going off when I woke up."

She nodded. "Did you dream?"

He opened his mouth to respond, and then closed it. Did he dream? Something about "Scooby-Doo?" The vision was murky, just random images without cohesion. He shook his head. "I think so, but I don't remember anything. Something about childhood. But—" He paused, frowning in the near darkness. "But I don't really remember it."

She nodded again. "What do you think about the ice cream man?" she asked.

The ice cream man. The fiend. The ghoul. The man in the gore covered, offal dripping jumpsuit. He shook the image away from his mind.

"He's not real," Trey said.

She blinked at him.

"I mean, he's real. He was there. And he called Alan. But he's not some...thing. He's a person."

"That's a good start," she whispered. "I want you to sleep now, if you can. I'm going to have the nurses wake you every couple of hours and check on you." She reached out a hand and patted his left arm. "I think you need to stay here a couple of days for observation, okay?"

Trey smiled. "No rubber room?"

"Not this time, mister." She rose from her chair. "The delusion has passed and I don't think you should be pissing in the corner if you know that." She leaned over and pulled the covers around him, readjusting the blanket on the bed. "Now, you looney," she said, "get some sleep. I'll come back later today and we'll talk again, okay?"

"Yeah," he whispered. She nodded to him and turned toward the door. "Thanks, doc."

"Have to keep you healthy," she said walking to the door. "You're my next paper in psychotics monthly."

Trey snorted as she disappeared into the hallway. He closed his eyes and drifted off to sleep.

Chapter
Twenty-Three

As she turned off the bathroom light, Carolyn stared into the bedroom's blackness. She heaved a sigh, pulled off the robe, and walked to the bed. She slipped beneath the sheets naked, shivering a little as she wrapped herself in the cold fabric. Trey was usually in bed before her, and the sheets were always warm with his heat.

She rolled onto her side, sniffing in the scent of his body still on his pillow. Another night with him gone. Another night without a partner.

This was the fourth time since they'd been married that he'd committed himself. The first two times were medication changes that backfired. But the last time was the scary one.

Carolyn still didn't quite understand what happened. She'd come home from work one day and found Alan inside the house, laying in the middle of the floor and surrounded by his toys. Scooby-Doo was playing on the television. Alan was four years old. "Where's Daddy?" she asked Alan.

"Hi, Mommy. Daddy's outside." He smiled up at her and giggled. "Daddy's pretending."

"Pretending?" she asked.

Alan nodded and giggled again.

She felt a cold stab of fear in the pit of her stomach. "What do you mean he's pretending?"

"He's pretending there's someone to talk to."

A shiver raced up her spine. "Okay, champ," she said in a broken voice. "Can you stay out of trouble for a few minutes?"

He nodded. "I've been a good boy. I want a popsicle."

"When I get back, we'll talk about it, okay?"

He went back to playing with his toys.

Carolyn took a deep breath and slipped out into the sunroom. She stopped as soon as she slid the glass door closed. Voices. Two distinct voices. She froze in the middle of the room. Trey and whomever he was talking to were around the corner and in the middle of the deck. She couldn't see them, and suddenly she didn't want to.

"I don't understand why you're so angry," Trey's voice said.

Without a pause, another voice spoke, sending chills down her spine. "You don't understand?" the alien voice growled. It's timbre was so unlike Trey's, deep beyond measure, somehow a mix of a growl and a scream. "You broke the rules"

Trey let out a sob. "No, I haven't broken—"

"You forfeit the boy."

"No, goddammit!" Trey screamed. "You leave him the fuck alone."

She shivered as the other voice, the thing that wasn't Trey, loosed a low chuckle. "You brought him here, Trey. You made him. And you didn't ask permission."

"Fuck you," Trey whispered. "I'm not giving him to you."

"It doesn't matter," the other whispered. "I'll take him anyway."

"Fuck you!" Trey yelled.

Carolyn took a step backward. There was the sound of flesh against metal and the tinkle of shattering glass.

Carolyn threw open the screen door with a single sharp palm to the latch. The pneumatic piston broke from the impact, but she didn't notice. She turned through the threshold and stopped, her mouth open.

Trey stood before the patio table, his hand pounding the metal frame. Shattered glass covered the deck in front of him, slivers of it caught in his hair. His right hand streamed blood from several open wounds. But it was the expression on his face that chilled her. His teeth were bared, saliva spitting from his mouth, as he let loose punch after punch into the twisted metal.

"Trey!"

"Die, you fucker!" he screamed at the table, smashing his fist again into the beige frame.

The metal bent further, screeching under the assault. The table wobbled and slid backwards until it rested against the house wall.

"Don't you dare fucking touch him!" he screamed again.

Carolyn ran forward, putting her arm around Trey's waist. Trey screamed again and turned, his elbow connecting with her chin and knocking her off balance.

The world went grey and she found herself falling, her ass hitting the unforgiving deck surface. The crash of pain knocked the breath from her lungs. She went down, head colliding with the deck, and for a moment, the world went away.

"Carolyn!" Trey's voice said in the distance. The blackness slowly receded. Her husband's face was inches from her own. His voice was choked with tears, droplets falling from the end of his nose and landing on her neck. "Carolyn, Goddammit, wake up," he whispered.

"Trey?" she asked, her voice groggy and broken.

A wan smile filled his face. "Goddammit, Carolyn. Goddammit," he whispered. He hugged her. "I called 9-1-1. They'll be here soon."

She wiped at her nose with a lazy hand, felt it come away wet. She turned slightly, staring at the bright crimson smear staining her fingers. "Trey?" she asked again.

"Yes, baby?" he sniffed back more tears.

"You called 9-1-1?"

"Yes, baby. I did."

"Help me up," she said softly.

"Baby, I don't think—"

"Help me up," she said in a low growl.

Trey stiffened, but said nothing. He stood from his kneeling position and bent at the waist. Bright red blood still dripped down his right hand.

As she put her hands in his, she felt the shards of glass caked in his skin, but he didn't wince when she pressed against him. She rose as he pulled her to her feet. Carolyn struggled to remain standing, her balance wavering. Trey tried to put his hands on her waist. She slapped at them, glaring into his eyes. The hurt and confused expression on his face increased her anger. She leaned forward and slapped his cheek. His right hand flew up to his face and he backed up a few steps.

"Carolyn?" he asked. "What—"

"You. Stay. The. Fuck. Away. From. Alan," she said, her finger punching into his stomach with each word. "And you stay the fuck away from me."

A fresh run of tears filled his eyes.

The furnace of anger within her made her feel as though she'd explode at any second. "You wait right fucking here and don't fucking move, or I'm sending you to fucking jail."

Trey sobbed, his legs wobbling. He moved to the deck banister, leaning hard against it.

She slowly backed away from him, heading toward the screen door. "Stay," she said, as though talking to a bad dog.

Trey said nothing and didn't move.

The ambulance and the cops arrived soon after. When the paramedics reached Trey, he was slumped in one of the deck chairs in shock. The blood loss from the open artery in his hand was too extreme for them to do anything besides rush him to the hospital.

She watched as they took him away on a stretcher, an oxygen mask on his face. As they put him in the ambulance, he reached out his left hand toward her. "Carolyn," he said through the mask. "What happened?"

She burst into tears as the doors closed and the ambulance left the street. When the cops tried to take her statement, she waved them off, telling them to meet her at the hospital. They left her there, still covered in Trey's blood. Alan had started crying the moment Carolyn had come in. She cooed at him, carrying him to the couch. They sat there, Alan in her arms, face buried in her shoulder, her head resting against his.

"Where's my Daddy?" Alan had asked. Carolyn started to answer him, but he cut her off. "I want my Daddy back," Alan sobbed.

The vision of Trey's horrified expression when she slapped him, his ashen face as he called to her through the oxygen mask, and the broken, lost, hurt sound of his voice, flashed through her mind. That was Trey. Not the man who'd been smashing the table, the man who'd elbowed her in the face, the screaming madman on the deck.

"I want Daddy back, too," she whispered.

Once she had calmed Alan, and herself, they left for the hospital. They found Trey in the ER, already in a bed with a blood bag hanging from a metal stand. One of the cops from the house stood by the bed. "Are you prepared to make a statement?"

She pulled a chair up to Trey's bed, and placed Alan in it.

Trey's eyes fluttered. "Alan?" he asked in a whisper.

"Daddy," the boy replied.

Trey smiled and then closed his eyes again.

Carolyn fought hard to keep her voice steady and forced a smile. "Alan?" He turned to her in the chair, his face sad, but calm. "Can you watch over Daddy for a minute?"

He smiled back at her. "Yes, Mommy."

She nodded to him and looked at the cop. "Can we talk outside?"

The cop smiled at the boy and then looked back at her. "Sure, Ma'am."

The two of them walked out into the hallway. A stretcher passed by them and the noise in the ER increased. The cop led her to a small out of the way corner.

"What do you need to know?" she asked as he pulled out a

battered notepad.

"Ma'am? Your husband called 9-1-1." She nodded to him. "Do you know why?"

"I— I passed out?" she asked.

The cop tapped a pen on the notepad. "You don't know?" She blinked at him and then shook her head. The sad smile on his face faded into a thin line. "Your husband said someone hit you."

Carolyn opened her mouth and then closed it. The officer stared at her, his pen still tapping against the notepad. "Did Trey say who?" The officer said nothing. What does he want me to say? she wondered. "Officer..."

"Hutchins," the humorless cop said.

"Officer Hutchins?" Carolyn asked. "Did Trey say who hit me?"

Hutchins said nothing.

With an exasperated sigh, Carolyn put her arms across her chest. "Okay. I get it," she whispered. "You think I've got battered woman syndrome or some shit like that."

"Did your husband strike you, Ma'am?"

She blinked at him again. "Whoever hit me was not my husband." She punctuated the last three words.

"Then who hit you?" Hutchins' eyes glittered.

Carolyn leaned forward. "I. Don't. Know."

The officer nodded. "You're not going to tell me the truth, are you?"

She smiled at him. "I already did, sir."

He nodded again. "Your husband," he said with another sigh, "called 9-1-1 and reported that you'd been attacked. He said the attacker was still in the house, and that we needed to help you." He paused. "I find that kind of interesting," Hutchins said. "Not that we needed to help him, but help you."

She shivered. "I don't see what's so important about that." Her voice trembled with each syllable.

He smiled at her. "Of course you don't. Do you know how your husband hurt his hand?"

Trey, screaming at the top of his lungs, fist battering into the table's broken glass and metal frame. His face filled with panic, fear and rage, his hand throwing up great loops of blood with each punishing blow.

"He accidentally put his hand through some glass."

"Accidentally," Hutchins said to himself and scrawled into his notepad. "That's very interesting, Ma'am. He told us he broke it," Hutchins said, flipping the notepad back a page, "while he was defending the boy from the attacker." Carolyn opened her mouth and then closed it again. Hutchins nodded. "Now," he said, placing the notepad in his front pocket, "you want to tell me what really happened, Ma'am? Because I'm getting a little frustrated with the run-around."

Carolyn dropped her eyes. "My husband is ill," she said softly. "He—" She swallowed hard. "He has a mental disorder and sometimes he sees things that aren't there."

Brows furrowed, Hutchins narrowed his eyes. "He hallucinates?" Hutchins whispered. She nodded. "Then he was—"

"Protecting us," she said softly.

"From what?" Hutchins asked.

"I don't know," Carolyn said, wiping a tear from her eye. "Look, I don't want to press charges—"

"Lady?" Hutchins said, hands on his hips, "that's your business. And maybe it's none of mine, but you should keep yourself and that kid as far away from that guy as possible."

A flush of anger filled her, her vision tinged with crimson. "It. Is. None. Of. Your. Business."

Hutchins took a step back, raising his hands. "Ma'am, you don't—"

"Fuck you," she growled. "That's the father of my son, and he is my husband. And don't you dare fucking judge me or my family."

"Okay, I—"

"So you write down whatever the fuck you want," she whispered. "But I won't press charges." She glared at him, breathing through her nostrils. "If you'll excuse me, I'm going to see my husband." She walked past Hutchins, her heels clicking on the tile floor.

"Ma'am?" he called to her.

Carolyn didn't turn around, and said nothing as she re-entered the room. Alan was sleeping in the chair, his tiny hand clasped in Trey's. She smiled at them.

"Carolyn?" Trey asked in a whisper.

She leaned down and brushed her hand against his cheek. "Yes, honey?"

"Love you," he whispered. He closed his eyes and started snoring again.

She reached for his side of the bed, knowing he wasn't there. That first episode was ten times more frightening than this latest one. He'd gone away for several weeks, and she'd barely been able to bring herself to see him.

The bruise on her cheek had faded with time, just as the pain in her nose.

Trey. Protecting them from something that wasn't there. Four years ago. Four years without any major incident. She held back a sob.

"I miss you," she murmured.

Carolyn fell asleep, remembering the frenzied expression on his face, the blood flying from his hands as he protected them from a monster only he could see.

Chapter
Twenty-Four

"Alan."

His eyes snapped open and he stared into the darkness.

The rain had stopped pattering against the sides of the house, leaving only the sound of the heater.

"Alan," a voice whispered from the side of the bed.

Alan shivered beneath the warm blankets. He knew if he looked toward the voice, he'd see nothing.

"Alan," the voice whispered again.

He scrunched his eyes together and listened to the mad drumbeat of his heart in his ears.

"There is no Closet Man," the voice chuckled in the darkness. "But there is an Ice Cream Man."

His eyes flew open and he turned his head to the left side of the bed. Two gleaming yellows globes glowed in the darkness.

Alan threw the covers off the bed and flung himself toward the nightstand. Unable to breathe, he snapped on the lamp. The darkness was obliterated in an instant, leaving him staring at an empty room.

"I'm under the bed," the thing whispered.

"No, you're not," Alan whispered back, his words broken by rapid breaths. "You're not here," he said. Fighting back the urge to run screaming from the room, he dropped to all fours, his eyes scanning beneath the bed. Nothing was there. "You're not real," Alan said and stood. Shivering from fear, Alan rolled up the blankets and dragged them toward the door. "You're not real," he whispered to the room, closing the door behind him.

Chapter
Twenty-Five

It was still dark in her bedroom when she opened her eyes. Her alarm hadn't gone off yet. Her hand reached for Trey but found only sheets and his pillow. "Not this morning," she said to herself and managed to choke back the sob.

Morning. Time to get up. Time to get Alan some breakfast and get him to school. Then she'd have to call about Trey.

She threw back the covers and stared at the ceiling. Cold air tingled across her bare legs and chest. She shivered. Hot shower. Yes, a hot shower was exactly the thing. Carolyn put her feet on the floor, slid out of bed, and started for the bathroom. A shape on the floor stopped her from putting her foot down.

Carolyn froze, unable to exhale. Covers? Blankets? The bundle twitched and rolled. Carolyn held back a scream. She stepped over the cloth-covered blob and into the bathroom. She flipped on the lights and turned, ready to face whatever it was.

A small hand rested on the floor, stretched outward from a Spiderman blanket. Carolyn finally managed to exhale, her heart beating so fast she thought it would explode. She moved toward

Alan, and then realized she was naked. Feeling embarrassed, she grabbed her robe from beside the bed and cinched it around herself.

She took a deep breath, forcing herself to calm down. Why the hell had that scared her? Just a bundle of blankets, dammit, with her sleeping son beneath it all.

Once she felt her heart rate had slowed to an acceptable rhythm, she knelt down beside Alan. She peeled back the blanket and stared into his sleeping face. He didn't look peaceful. Instead, his teeth were locked tight, his eyes scrunched together.

"Alan?" she whispered.

The boy didn't move.

Knowing it was going to hurt, she slipped her arms beneath him and lifted. She grunted with the effort and ignored the pain in her lower back as she placed him on the bed.

"Alan?" she asked again.

The boy said nothing. With a sigh, she straightened him on the bed, practically dragging his head toward Trey's pillow. She covered him in blankets and turned back to the bathroom.

"Want Daddy to protect me from the ice cream man," Alan mumbled from behind her.

She spun on her heel and stared at the bed. Alan rolled over onto his side, his breathing deep and level. Her heart rate had risen again, hammering in her chest.

"Alan?" she asked.

He didn't respond.

She closed the bathroom door with care, ensuring it wouldn't bang and wake him up. He had at least another hour of sleep before she needed to push him out of bed.

The ice cream man.

"Fuck," she whispered.

Was Alan already starting to see the same things Trey did? Was he going to end up in an institution talking to people who weren't there?

She shivered. "Just sleep talk," she whispered to herself.

She pulled off the robe and stepped into the shower, trying to take deep, even breaths.

Chapter

Twenty-Six

She'd awakened Alan from her bed by stroking his cheek and saying his name. The boy's eyes fluttered open and he stared into her face, a look of surprise that transformed into a thin smile.

"Good morning, Mommy," he said.

"Good morning, baby." Her hand still brushed his cheek. "Do you know where you are?"

"In your room," he blushed.

"Yes, you are," she giggled. "Do you remember why?"

Alan yawned and put his small hands over his face. "No," he said through his fingers, the word muddled and muffled.

She nodded and squeezed his shoulder. "It's time for you to get dressed and ready for school."

He dropped his hands from his face. "Okay, Mommy." Carolyn stood up from the bed to leave just as his hand reached and grabbed the hem of her robe. "Mommy?" he asked.

She turned back to him with a sigh. "Yes, Alan?"

"Will Daddy come back to keep us safe?"

Her brow furrowed. "Keep us safe. From what?"

Alan frowned. "I don't know."

"Get dressed, kiddo. Have to get some breakfast in you."

Alan smiled and slid off the bed.

She watched him leave the room and then closed the bedroom door. As she turned from the door, the smile faded. "Will Daddy keep us safe?" Alan had asked. She shivered.

While she dressed, she thought of all the things she had to do. First, call work and tell them she wouldn't be in. Second, get Alan to school. Third...

It was the third one that worried her. She had to call Kinkaid, find out Trey's condition, and whether or not she could see him. But even if Kinkaid said no, she was going to be there, dammit.

Not like last time.

Carolyn picked out a clean pair of jeans and a sweatshirt. No makeup. Well, maybe a little. She slipped on the jeans, a practical bra, and then the sweatshirt.

With a sigh, she stared at herself in the mirror. A worry line was forming and her eyes had dark circles. Four hours of sleep. Fuck. She wondered how much sleep Trey had managed.

Would he still be in the hospital bed, his skull wrapped in bandages? She took in a sharp breath and then let it out slowly. "I'll see you, Trey," she whispered. "I promise."

Carolyn braided her long hair, tying the end with expert fingers. She stared at herself in the mirror. She looked like shit, but she knew Trey wouldn't care and on a morning like this, she didn't give a damn who saw her. She flipped off the light and headed downstairs.

Alan was at the breakfast table, munching on cereal. She walked up behind him, and squeezed his shoulder. He turned around to her, his teeth still crunching.

"Are you going to see Daddy today?"

"Don't talk with your mouth full, son," she said with a smile. "Yes." She headed to the coffee maker. "I'll see him while you're at school."

Alan clinked his spoon against the glass bowl. "Can I see him tonight?"

She paused and then clicked the coffee maker button. "I don't know if you can see him tonight, baby."

"But—"

"I know, Alan." She turned toward him. "I'll ask."

Alan nodded, his smile creeping back. "You'll tell Daddy I love him?"

"Of course." She turned back to the coffee maker and then stopped. "Alan?"

He looked up at her as he put another spoonful in his mouth.

"Do you know what Daddy is supposed to protect us from?"

He opened his mouth to speak, then closed it, continued crunching, and swallowed. "The Ice Cream Man," Alan whispered.

"Who?" she asked, her heart rate rising and thumping in her ears. "The Ice Cream Man, Mommy. Daddy doesn't like him." Alan frowned. "I don't like him either."

She stepped away from the coffee maker and sat down at the breakfast table. She thrummed her fingers on the glass surface. "You've never met the Ice Cream Man."

Alan shook his head. "I saw him. When we picked up Daddy yesterday." Alan frowned. "I don't like him."

The Ice Cream Man.

Carolyn barely remembered the guy. She had driven the car as fast as she dared through the winding main drag of the subdivision. When she reached the intersection of Pine and Crystal, the ice cream van was parked at the side of the tree-lined road.

A few people stood around the white Econoline van. She pulled into the side street and parked the car.

"Alan, stay here," she whispered and opened the door. She ran toward the van.

The man in the cream colored overalls stood at least a head above everyone else. He stared down at the prone figure at his feet, his white pie hat swept forward so that it nearly covered his eyes. He looked up at her as she ran toward him.

"Ma'am?" the man said in a high-pitched voice. "Are you the

wife?"

She knelt down before Trey without looking up at the man in the overalls. "Yes," she said. Trey lay on the concrete, eyes closed. "Trey?" she asked. His eyes fluttered. Blood trickled down his scalp from where his head had hit the ground. "Trey?"

"He ran at me," the man said.

Carolyn glanced upward. She had difficulty making out the man's face beneath the shadow of the pork pie hat. His long nose and pouty lips were all she could see, besides his fat jowls. His eyes were perfectly hidden.

"He gave me quite a fright," the Ice Cream Man said in a monotone.

She glanced back down at Trey. "How long has he been like this?"

"About ten minutes," the man said in that same expressionless voice. "Lady? I have to go," the man said. "I'm a little out of sorts."

She looked up at him. The man rubbed his hands together, the friction against his palms sounding like sandpaper.

"Yes, of course," she said softly. "I'll take him to the hospital. If you can help me get him to the car?"

"Sorry, ma'am," the man said. "Hurt my back years ago. Can't help you there." He looked into the crowd of people. "Can one of you help this lady?" he asked in that same flat voice.

"Yeah," a young man said. "Here," he stepped forward to Carolyn and grabbed one of Trey's arms. "I got him," he said.

Carolyn looked up at the goateed teenager and smiled at him as best she could. "Thank you," she said.

They lifted Trey by his arms, bringing him to his feet. Trey's eyelids fluttered again, enough for him to hold Carolyn's stare. His legs took some of the weight as they walked to the car.

Carolyn turned her head to thank the Ice Cream Man, but he was already in his van. The word "YUMMY" was spelled in bright, crimson letters on the back of the van. She felt a chill as it made its way up the street, a thin, broken line of blue exhaust spitting from the tailpipe.

She stared at Alan across the breakfast table. "Did you see

something, Alan?"

Alan shrugged. "He hides his eyes," the boy said softly. "He doesn't look like somebody nice."

With a nod, Carolyn forced a smile. "You're a smart kid." He'd smiled back at her. "Now hurry up and finish breakfast. We're going to be late."

The drive to the hospital had been quiet and uneventful. She pulled into the parking lot and realized she couldn't remember the drive at all, only the thoughts in her head. Alan had kissed her goodbye as he left the car, making her once again promise to tell Daddy he loved him. The hospital sat before her, its lights visible in the darkness of the overcast day. The weather was finally supposed to break later that afternoon, but Carolyn could scarcely believe it.

She pulled out her phone, unlocked it, and found Kinkaid's number. With a tap, she brought the phone to her ear. It rang twice.

"This is Doctor Kinkaid."

"Hi," Carolyn said, "this is Carolyn Leger, I—"

"Carolyn," the doctor's voice answered. She could hear the smile in the woman's voice. "I suppose you're calling about Trey."

She nodded and said "Yes, I am."

"Trey's okay. He's been quiet this morning. His concussion isn't as bad as we thought. I haven't really had a chance to assess his state this morning, but the nurses say he's doing okay."

"I'm here at the hospital," she said. "I was hoping I could see him."

There was a pause. "Okay. I'll, um, call the nurses' station in a minute and let them know."

Carolyn frowned. "You sounded a little hesitant there. Is there a problem?"

"Um, not really," Kinkaid said. "I just want you to be prepared. I know what kind of...hallucinations he's had. I assume he told you as well."

"Yes."

"Okay. Then I want you to be prepared that he may see those

again. I'm just not sure what kicked them off. So do me a favor,"
Kinkaid said, taking a deep breath, "let's try not to get him excited
for the moment. Okay?"

"Okay," Carolyn agreed.

"Keep the visit pretty short, please. I'm going to come in later this
morning and talk to him."

Carolyn felt a sob trying to break its way past her throat. She
managed to choke it back. When she spoke again, her voice quivered.
"Okay," she sniffed.

"Carolyn? It's going to be okay. He's been resilient in the past and
you and Alan have a lot to do with that."

"I abandoned him last time," Carolyn said, unable to hide the
tears in her voice.

Kinkaid sighed on the other end of the line. "No, Carolyn. You
didn't. If you'd abandoned him, you never would have allowed him
back in your house. And I can't tell you how much courage that took."

Carolyn stifled another sob.

"Carolyn? Be strong, dear. You're doing fine. He's going to get
better and he'll be back home before you know it."

"Okay," Carolyn said, wiping her eyes. "Just a little visit."

"Yes," Kinkaid said back to her. "Just a little one."

"Okay."

"You all right?"

"Yes," Carolyn lied, wiping at her eyes again. "I'm okay."

"All right. Call me anytime, okay?"

"Yes," Carolyn said.

"Good. I'll call the nurses' station and let them know, all right?"
"Yes."

"Have a good visit. Trey loves you. Help him get better, okay?"
Carolyn didn't respond. "Bye, Carolyn." The phone beeped as the
connection ended.

For a moment, Carolyn sat in the seat, the phone still held to her
ear. She lowered the phone to her lap and stared at the hospital.

Short visit, she thought to herself. Short visit. Wasn't that like abandoning him all over again? Just walking in and saying hello?

"Christ," she muttered aloud.

She unfastened the seat belt, opened the door, and stepped out into the humid winter air.

Chapter
Twenty-Seven

Trey opened his eyes and immediately felt ice cold. The temperature in the room seemed to have dropped at least thirty degrees. The blankets wrapped around his legs were little protection. He'd come awake because of the sound near his left ear.

Click. Click. Grind. Trey turned to his left and choked back a scream. It stood there, towering above him, its shadow swallowing him whole.

"What—" he asked in a breathy whisper.

The ghoul. Its misshapen jaws clacked together and then ground, the canines protruding from gray lips. Drops of saliva fell as its mottled tongue flicked in and out.

"I told you I'd come for you," the thing said. It wore the ice cream man's uniform, cream colored overalls, pork pie hat sitting jauntily on its crusted and matted scalp. The yellow eyes danced with crimson in their centers, the color swirling like flame. "You didn't ask permission, boy," the thing said.

Trey choked back another scream. "I'm sorry," he whimpered. "Don't put me—"

The thing smiled and leered. It bent down, close to him, cutting off his thoughts, his speech.

"You're going back with me," it breathed. "You're going back with me and this time I won't let you out." The crimson pupils faded and turned black.

"No," Trey whispered. "I won't—"

The thing laughed, its eyes turning green. "Yes, you will. You'll do everything I tell you," the ghoul said, stretching out a taloned finger to scrape against Trey's chest. "Or I'll split you in half like I should have all those years ago. Bad boy," the thing growled. "Bad, dirty little boy."

"No," he whispered. He closed his eyes. "You're not real." He felt its hot, rancid breath against his ear. Its jaws clicked. A single drop of saliva wet his cheek, stinging his flesh. "You're not real!" he screamed aloud.

"You," it tittered, "you are the one who's not real."

"Fuck you!" his voice broke on the last syllable. He opened his eyes, his fists ready to strike, and stared into the ghoul's rotted face. "Fuck—" The overhead lights flipped on.

"Trey!" a voice yelled from the doorway.

Trey whipped his head around, fists still raised. Carolyn stood in the doorway with one of the many nurses that had checked on him during the night. "It's here!" he yelled and whipped back toward the left side of the bed.

There was nothing there. Nothing.

Carolyn and the nurse walked in. He turned around to face them. "It was right there," he whispered.

"What was, Mr. Leger?" the nurse asked. She had reached the IV cart and picked up the clipboard at the base of his bed. Her deft fingers reached around his wrist, checking his pulse against her watch. "Can you tell me?" she asked softly.

"The—" He looked over the nurse's shoulder at Carolyn. Her face was ashen. Trey thought he saw a tear hiding at the edge of her eyes. "It—" He swallowed hard. "It was just a dream." He let his head fall back into the pillow.

"You're very cold," the nurse said, pulling the blankets back atop him. "You may have a fever. I'll come back in a few minutes and check your temperature," she said, marking something on the chart. She looked at Carolyn. "Short visit, okay?"

Carolyn nodded to her and the nurse walked out of the room. She stared at Trey, a weak smile breaking through her deep frown.

"Hello, baby," she said softly.

He smiled back at her, his forehead still covered in sweat.

Carolyn walked to the side of his bed and pulled up a chair. She sat down and placed a hand in his. He gently squeezed her. "You have a bad dream?"

Trey nodded. "Yeah. Bad dream."

"Can you tell me about it?"

Trey opened his mouth, and then closed it. "No, honey, I can't." He could have. He wanted to. But she had seen enough already. She didn't need to know he saw the damned ice cream man in the room. She didn't need to know that. Not now. "How are you?" he whispered.

"I'm okay," Carolyn said with a smile. "Just worried about you." She gave his hand a healthy squeeze. "Alan said to tell you he loves you." She laughed a little. "He was very adamant."

The smile on Trey's face didn't feel awkward or fake. He imagined the boy telling his mother that, face stern and serious. "You'll tell him I said I love him too. Won't you?" She nodded. "Okay, good."

"He wants to come see you," she whispered.

Trey broke her stare and looked down at the cast on his arm. "I don't think that's a good idea right now." He heard her sigh and turned back to her. "Maybe in a day or two."

She nodded. "Dr. Kinkaid said she's going to check on you later this morning."

"I'm sure she will," Trey said.

Carolyn giggled. "She's your girlfriend, isn't she?"

Trey snorted. "Yeah, I'm her centerfold for psycho weekly." He watched her laugh, loving the way her lips curved upward and the sound of her voice. So many things he wanted to tell her. So many things. "She's a good quack." Trey grinned.

She nodded. "Yeah, I like her, Trey." Carolyn paused, staring down at their clasped hands. "I'm not leaving you." She slowly raised her eyes to his. "You know that, right?"

"Yes, baby," he whispered. "You never have."

"Before," she said, "last time. I stopped—"

Trey shook his head. "Baby? I— I hurt you last time. There's no reason to—"

"I was afraid," her voice choked. "I was afraid—"

"I know you were." He squeezed her hand, but she didn't look at him. "Carolyn?"

She nodded, but didn't meet his eyes.

"Carolyn? Please look at me?" Slowly, she raised her head. He smiled at her. "It's okay, baby. I know you were scared. I'm just happy you brought me home again."

"I will this time, too," she whispered. She leaned over and kissed his damp forehead.

"Mrs. Leger?" the nurse called to her from the doorway. Carolyn turned around. The nurse tapped her watch.

Carolyn nodded to her and then turned back to Trey. "I'm being kicked out."

Trey sighed. "I know. Goddamned Nurse Ratchet clones," he whispered. He paused for a moment, and then leered. "You think they'd let us get freaky in the bed?"

She laughed. "Maybe later." She kissed his forehead again. "Maybe I'll wear something more appropriate next time."

"Sure, baby. Sure. We can try and find a use for the bedpan."

"Eewww," she said. "I'm not sure I want to come back after that!"

They laughed together. "Go on, get out of here." He waved his good hand.

"Okay, baby. Call me when you have a chance?"

He nodded. "Assuming they don't put me in the rubber room, I will."

Carolyn stood and walked to the door. She turned back to him. "Alan misses you, baby. And so do I."

"I'll make sure to call you when I'm—" He swallowed hard. "When I'm ready to see Alan."

She nodded to him and waved. With that, she left the room.

Chapter
Twenty-Eight

A s with the ride to the hospital, she barely remembered the ride back. The moment she'd walked out of Trey's room, his terrified and shocked face flitted into her mind. He'd looked so lost, so desperate. What did he see to cause that, she wondered. He'd told her what he'd seen, but she couldn't really imagine it. Not what it looked like through his eyes.

For years, he'd rolled about the bed at night, dreaming his dark dreams and muttering in his sleep. Every time she woke at night from his moans and whispers, she'd see that same terrified expression on his face. But with him awake— Christ. What the fuck was so bad that it left him so shaken?

Carolyn pulled into the neighborhood and made her way down Pine. The tall pine trees, for which the road was named, swayed gently in the wind. She wound past Crystal, the intersection where Trey had collapsed. Carolyn forced herself to keep her eyes on the road. She didn't want to remember the blood on the concrete, or the crowd standing around Trey like he was some kind of circus attraction.

Alan had watched all that from the car. She choked back a sob.

He shouldn't have been exposed to that.

As she turned on to Moss, she slowed to a crawl. The van. The white van was in front of her house. Its back faced her, the scarlet word "YUMMY!" staring at her with gleeful malice.

She shivered as she pulled around the van. She didn't dare look through the darkened windshield as she pulled into the driveway. Once the car was off, she looked in the rearview mirror. There was no movement inside the van. Carolyn pulled out her cellphone, hands shaking.

She typed in the code to unlock the phone three times before she got it right and scrolled through the address book. She pressed on the phone's screen and put the phone to her ear. "Please be home, please be home, please be home," she whispered to herself with each ring.

"Hey, Carolyn. How are you?"

"Dick," she whispered.

There was a pause. "Are you okay, dear?"

"You home?" she asked.

"Yeah. Carolyn, you sound scared. What's going on? Something happen to—"

"That van is in front of my house."

She heard Dick take a deep breath. "Where are you?" he said, his voice stern.

"In the driveway."

"Okay, Carolyn. I'm coming, okay?" She heard the jingle of a jacket zipper. "Stay put and keep the car doors locked." The line went dead.

Carolyn glued her eyes to the rearview mirror. The van sat silent at the curb, bright decals showing smiling children and pictures of candy and ice cream treats. There was a blur at the tinted driver side window. The tiniest movement.

She sucked in a deep breath. What if he was in her backyard? Or in the house? She shivered again. The idea of the tall man with the shadowed eyes hiding in her closet, under her bed, anywhere—

The van's door opened. The tall man stepped out. Carolyn sucked in a shuddering breath. The man closed the door and turned toward her. The ice cream man's clean, cream overalls seemed to glow in the dim sunlight. He stepped toward her, his hat slung low over his forehead, once again hiding his eyes.

As she watched, the man stopped and turned. Dick was walking across the street, a smile on his face. His blue windbreaker bulged at the side. Carolyn blew out a shuddering breath and unlocked the car door.

As she stepped from the vehicle, she heard Dick talking to the man. "How you doing?"

She watched the ice cream man shrug. His voice was raspy, choked with phlegm. "All right, I guess."

Dick walked to the man and offered his hand. "I'm Dick Dickerson."

Carolyn walked down the driveway to the side of the ice cream man. She watched as the two shook hands. "Reggie," the man said in his raspy voice.

"Hi," Carolyn said, walking to stand beside Dick. She still couldn't quite make out Reggie's eyes. "I'm Carolyn," she said, extending her hand. The man dropped Dick's and immediately placed his large hand around hers. "You're Reggie?"

The man nodded, releasing her hand after a gentle shake. "Yes, ma'am."

Carolyn tried hard not to glance at Dick. She didn't want the ice cream man to see the look, to know she'd called Dick. "Nice to meet you," she said.

Reggie nodded. "Nice to meet you too."

"So," Dick said, causing Reggie to turn toward him, "what brings you here? Kids aren't out for another couple of hours yet."

There was an awkward pause as Reggie stared at him. The man's gloved hands rubbed together, sounding like sandpaper. "I came here," he said, turning toward Carolyn, "to apologize for taking off so fast yesterday." Carolyn blinked at him. "And to make sure your husband was okay."

She opened her mouth, but Dick spoke first. "What do you mean 'take off'?" he asked.

Reggie turned back to him with a sigh. "Her husband kind of... had a fit or something. He fell and hit his head on the concrete." The cream clad man sighed. "I, um, noticed he wore a medical bracelet. So I called the number on it." Neither Carolyn nor Dick said anything in the awkward silence. "I got word to Mrs. Carolyn—"

"Leger," she said softly.

Reggie turned toward her, the barest smile visible beneath the shade of his hat. "Mrs. Leger, that her husband had an accident."

Dick nodded. "So you—"

"Let me finish," the man said, his voice flat. "I waited until she got there. I wanted to make sure Mr. Leger was okay, but I was a little freaked out." He lowered his head. "He, um, looked like he was going to attack me or something."

Carolyn exchanged a quick glance with Dick. He blinked at her. She could tell he wanted to ask a question, but would hold it until after this. "I'm sure it was a little unsettling," she said. "I do appreciate your calling me, Mr.—"

"Reggie," the man said simply.

"Reggie," she agreed. "I appreciate your calling us and letting us know."

"Is your husband okay?" he asked, lifting his head just the slightest bit.

Through the shadow cast down upon his face, she saw that long nose again, the gray lips. "He broke his arm," she said. "And he has a concussion."

"What's wrong with him?" Reggie asked.

Dick laughed. "I'm sure that's none of your business."

"Oh," Reggie said. "My mistake."

For a moment, no one said anything. Carolyn and Dick exchanged glances again.

Reggie shuffled his feet. "All right," Reggie said, "I just wanted to make sure the man was okay." He extended his hand to Carolyn again. "Sorry it happened, ma'am. But it was nice to meet you."

Carolyn managed to put her hand in his again and shake it. "Both of you." Reggie offered his hand to Dick.

Dick was slow to take it, but squeezed hard once he did. Carolyn noticed Dick's eyes and knew there was little question as to whether or not he liked the ice cream man. "I'm sure," Dick said. He grinned at Reggie, but his eyes still burned.

"I'll be going," Reggie said. He headed back to the van and stepped inside. The engine started up, the tail pipe blowing a small puff of blue smoke into the winter morning. The two of them watched as the van drove into the cul-de-sac, rounded it, and headed back out into the neighborhood. They saw the barest glimmer of a wave through the passenger-side window as it passed.

"I don't like that guy," Dick whispered as the van disappeared.

Carolyn shivered. "Buy you a cup of coffee?" she said.

"Your place or mine?" he asked.

"Definitely mine," she said.

Dick placed a hand on her shoulder. "Yeah," he chuckled. "Your coffee rocks, mine always sucks."

She turned her head toward him and smiled.

"Come on," he said, "let's get out of this cold."

Chapter Twenty-Nine

"So he just collapsed?" Dick asked, a chocolate coffee biscuit rising to his mouth. He munched on the cookie with a satisfied "hmmm."

Carolyn sipped her coffee. "Yeah, I guess. He doesn't quite remember falling down."

Dick nodded. "Does he remember passing out in front of the house?"

Her fingers picked out one of the biscuits, sliding it into her mouth. She crunched the end and swallowed it. "Yeah, he does."

"Is it that guy? That Reggie?" Dick asked with a look of distaste.

"Yes," she said, wiping crumbs from her lips.

"Guy creeps me out," Dick said, pushing the rest of the cookie into his mouth. He brushed crumbs from his jacket and took a sip of coffee. "I think we should call the HOA, get him banned."

She harrumphed. "Good luck with that. Trey said the elementary school kids flock to him."

"Sure," Dick agreed. "But those damned bells. Man, they could wake the dead." He paused, staring into his coffee cup. "Think we could file a noise complaint"?

Carolyn stared past him to the window overlooking the deck. Fall leaves, brown and dead, littered its wooden surface. "I don't know. Is it really worth it?"

He shrugged. "Don't know. But that guy creeps me out," he said. "Just creeps me out."

She laughed. "You need a thesaurus."

With a grin, he picked up another coffee biscuit. "That's gonna cost you," he said, lifting it and then consuming it in one bite.

"Small price for the zing." She put her elbows on the table, resting her head on clenched fists. "What is it about him that creeps you out?"

Dick shrugged. "Don't know, exactly. But those tinted windows on the van... Who the hell does that? I mean, it's just— Well, it just makes me distrust him." Dick shook his head. "After meeting him today, I like him even less."

"The hat?"

Dick nodded. "Yeah, the way he keeps it down so low over his forehead you can barely see his eyes. And," Dick said, raising his hands in the air, "who the hell wears gloves like that? Did you feel his fingers through them? Christ," Dick said, "something wrong with that guy."

"What do you mean about his fingers?"

"I held him a bit tighter than you," Dick said, "they felt...wrong. I don't know how else to say it. Plus," he said, taking another cookie, "his voice sounds all jacked up. Like he's on the verge of dying or something." Dick shook his head. "Diseased."

Carolyn nodded. She'd heard the rattle in the man's chest as well, breathing as if through cheesecloth. "Okay, yeah, I don't like him either," Carolyn said.

Dick munched, holding up a finger, and then swallowed. "So, Trey's in the hospital?" he asked.

The tension from meeting the ice cream man had faded a bit, but it suddenly returned. When Dick left, she'd be all alone in the house until Alan came home. She nodded. "Yeah."

He clasped his hands around the coffee cup. "For the broken arm?"

"And for the...episode," she whispered.

Dick nodded. "None of my business, Carolyn. I like you guys a lot and just want to know you're safe." He thrummed his fingers on the table's surface. "Okay?"

"I appreciate that. I really do."

He leaned back in his chair. "Okay, so here's the deal," he said, crossing his arms across his ample chest. "I want you to call me if anything strange happens. I don't care if it's a false alarm, you just call me. I'll keep watch." He chuckled. "Hell, I'm almost always home anyway."

Carolyn nodded. "Thank you."

He smiled. "Now," he said as he reached for the packet of biscuits, his face set in a manic grin, "may I have another?"

Chapter
Thirty

The hospital room was still dark, but the sunlight had managed to break through the clouds enough to clothe the room in twilight. Through the half-open door, he heard nurses walking past, medicine carts traveling through the hallway on squeaky wheels and the occasional conversational fragment.

Trey lay with his eyes closed, focused on his breathing. They had given him another sedative after Carolyn left.

"Something to help you sleep," the nurse had said.

Sleep? Shit, the stuff had knocked him flat. He didn't so much sleep as pass out. The next time he opened his eyes, the sunlight had shifted. A look at the clock on the wall told him it was already 3 p.m. Alan's school day would soon be at an end.

Trey felt his heart rate rise. He closed his eyes again, and imagined Alan's happy face. His heartbeat slowed a bit.

Carolyn would pick him up. Carolyn would walk or drive him home. It would all be okay.

The thing at his bedside. The ghoul dressed in the the ice cream man's uniform. It had surprised and scared the hell out of him. But hadn't there been something else? Something familiar? The thing had... rasped.

Trey felt something click in his mind. Raspy voice. The long nose. The eyes. They had been yellow and then turned green. Closet Man green. Something was so—

"You sleeping, Trey?"

He didn't bother opening his eyes, but smiled. "I've been lying here for hours waiting for you to show up."

"Uh-huh," Kinkaid said.

Trey opened his eyes and watched as she entered the room.

"I wanted to make sure we weren't going to need the rubber room."

"Oh," he growled, "you tell that to all the crazy people?"

"Only the ones that need to hear it."

"Quack," he said.

Kinkaid stared at him, a mischievous grin on her face. It was infectious.

"So, what do you have to say for yourself?"

She bent down and looked at his chart. "Nothing serious. Been getting updates on you from the nurses every couple of hours. They say you slept like a baby."

"Slept? Fuck," he whispered, "more like they kicked my head in. What the fuck was that shit?"

"Just something to keep my favorite psycho asleep until I got here."

"Ah," Trey said. "So your bedside manner is only at your convenience?"

She put the clipboard down, her smile fading a bit. "You aren't my only patient, Trey. Just the only patient I'm currently interested in."

"Quack," he growled.

Kinkaid pulled over a chair and sat down beside him. "They've cleared your concussion. You're out of the woods."

"Just like that?"

She nodded. "Just like that. Last time the nurse peered in your eyes and asked you your name, you actually passed the test." She licked her lips. "Now let's talk about the hard stuff."

He sighed. "You're going to commit me."

The grin on her face disappeared. She sucked in a breath. "Trey? You checked yourself in. Even though you're in the hospital ward, that doesn't really mean much. You asked me to more or less admit you for treatment, and that's what we're doing." Trey said nothing. "Do you remember the last time we did this?"

"Yes," Trey said, his voice flat. "You asked me to admit myself. And I did."

She nodded. "And I let you out again, didn't I?" He said nothing. "Last time you'd hurt yourself. You'd hurt your wife." She paused. "Do you want to do that again?"

"Fuck no," Trey said at once, his voice loud in the quiet room.

Kinkaid didn't flinch, but her smile returned. "Good. Now. Do you have any questions?"

"Just until the delusions pass?"

She nodded, her smile growing sad. "Yes. Once we're sure you're not going to have any more hallucinations, I'll kick your ass out of here." She chuckled. "I like my favorite psycho being on the streets. It's good for my reputation."

"Uh-huh."

"Trey, there's someone I would like to bring in on your treatment." She paused again, staring into his eyes, unblinking. "Is that okay?"

"Who?"

"You'll meet him tomorrow, if you agree. I think you'll like him."

"Okay," he said. "Guess I'm going to have to sign something?"

She shrugged. "Actually, I'm going to have Carolyn sign something. Although it's really just a formality. I wanted to get your consent, though. Don't want you wasting anybody's time by being more of a pain in the ass than you already are."

"Okay, fine. I give you my verbal consent to bring in someone else to fuck with my brain."

"Good," she said with a laugh. "The more quacks, the better, right?"

The smile was getting to him again. His lips turned upward of their own accord. "Bring in a fucking flock of geese if you think it's going to help."

"Sure. I will, believe me. Now," she said and pulled a notebook from her valise, "can you talk to me about your visitor?"

He shivered and turned away from her toward the side of the bed where the thing had been. "What do you want to know?"

"Can you describe him to me?"

Trey shrugged and looked back at her. "It was the ice cream man, again. But..."

"But, what? What did he say to you?"

That voice. The rasping voice. The green eyes. "You dirty, little boy! You're coming back with me! Or I'll split you in half like I should have!"

The shiver wracked his entire body. The voice echoed in his brain. "He told me he was going to take me back."

She furrowed a brow. "Back? He was going to take you back? Where?" she asked.

"I— I don't know," he whispered.

She nodded and scribbled in the notebook. She dropped it to her knees, her hands clasped atop it. "You remembered something this time, didn't you?"

"Yes," he said. "The voice. It was— I've heard it before." He looked away from her again, staring at the half-open door. "I just can't remember where," Trey whispered.

"Shhh. It's okay, Trey." She clucked her tongue. "Do you remember who you were talking to last time you had an incident?" He shook his head. She picked up the notebook, thumbed through the pages until she encountered a sticky note. "According to Carolyn, you said 'You leave him the fuck alone.'" She looked up at him. "Does that mean anything to you?"

Trey thought for a moment. Who the hell had he been talking to? That voice. The rasp.

"I was telling him to leave Alan alone."

She inched forward in the chair, leaning toward him. "Who were you telling, Trey? Who?"

"The— The man," he whispered.

A tall figure, dressed in jeans that smelled like dirt and oil, a soiled denim jacket covering broad shoulders. Dirt encrusted work boots. A belt swinging from one hand. Frantic green eyes staring with malevolence.

The sound of snapping fingers caught his attention and he looked over at her. "Still with me?" she asked, her brows furrowed. "Still with me, Trey?"

He swallowed hard. "How long this time?"

She shrugged. "About a minute. What did you see?"

"The— The man." His vision began to blur..

"Stay with me, Trey," she whispered.

His vision snapped back, the world once again solidifying around him.

"I need you to take some deep breaths, okay? Deep breath." She pulled in a lungful of air and held it. As he watched her, he found himself doing the same. She exhaled slowly, Trey following suit. "Good," she said. "Keep doing that for a moment, okay?" Trey nodded. "Now close your eyes."

The room disappeared behind his lids. He heard her shift in her chair, but continued the breathing. The world spun a little and then righted itself. Alan's face floated across his mind.

"Now," she said, "can you picture the man?"

Alan's face melted, a long nose pushing its way through the boy's smile, long teeth crunching through his cheeks. Trey opened his eyes and sat up in bed, screaming.

Chapter
Thirty-One

The final bell rang. The twenty children in the room had been shifting in their seats the last ten minutes. Even as the teacher read aloud from their history text, Alan knew none of the class was listening.

All he'd heard at lunch that day was about the Ice Cream Man. Kids talking about how nice he was, how he helped them count out the change, and always had something to recommend.

Alan said nothing while his classmates blathered on about the Ice Cream Man. When they asked why he hadn't met the Ice Cream Man, Alan had only shrugged— he didn't want to tell them.

It was at recess, though, when the day had gotten bad. He was playing on the monkey bars, throwing one hand in front of the other, swinging across them in the darkened afternoon when Jimmy Keel walked over with his three friends. The rest of the children knew they were the bullies, the ones who would trip you when you were late to class, or steal your lunch. They were bigger. Mean. Jimmy was the largest of the group and by far the worst.

"Hey, freak," Keel called to him as Alan stepped off the monkey bars. Alan said nothing, ignoring him and going to the other end to start again. "Hey, freak, I'm talking to you," Keel said from behind him.

Alan continued to say nothing. He just put one hand in front of the other, swinging from one metal bar to the next.

"Your dad is shit-house nuts," Keel growled.

Alan dropped from the monkey bars, landing on his feet beneath the horizontal metal ladder. A sudden flush of heat had filled him. His skin had become volcanic, cheeks burning with... What? Rage? Embarrassment? He turned, listening to Keel's laughter.

The other three boys with him looked at one another, giggling.

"What did you say?" Alan asked in his high-pitched voice.

Keel stepped forward with slow, deliberate steps. His savage smile displayed all of his ivory teeth. "I said your dad is shit-house nuts." Keel advanced a few more steps until he stood just in front of Alan, his face staring down into Alan's flushed face. "What do you say to that?"

"I don't know what you're talking about," Alan said.

Alan tried to step around Keel, but the boy moved back in front of him. "My brother saw your old man yesterday, freak." Keel chuckled. "Said your old man freaked out and then went face first into the fucking pavement." The boy spat into the dirt, right next to Alan's shoe. "Your dad's afraid of the Ice Cream Man, you wuss," Keel said.

Alan tried to step around him again. Keel matched the move. "Leave me alone," Alan whispered.

"Ah, little sissy boy. You afraid of the Ice Cream Man, too?" The other three boys behind Keel giggled again. Jimmy turned back to them, laughing. "See," he said to them, "he's afraid too." Jimmy turned back to Alan, bending down so his foul breath chuffed into Alan's face. "A crazy little pussy, just like your dad."

The lava of rage that had been building in his stomach overflowed. Alan's left leg shot up in a soccer kick that connected with Keel's balls. Keel let out a whimpering breath and fell to his knees. The three boys behind him all winced, their faces surprised o's.

The memory of his father, laying on the pavement, his mother kneeling over him, and the Ice Cream Man standing above them filled his mind. A single tear welled up in his eye and he wiped it away. "Don't you ever talk about my dad that way again," Alan whispered.

He walked past Jimmy's kneeling form. Keel's bully buddies moved out of his way to let him pass. "I'm going to get you for that," Keel shrieked from behind him.

Alan didn't turn around. He just continued walking toward the swings where he knew Mrs. Sinclair would be.

The rest of the afternoon, the children whispered. They wouldn't talk to him. Some looked at him with a new found reverence. Others practically crossed themselves.

He knew what they were thinking: he was a dead man. Jimmy Keel and his friends would catch him. Not today, since his mother was coming to pick him up. But one day soon. They'd catch him, and they'd beat him up.

When the school bell sounded, Alan stuffed his small notebook in his backpack and pulled it up. The teacher was babbling something, but Alan didn't pay attention. He made his way through the doors and into the hallway.

Sure enough, Keel and his boys were standing at the wall near the school exit. The four of them glowered at him as he passed, but said nothing. He knew why, too. The Assistant Principal, Mr. Herman, was within earshot. Alan didn't bother making eye contact with them. He knew he'd pay for what he did, but not that day.

Alan walked through the school doors while the smaller kids ran past him. The ice cream van's cheery, loud bells rang across the playground. A crowd had already gathered in front of the white van. Alan walked toward the parking lot and stopped. His mother wasn't there yet.

He turned and stared back toward the ice cream van. Even through the trees, he could make out the Ice Cream Man's bobbing head as he exchanged treats for the pocket money.

"You're fucking dead," a voice from behind him said.

Startled, Alan turned. Jimmy Keel stood alone, his feet on the parking lot's cement curb. His grim face highlighted the hate in his eyes.

Alan felt a pang of fear, and then remembered what the boy had said about his father. "Not today," Alan whispered.

Keel grinned. "No," he said, "not today. But I'll get you, you little shit." Keel walked past him, purposely bumping him hard with his elbow.

Alan's ribs screamed in pain but he forced himself to stay quiet. "I'm going to see the Ice Cream Man," he said. He turned around and glared at Alan. "I'm not a pussy like your daddy." He smiled at Alan, his eyes still filled with that glittering rage. He flipped Alan off and then made his way toward the van.

Alan watched the boy make his way toward the Ice Cream Van. The Ice Cream Man had made short work of the crowd and most of the children had left, heading home. Jimmy Keel's tall, bulky form strutted through the copse of trees.

"Alan!" a voice yelled behind him. He turned. His mother's car was behind him now, parked in the space. "You ready?"

He took one look back and watched Jimmy Keel standing at the edge of the curb, staring into the Ice Cream Van.

"Yeah, Mom." He turned back toward her. She looked like she'd had a rough day. He felt...like crying. She looked a little lost, a little scared. He choked back the feeling and forced himself to smile. *Daddy isn't here to make her smile*, he thought, *so it's my job now*.

Chapter
Thirty-Two

D inner was blessedly short. Mommy took Alan to Chipotle where they each had a burrito, although Alan didn't feel much like eating. He knew from the moment she picked him up that she'd seen Daddy. The worried look on her face and the way her eyes didn't make contact with his told him everything he needed to know. But Mommy still tried to talk to him, as best she could.

In as few words as possible, he related his day, leaving out the confrontation with Jimmy Keel and the hallway whispers. She didn't need to know any of that.

When he asked how her day was, her face grew pale. "It was a day," she'd told him. "Daddy said he loves you."

Alan had smiled at that. "Is Daddy okay?"

Mommy nodded. "Dr. Kinkaid is taking care of him. They've got his broken arm all fixed up and he's sleeping a lot."

Although he didn't say it, Alan knew what that meant. Daddy was sleeping a lot because they were making him sleep. Daddy had looked so lost in the hospital. Lost and in pain. Alan had wiped at his eyes, but said nothing.

Sitting in the living room with his math book in front of him, Alan read the word problem again and again, but none of it made sense. His mother sat on the couch, a book splayed open on her lap. He didn't think she was really reading either

"Mommy?"

She looked up from the book. "Yes, dear?"

"When can I see Daddy?"

Her face froze and then slowly relaxed. "Daddy will let us know."

Alan nodded. "Is it bad?" Mommy didn't answer. She broke eye contact with him, staring down again at the book in her lap. Alan felt a wave of depression wash over him.

"Is it as bad as last time?"

She didn't look up. "I don't know," she whispered. "I just don't know." A tear slid down her face.

"Mommy?" She wiped her face and looked at him. "It's going to be okay. Daddy will be back. Right?"

A reluctant smile spread across her face. "Yes, honey. Daddy will be back."

Alan let the conversation drop and stared back down into his book.

"Alan?" she said after a few minutes.

"Yes, Mommy?"

She cleared her throat. "I want you to stay away from the Ice Cream Man."

The shiver in her voice caught his attention. "I will, Mommy. I don't like him."

"Good," she said, staring back into her book. "Now finish your homework, kiddo. It's getting late."

Alan stared back down at the numbers on the page.

The Ice Cream Man.

He looked up at his mother.

The whispers. The eyes. Should he tell her? He looked back down at the page, feeling his heart race. It wasn't real. No more real than The Closet Man. Mommy didn't need to hear about the whispers. She didn't need to know about the eyes.

The pencil moved on the notebook next to the book as he scrawled answers, showing his work as always. Ten more math problems, and then he could... what? Go to sleep? Read more Harry Potter? He looked up at Mommy again. She was staring into her book, but her eyes weren't moving across the page.

As fast as he could, Alan ran through the problems. His pencil raced down the page. As he wrote the answer to the last homework problem, he put the pencil down and took a deep breath.

"I'm done, Mommy," he said in a breathy whisper.

She looked up from the book. "What, honey?"

"I'm done."

"That's my boy," she said. "Why don't you go and get ready for bed?"

His heart beat faster in his chest. "You'll come tuck me in?"

"Of course," she said.

Alan grinned. "Okay," he said. He closed the book and shoved it into his pack. With a yawn, he carried the pack to the front door and hung it from the credenza hook. He turned to the dark stairway.

He reached for the light switch.

"Alan," a voice whispered in his mind.

Alan closed his eyes.

"Alan," it whispered again. "I'm waiting for you."

Alan flicked the light switch and took a deep breath. He opened his eyes. The stairwell was lit, the shadows and darkness had retreated. With a shuddering exhale, he trudged up the stairs and into the hallway. He walked forward and then stopped. His parents' bedroom was to his left, the open door leaving a gaping rectangle of darkness.

"Won't be there if I don't look," he whispered. He took another deep breath and walked past the bedroom without glancing inside.

With the hall light, the bathroom light, and that of his bedroom, few shadows remained. He brushed his teeth and made his way back to his room. He left the door open as he undressed and put on his pajamas. He turned on his lamp and then turned off the overhead light. As he crawled between the sheets, he heard the sound of his mother's footsteps on the stairs. He pulled the blankets up to his neck and stared at the ceiling.

"Alan?" she called from the hallway with a laugh, "did you have to turn on every light in the house?"

Alan blushed as she entered the room. "Sorry, Mommy. Forgot to turn them off," he lied.

She nodded to him. She sat on the edge of his bed and gave him a quick peck on the cheek. "You going to sleep now?"

He nodded. "I'm tired."

"So am I" she yawned. "Get some sleep, kiddo. I'll take you to school tomorrow, okay?"

"Yes, Mommy," Alan said.

She smiled at him. "Good night, baby." She kissed his cheek, rose from the bed, and headed for the door.

"Mommy?" She stopped and turned, her brows raised. He opened his mouth and then closed it. "Good night."

She smiled at him and walked out of the bedroom. The lights in the hallway went out. He took a deep breath and then snapped off the lamp. The room instantly fell into darkness. Alan lay on his back, the covers up to his neck, and closed his eyes.

You afraid of the Ice Cream Man too? Jimmy Keel's hateful voice whispered in his mind.

"Yes," Alan whispered, "I am."

You should be, a rasping voice answered back.

Alan opened his eyes and stared around the room, but nothing was there. No yellow eyes staring back at him. No menacing silhouette in the darkness. He took in a shuddering breath, closed his eyes and tried to keep the whispers at bay.

Chapter
Thirty-Three

She'd checked her work email the night before. She was going to have to go in. There was no question about it, really. A pain in the ass client was demanding another meeting to go through the final contract details. Carolyn was going to have to placate the asshole, again.

She surely wasn't going to tell Trey about Alan having to walk home by himself. That wasn't something he'd be able to handle right now. She made a mental note to call Kinkaid when she got to the office the next morning and find out how he was doing.

Alan had been very quiet. The two of them had shared the living room in silence while she pretended to read a book and he pretended to study. She knew he wasn't able to concentrate. She wanted to talk to him about it, but she just didn't have the energy.

He went to bed without a fuss. She'd managed some sleep, but not much. Trey's frightened, haggard face kept flashing through her mind. The shadowy face of Reggie the Ice Cream Man did the same.

Even in her dreams, she heard Alan saying "I want Daddy to protect us from the Ice Cream Man."

When her alarm finally screeched in the darkness, she was glad. Once she made sure Alan was awake, she returned to her normal work ritual: shower, make-up, the choosing of clothes from the closet, the hunt for hose that didn't have a run, and the frantic effort to get coffee made and swallow down some breakfast before having to jump in the car and head for work. On top of all that, she'd also have to get Alan to school.

As they made their way toward the school, she glanced at him. "You going to be okay walking home from school?"

Alan nodded, his face pressed against the window. The clouds had disappeared leaving a bright, blue sky in their place. "Yes, Mommy."

"Good. I want you to come straight home, okay?"

He turned to her. "Okay. I'll come home and get my homework done, in case we get to see Daddy tonight."

She pulled into the side street and parked near the thicket of pines. "You okay to walk from here?"

"Oh, yeah," he said with a smile. He leaned over and kissed her cheek. "Bye, Mommy."

"Love you," she said. "Have a good day."

He opened the door and bounded out, his backpack slapping against his back as he ran up the curb.

She shook her head and drove down the side street away from the school.

Chapter
Thirty-Four

The small windowless room was dark. Light from the hallway streamed through the small glass rectangle set into the door, barely illuminating the bottom of the sheets. Trey turned his head, looking for a clock he knew wasn't there.

Day. Night. Didn't matter anymore. Every waking moment was just a brief interlude before the next descent into dreamless sleep. He didn't know how long he'd been awake, only that the light in the hallway had been disturbed three times by people walking past it.

Carolyn. He wanted to call Carolyn. He wanted to talk to Alan. He wanted—

The lights in the room began to glow. Soft. Even the gradual change from darkness to twilight stung his eyes. Trey forced them to stay open. The pain slowly subsided as the light grew and grew. After a minute or so, the darkness had fled the room. He took a deep breath and stared at the door. Was this real? Would the thing come through the door?

As if on cue, the rectangle darkened. Someone was in the hallway. Trey took a deep breath, not knowing what to expect. His diaphragm primed itself for another throat-shredding scream.

The door opened and a man rolled a wheelchair into the room. "Good afternoon, Mr. Leger. You have visitors."

Trey blinked at the man. He couldn't remember the orderly's name, although he'd seen him more than once. "Visitors?" The man nodded. "my little boy?"

The man's brow furrowed. He dropped his eyes and finished rolling the wheelchair next to the bed. "Let's go, Mr. Leger."

Alan. Seeing Alan would make all this more real. It would banish the boogeyman, make the Ice Cream Man rest in peace. Somehow. Alan would—

"Mr. Leger?" the orderly said again. Trey swiveled his eyes toward him, blinking. "You all right?"

He smiled. "Sorry. That happens sometimes." The man nodded to him. Trey made his way off the bed and dropped into the chair. They'd removed his restraints sometime during the night. Although his wrists still itched, at least he no longer felt like a prisoner.

The orderly said nothing as he rolled Trey out of the room and into the hallway.

They passed a number of other rooms. Some were quiet; others buzzed with whispered ramblings. Trey shivered. Was that what he sounded like when the Ice Cream Man came to visit? *Am I really that insane?*

The hallway curved around to a much more friendly part of the ward. The walls weren't painted white, but blue. Trey smelled coffee, lunches being eaten at desks. The scents of normalcy. He sighed aloud, eyes closed, letting the aromas fill his nostrils.

The wheelchair turned. Trey opened his eyes. The orderly wheeled him into a large room with a steel table bolted to the floor. A goateed man stood from his chair at the table, a smile on his face. Dark hair, tied back in a loose pony tail. Stylish, silver rectangular glasses glinting beneath the bright fluorescents.

"Hello, Trey," the man said.

Trey blinked at him.

The man's voice was smooth, a medium tone, a slight lilt in the syllables. "My name is Tony Downs."

Trey said nothing as the wheelchair stopped in front of the metal table.

"Thank you, Stephen," Tony said to the orderly.

Trey didn't turn, but heard the padded footsteps as the man left the room, closing the door behind him. Tony offered Trey his hand. Trey tepidly shook with his good hand.

"Dr. Kinkaid asked if I'd look in on you."

"That quack," Trey said. "She too busy to see her favorite psycho?"

Tony laughed, his eyes dancing behind the lenses. "Not at all," Tony said. "Think of this as more of a consult."

Trey turned toward the glass on one wall. He waved his good hand at it. "Hi, doc!" he yelled with a smile.

"Right," Tony said. "Crazy, not stupid."

Trey returned Tony's smile and placed his good hand on the table.

Trey tapped his foot and stared into Tony's face. The man exuded intelligence, but also a kind of sadness. He furrowed a brow.

"So, Tony, there something on your mind?"

Leaning back in his chair, Tony crossed his arms in front of his chest. He tilted his head slightly, the smile disappearing from his face. "As a matter of fact, yes."

The man stopped speaking. If not for the occasional blink of his eyes and the nearly imperceptible rise and fall of his chest, it would have been difficult to tell he was alive. The silence was broken only by muffled hallway conversations and the occasional squeak of a gurney. Trey sighed. "You going to tell me what?"

"Glad you asked," Tony said, his lips pursing into a reserved smile. "I have a question for you. I've had it since Dr. Kinkaid told me about you."

"Okay," Trey said. "Shoot."

Tony nodded. "I want to know who your Ice Cream Man is."

Trey blinked. "I— He's the guy who drives around my neighborhood. I know he's just a delusion, but—" Trey stopped speaking.

Tony was shaking his head, the smile wiped from his face.

"What?" Trey asked.

"That Ice Cream Man isn't who I'm talking about," Tony said. He drummed his fingers on the metal table, and turned in his chair. "I've read your file, Trey. I know there's some information missing from it." Tony paused, leaning forward in the chair. His breath smelled of cigarettes and coffee. "Do you?"

"I—" Trey frowned. "I don't know what you mean." The pace of his breathing increased, but he didn't know why.

"Do you know?" Tony said again. "Do you know what's missing?"

"I—" Trey felt something crack the slightest bit in his mind. Something... "I don't know."

Tony smiled, leaning back in his chair once again. Trey noticed the man's face was flushed as though he'd done something difficult. "There's nothing in your file describing your earliest childhood. Nothing but bullshit about it being a happy childhood."

"It's not bullshit, it's—"

"It's bullshit." Tony stood. His palms rested on the table, his face leaning closer to Trey's. The man's eyes were glittering, dancing with something malevolent.

Trey shuddered.

"You know it's bullshit, Trey."

Trey leaned back in the wheelchair. "I don't want to—" He stopped speaking as he stared into Tony's manic grin. "I don't want to talk about this anymore," he said.

Tony shook his head. "We are going to talk, Trey," Tony said with a leer.

The image of the thing at his bedside, the thing standing over him, promising to punish him for having a child without asking permission. The thing. The Ice Cream Man. The Closet Man. It flooded his vision, saliva dripping from its canines and carrion crusted maw, razor sharp talons dangling just above its chest.

Trey put his hand to his head. "I don't want to—"

"Remember?" Tony asked. His voice was savage, on the verge of a shout. His eyes were changing color, turning green. "Remember? Good little boys remember," Tony said in a low growl. "Good little boys tell the truth."

The Ice Cream Man. Long nose. White stained uniform replaced by soiled jeans, soiled black boots, a red-checkered torn flannel shirt. The Closet Man. Crooked teeth in a jaw that didn't quite close. Bright green eyes leering down at him from a smiling face.

"Good little boys—" Trey muttered. "Good little boys ask permission." Trey wept.

"Ask permission for what?" Tony's voice was still edged, but quieter. Tony's eyes returned to their brown color. When Trey didn't answer, the booming voice returned. "Good little boys ask permission for what?"

"I can't!" Trey screamed, his eyes glaring up at Tony. "I can't say—"

Tony growled, his face a mask of violence as he stepped around the table. He stood in front of Trey, leaning over him. "Ask permission!" Tony yelled at him. "Ask permission now!"

The man before him melted, the nose growing longer, hair dripping into a crew cut, brows lengthening, cheekbones narrowing. Perfect white teeth shifted, the jaw offset. Dockers and the polo shirt morphed into the dirty, filthy thing's outfit.

"ASK PERMISSION," it growled.

"Don't hit me," Trey sobbed. He put his hands over his head. "I didn't mean to pee in the corner!"

"You must ask permission," the man before him said, its fist mere inches from him. "Ask permission for everything. To eat. Even to breathe, you dirty boy. Dirty little boy." It paused, foul breath steaming into Trey's face. "Look at me, dirty little boy!"

Trey dropped his hands, staring up into the giant, leering form.

"You will ask permission, boy. You are never going to say anything." The man slapped a fist into his palm, the sound like a belt cracking. "You will ask permission."

"I—" Trey sobbed. "I will ask permission," he said in a shuddering voice.

"Ask permission to save your son!" the man screamed at him. Saliva dripped from the side of the man's mouth, droplets hitting the tile floor.

Something fractured in Trey's mind. Alan. Alan's in trouble?

"My son?" he breathed.

The man before him grew a little smaller. "What have you done to Alan?"

Rage. Pure rage. The thing wasn't a thing. It was a man. The man before him had done something to Alan. Touched his boy. Hurt his boy. Savaged his boy. Trey stood from the chair. The thing had grown shorter, almost to Trey's height.

"Ask permission, boy."

The fear rose again in his mind, but the rage tamped it down, overwhelming the icy feel with wrathful fire. "No," Trey whispered. He took a step toward the man. "Tell me what you did to Alan." He took another step.

The man grinned. "Ask permission, boy, and I'll tell you." The man licked his gray lips, the stench of unwashed teeth filling Trey's nose. "Ask," the man said and chuckled. "Ask now, or I tell you nothing."

Trey's hate rose another notch. He spat the words, saliva flying with each syllable. "I ask permission to ask a question."

"That's better," the man replied, a smile exposing crooked teeth. "Ask."

The noxious odor. The smile. The rage. Trey took another step closer, his nose nearly touching the ugly face of the man in front of him. "What have you done to my son?"

In an instant, the smile disappeared into a flat expressionless line. The man leaned forward, eyes filled with malice. "You. Tell. Me."

The closet. The black. The unending darkness. The fetid smell of sour shit and stale urine. The feel of dirty carpet beneath a bare bottom. Hugging himself in the cold, the sting of endless tears down his face. The hurt in his throat from crying, from screaming. The fear. The pain. Alan. Alan was in the closet.

Trey screamed and swung his cast toward the man's face. The man jumped backward, but too late to completely miss the blow. The cast bounced off a shoulder blade and connected with the man's chin.

Searing pain split through Trey's mind and he crumpled to the floor. He looked up through his wavering vision, expecting to see dirty boots, soiled jeans, and that leering grin. But there were only sneakers. Dockers. And Tony Downs.

The door swung open. Two orderlies appeared in the room, followed by Dr. Kinkaid. "Trey!" she shouted as he tried to get up. "Stay down!"

The pain in his arm was a screaming hot needle. He fell to one knee and felt arms grab his waist. Trey collapsed into the chair, his good arm holding his bad one.

Tears welled up from his eyes, but he smiled through it. "I'll tell you, you fucker."

As they wheeled him out of the room, he heard Tony's soft voice. "Nice to meet you, Trey."

Chapter
Thirty-Five

Back in his room, Trey felt drained. His broken arm throbbed and he gritted his teeth against the pain. The scuffle with Tony had set his entire body into an adrenaline overdrive, but it was fading and there was little left except pain and confusion.

He wondered how soon Kinkaid would come into the room brandishing a sedative and kind words as they drugged him back into a dreamless stupor.

Tony. That fucker. He'd— Trey stopped grinding his teeth. The man. The man with the soiled clothes, the foul breath. A man. Just a man.

"You have to ask permission," the man had said, his fists dangling near his waist, fingers twitching.

Trey shivered. Permission. He felt something unlock in his mind. Something about Scooby-Doo. A grubby hand reaching out with a plastic lunch box, Scooby-Doo in the foreground, his tongue lolling happily from his mouth, the Mystery Machine in the background. Flashlights. Shaggy. Fred. Wilma. Daphne. The grubby hand was attached to a grubby man who smiled with all his crooked teeth.

The looming giant offered the lunchbox. Scooby-Doo. Unafraid, laughing, Trey reached for the plastic container.

The grubby man took a step backwards. "Come get it. Dontcha want it?"

Still laughing, Trey scampered forward toward it. The man was playing keep away, the same game Daddy always played with him.

Trey staggered forward from the lawn, heading toward the man. The grubby man opened the door to his car, his white car, and tossed the lunchbox inside. Trey scrambled into the car after the lunchbox, his small hands clutching it to his chest in victory. The door shut with a quiet *chunk*, the click of electric door locks following close behind.

The driver side door closed, the giant now inside. The grubby man turned toward him. "I have more," he said softly. "I have more."

Trey looked up into the man's green eyes. The man turned back to the steering wheel and started the car. Trey held the lunchbox, turning it over and over again. "It's yours," the man said.

"Show it to Mommy?"

With a laugh, the man looked at him from the rearview mirror. "We'll show Mommy all your goodies," the man said. "In just a little while." The smile on the face. That face. The long nose. The parched lips. The glittering green eyes.

"Trey?" He flinched and looked up at the doorway. Kinkaid stood there, notebook in hand, a concerned expression on her face. "You here?"

Trey opened his mouth and then closed it. He realized a tear had fallen from his eye. He wiped at it and groaned a little as the movement brought the pain in his arm back. He nodded to her and waved her in with his undamaged hand.

She grabbed a chair and pulled it toward the bed. "Can you talk?" she asked.

He nodded again.

She pursed her lips. "Now you're just fucking with me," she whispered.

A thin smile broke out on his face. "Yes and no," he said in a soft voice.

"Thought that might make you smile."

He nodded. "You always know how." He said. He paused for a moment, scanning her face. "Is that asshole okay?"

"Who, Tony?" Trey nodded. She laughed. "You're not the first patient to deck him, Trey. Not at all." She tapped her pen on the notebook. "I'll bet you won't be the last either."

Trey shook his head. "What the fuck did he do?"

She shrugged. "You tell me. What did you see?"

"I—" Trey closed his mouth again, teeth clicking shut. For a moment he tried to string the words together. "I saw him," was all he managed. Kinkaid said nothing. Her pen tapping had stopped, leaving the room silent except for the occasional footstep in the hall and muffled, distant conversation. Words flashed in Trey's mind. Permission. Want. Need. Trey shivered. "I saw the grubby man."

"Who's the grubby man?"

He stared at her. "I—" He stopped.

She nodded to him. "How old were you, Trey?"

"Four," he said. "I think I was four."

Four years old. Mommy was on the phone. Trey wanted to play in the front yard. Holding his bright orange Tonka truck under one arm, he swiveled the dead bolt on the door just like he'd seen Mommy and Daddy do so many times in the past. It clicked and he stepped out of the house.

The smell of the neighbor's freshly mown grass. Trey sat halfway down the lawn, his orange truck rolling over the bright green blades of grass. The sun was rising higher in the sky, the summer morning already warm and muggy. But Trey's truck didn't mind, so Trey didn't either. The sound of a car stopping in front of the curb with a soft squeal of its brakes.

"Can you tell me what happened?" Kinkaid asked.

Trey nodded. "I was playing in the front yard. The grubby man—" He paused, staring down at the table. "The grubby man tricked me into his car."

Kinkaid opened the notebook. She grabbed the edge of a sticky note jutting out and pulled the notebook open to the page. "Can you tell me what happened?" she asked again.

The drive. The long drive. Trey played with the lunchbox. Something inside rattled as he shook it. Smiling, he asked the grubby man what it was.

"Open it and find out," the grubby man said.

Frustration faded into glee as the plastic snaps finally gave under his tiny fingers. The lunchbox lid flipped open. Trey laughed. A Scooby-Doo sippy cup stared back at him, the dog's face screwed up in an expression of fear, a shambling mummy running behind him. He grasped the cup and shook it, listening to the liquid sloshing inside. "What's in it?" he asked the man.

"Something good," the man said and smiled at him from the rearview mirror.

Trey laughed and swiveled off the top. He smelled it. Cherry Kool-aid. "I like Kool-aid," Trey muttered and drank.

"Good boy," the man said from the front seat. Trey put the cap back on the cup and turned toward the front. "But," he said with a snarl, "you didn't ask permission, you little shit."

Kinkaid leaned in toward him. "The man drugged you?"

"I fell asleep," Trey whispered. Another tear sprang to the corner of his eye. "And, when I woke—"

Darkness. A thin slit of light from beneath a door. Trey was cold and his head hurt. He was naked. "Mommy?" Trey asked in the darkness. "Daddy?" Nothing. He started to cry and then heard a sound from outside the door. A sound like— Like people talking on a radio. "Mommy!" Trey cried out again. "Mommy! Let me out!"

The voices on the radio quieted. The clomp clomp of work boots. The sound of heavy breathing. Trey's bladder let go and he cried as urine splattered on the floor. Daddy would yell at him for that. Mommy would—

"Boy," something growled from beyond the door, "you're not

allowed to speak."

"I want my—" Trey started to scream.

The man behind the door growled again, a sound that shocked Trey into silence. He wrapped his arms around himself, still crying. "You're not allowed to talk without my permission, boy." Something scraped at the door, a sound like nails on a chalkboard. "Or you'll be very fucking sorry." The heavily breathing thing on the other side of the door paused and then growled "Do you understand, you little shit?"

Trey nodded to himself, but said nothing.

A harsh chuckle from behind the door. "Good," the man growled.

"Do you know how long you were there?" Kinkaid asked.

Trey shook his head and shivered. "I— I don't remember."

Kinkaid nodded. "He made you ask permission for everything."

"Yes," Trey whispered. "Everything."

She nodded again. "Trey? You don't have to tell me anything you don't want to." She tapped the pen against the notebook once more. "Do you know how you got out of there?"

The stinging tang of stale urine, sour shit, and vomit. Trey was caked in it. The dark closet had been his home for days. The growling man didn't give him food or drink. The constant darkness had broken something. Voices inside his head whispered. The voices on the radio outside whispered, too.

The grubby man. He was always in the closet with him. The grubby man with his long arms and long nose and bright, green eyes. The grubby man. The Closet Man.

Trey couldn't cry anymore, couldn't move anymore. There was nothing left. All spent. Mommy wasn't coming for him. Daddy wasn't coming for him. The grubby man had told him that, and he believed it. There was only the grubby man. The grubby man and darkness.

He didn't even hear the clomping of the boots, or the key in the lock jiggling. The closet door opened and wan light washed in. For Trey, it was like bright sunlight. It stung his eyes, but he was too exhausted to lift a hand to shield them.

The grubby man stood just outside the closet. His fists clenched and unclenched. The baseball cap on his head shielded his eyes, leaving only his long nose protruding from its shadow. The heavily breathing figure reached around to his back and brought out a hammer, its wooden handle deeply scratched and pitted. "You are a dirty boy," he growled.

Trey closed his eyes. He wanted to sleep again. Sleep and wake up at home. Not feel this anymore. Not smell this anymore. Just—

"Dirty, stinking little boy," the grubby man said. The man leaned down toward him, the hammer clutched tightly in one fist.

"Please," Trey whispered through swollen, chapped lips, "let me go home. Please, let me go home. Please—"

The man had raised the hammer, his eyes glittering with hate. Trey stared up at the man through his bruised, hurt eyes. "You," he growled, "ask permission?"

"Please," Trey managed to say once more. His voice was gone now, dehydration locking the words in his throat. His lips continued moving, but no sound emerged.

The man dropped the hammer to the closet floor. It splattered into a day old pile of shit. He reached down and grabbed Trey by the waist. The grubby man's breath was foul, even when compared to the stench of the closet. The man's face smiled, but his eyes didn't.

"You," he growled, leaning in closer, nose nearly to Trey's, "will ask my permission for everything you do, you little shit."

Trey watched as the man's nose grew longer still, fangs sliding out from the misshapen jaw. Saliva fell in ropes from the slavering thing before him. The hands grabbing him by the waist grew talons. Trey tried to scream, but there was no sound.

"Trey?" Kinkaid's voice said. "Trey?"

"How long?" he asked, his face set in a mask of fear.

She cleared her throat. "About five minutes or so."

Trey nodded. "He became...that thing at the end. The ghoul. The grubby man turned—" He choked back a sob. "Turned," he whispered. "Just, turned." Trey shook his head. "But that's not what happened." He swallowed hard and ran his good hand through his hair. "He became the Closet Man. In my mind."

Kinkaid closed the notebook with her delicate fingers. She smiled at him. "You don't remember how you got home, do you?"

Trey shook his head.

"He let you go, Trey, because you asked permission." She placed a hand on his arm. "He could have killed you. You know that, right?"

"I think he was going to," Trey whispered. "I think—" Tears flowed from his eyes. "Why did he—" Trey closed his eyes and convulsed, his body shaking with all the stress and fear.

Kinkaid held his hand for a long time.

Chapter
Thirty-Six

The cold felt invigorating. Sitting in one of the benches beneath the hospital's overhang, the winter chill was unchecked by the sun. Trey shivered a little. He was wearing the same clothes as the night he'd been admitted. His shirt still had droplets of blood on it from where he'd smacked into the concrete. As people walked in and out of the hospital, some saw those stains and gawked. He didn't mind. His arm throbbed. The scuffle with Tony hadn't rebroken it or harmed the cast, but it had certainly hurt like hell.

Carolyn would be there relatively soon. He might have to wait another thirty minutes or so. But again, he didn't mind. The envelope they'd given him with his statement, insurance receipts, prescriptions for pain killers and Dr. Kinkaid's new drug regimen, sat beside him on the bench. Just more stuff to file. More slips of paper to take to the pharmacy.

He and Kinkaid had talked about the Closet Man, the grubby man. Trey knew they were the same, knew that one was in the past and the other in his mind. The green eyes were nothing more than illusion.

"I think I'm ready to go home now," Trey had told Kinkaid.

She'd stared at him, unblinking for a moment. "You want to go home." She sighed. "Are you sure?"

"I'm not—" His voice broke. He cleared his throat and started again. "I need to get home. I need to see Alan and Carolyn. At home."

Kinkaid had nodded. "Why are you in such a hurry to get home?"

"I just," Trey whispered, "have to get home. I," he said, motioning to the room, "don't feel right here. Need to be with my family."

She bit her lip, the same way Carolyn always did when unsure of something. "I think you should probably stay a while longer."

He shook his head. "Doc, I promise that if I have any other problems, I'll come right back here." She bit her lip again and he sighed. "I promise. I may be crazy, but I keep my promises."

"Can I call Carolyn?" Kinkaid had asked.

That was how they'd left it. Kinkaid had called Carolyn, allowed Trey to check himself out on the grounds that, psycho or no, he kept his promise.

"Hello, Trey," a voice said from his left. Trey turned. Tony Downs smiled down at him. The man wore a leather duster that hid his long sleeve shirt. "How are you feeling?"

Trey blinked. A flash of anger rose within him, but he managed to batten it down. This wasn't the man. This wasn't the grubby man. He'd only become the grubby man for a moment.

Trey cocked his head. "I'm fine. How's your, um—" Trey said rubbing his chin.

"Oh, that," Tony laughed, "I've had much worse. Much worse."

"I'm sorry," Trey said.

Tony waved his hands. "No worries, Trey. It happens." Tony gestured toward the bench. "Mind if I sit for a moment?"

"Um," Trey stammered, "um, sure."

"Cool," Tony said. The man walked past him to the empty part of the bench. He blew a sigh between his teeth. "Afraid I hate hospitals. I'd much rather freeze to death than stay in there any longer than I need to."

Trey turned to him. "Um, then why are you still here?"

"Because," Tony grinned without looking at him, "I was hoping to have a moment of your time."

Trey blinked. "Um, okay. But shouldn't you have done that—"

Tony turned toward him. Tony's deep, brown eyes had no pupils; they had become a sea of color. Trey felt for a moment like he was drowning in them. The concern he'd felt at this man being so close to him evaporated, as did the thoughts of the grubby man.

"I wanted to speak to you alone, Trey."

Time seemed to slow, or maybe it was just that his calm, the old calm, was back. As long as he'd been taking meds, the world around him had moved fast. But this was more like what he remembered as a child— lazy, time to think. "Okay," Trey said.

"Good," Tony said. He shifted his weight on the bench, turning more to face Trey. "I want you to understand something, Trey." Tony leaned in just the slightest bit. The scent of coffee and cigarettes filled Trey's nostrils as Tony spoke. "The drugs are never going to cure you. The drugs are never going to remove memory. The drugs and therapy are never going to heal you." Tony leaned closer still, his eyes growing large. "You have to face your fears, Trey. And your past."

Trey felt something click inside his mind and suddenly the world started moving in that rapid-fire manner again. Tony was no longer leaning toward him, but facing outward back toward the circle.

"They say it's going to get really cold tonight," Tony said with a shiver. "Well," Tony said as he removed a pack of cigarettes from his duster pocket, "I guess I've had enough fresh air." He stood, turning toward Trey. Tony slipped something from the pack of cigarettes and handed it to Trey. "Here's my card, Mr. Leger. Please call me if you need to talk about—" He paused as Trey took the card. "About today." Tony popped open the pack and lifted out a cigarette. He placed it between his index and middle finger, holding it by the filter. "Nice to have met you, Mr. Leger," Tony said. He tipped an imaginary hat and walked away toward the parking lot.

Still holding the card in his hand, Trey watched as Tony crossed the circle. "What the fuck—" Trey mumbled aloud. He stared at the card.

"Tony Downs," Trey said aloud. The face of the grubby man flitted into his mind. He felt cold all over, bone-chilling cold. He opened the envelope and placed the card inside.

As Kinkaid had been signing Trey's release papers, Trey had asked her who Tony Downs was.

She'd looked up at him, a smile on her face. "He's a friend of mine."

"Yeah, I got that," Trey said, "but what does he do?"

She shrugged. "He's a psychologist. Forensic. He consults for the police department, teaches classes, writes strange papers." She chuckled. "He's just a guy."

Trey had nodded. "How did he know—"

"He just does, Trey," Kinkaid said, her eyes glancing back down at the papers. Her pen scratched at it, ticking boxes and writing initials. "What he does is nothing more than a parlor trick, really."

"What do you mean?"

Kinkaid tapped her pen against the table. "You told him where to go, Trey. He asked you questions and guessed. When he was wrong, you put him on the right path."

Trey frowned. "He was never wrong, Doc."

She shrugged again. "It's nothing, Trey. Do you feel better?"

He thought for a moment. "Yeah, I guess I do." She smiled at him.

"But, I, I don't know what to do now."

Kinkaid nodded, her smile fading a bit. "Yeah, you do, Trey. You live. You cope. You deal." She finished signing the paper work, shuffled the papers into one neat stack, and put the pen back in her valise. "And, of course, you keep coming to see me."

"Of course," he chuckled.

"Starting next week, I want you in my office every Tuesday. I'll get Vivian to set it up. But I want to make sure you're doing okay." She turned from the papers, locking eyes with him. "Are you really sure you're ready to go home?"

He'd smiled at her. "Yes, I'm ready." That was more than an hour earlier. "Doing okay," he mumbled.

As Carolyn pulled into the circle, the conversations and worries evaporated. Her smile was all he needed to see.

Chapter
Thirty-Seven

Jimmy wasn't at recess. His three friends didn't bother Alan. Alan was smart enough to know the two were connected. Without their large leader, they were just like the other children they regularly terrorized.

When the school day ended, Alan stepped out into the brisk air. The winter sky was bright, clear, and warm enough to make a jacket unnecessary. Alan walked with a measured pace as the other children flooded past him and into the schoolyard. Most were headed toward the copse of trees. He stopped for a moment, watching his classmates run with reckless abandon, backpacks slapping against their shoulders, to be first in the queue.

The ice cream man was there, of course. The van's side door was already open. From this far away, he was just a cream colored figure, the hat slung low over his face.

The first kids made it to the van. For a moment, nothing happened. Then there was the sound of children shouting orders, their voices a disjointed shout. Alan heard a laugh that set his teeth on edge. The ice cream man.

Why was Daddy so afraid of the Ice Cream Man? "Why am I?" he mumbled aloud.

In reflex, Alan looked toward the parking lot, expecting to see his father standing there with that bright smile on his face, the one he always had when he saw his son.

No Daddy. Not today. Alan looked back toward the tight knit pines. Was it the Ice Cream Man whispering to him at night? Alan shivered. He had to know. He started walking.

With each step, the words became more clear. "Icy Pop" "Zots" "—Sandwich!" "—Taffy!" Names of different treats shouted at the vendor who deftly kept up with each request, palming money, making change, and handing out each desired item like an automaton.

As Alan approached, small groups of children brushed past him, opening their candy or already enjoying their treats. The crowd was thinning. Five minutes had passed and Alan wasn't sure just how many of his classmates had already been served.

No more than ten feet away from the van, Alan peered at the Ice Cream Man. The long sleeves of his uniform covered his arms. Skin-tight gloves, the exact same color as his suit, covered his hands. The man's neck, chin, his smile, and long nose were the only features visible. Alan stared at the man. The smile was wide and inviting, yet it could have been a dog's face set in a snarl.

The Ice Cream Man's falsetto voice brimmed with exuberance as he repeated back the orders. He reached down, his fingers gingerly sliding dollar bills from hands. "Oh, that's too much," he told one of the children, handing back an errant dollar and some change.

Alan couldn't help but smile at the man. It was just a man after all. Just a man making a living. One who liked kids.

"Then why am I so afraid of him?" Alan wondered.

He watched the crowd until there were only a few kids left. The Ice Cream Man looked at him as he counted out some more change. The smile grew wider. He nodded to Alan. Confused, Alan took another step forward. The Ice Cream Man knew him?

The last child at the counter received his treat and walked past Alan. Alan stared up at the Ice Cream Man. The man leaned over, his hands on the counter. His smile dropped a bit. "Hey, kid. You, um, Trey Legett's son?"

A shiver ran up his spine. That falsetto voice saying his father's name jarred him. "Leger, sir" Alan corrected.

"Ah," the man nodded, "yeah, Leger. I remember now." The man blinked at Alan and then looked around the playground as if to see if any more customers were coming. "Um, how's your Dad?"

Alan shrugged. "Okay, I guess. He broke his arm, sir."

The Ice Cream Man laughed. "You can call me Reggie, son." The man leaned forward, offering his hand.

"Reggie," Alan repeated back. He grabbed the offered hand and squeezed, just as his father had taught him. "Nice to meet you, Reggie." The man's hands felt thin and bony beneath the gloves.

"Likewise," the man said. They shook. Alan let go and the man laughed. "Quite a grip you got there, partner. Your Dad teach you that?"

Alan nodded. "Told me it's how men greet one another."

Reggie laughed again. It was an infectious belly laugh and Alan couldn't help but smile. He didn't want to like this man. He didn't want to. "Your Dad's right," the man said. Reggie paused, his eyes staring into Alan's. "So," Reggie's voice dropped in tone, "what can I get you?"

Alan blushed. "Oh, I don't want anything, Reggie." Reggie's smile dimmed. "I just wanted to meet you. Thank you for helping my Dad."

The man nodded. "You're a good kid," Reggie said, his voice dropping again, the tone now barely recognizable. Alan shivered. "Time for me to pack up." Reggie held one hand beneath the overhang as he punched a button with the other. Alan heard a click and saw the door shudder. "Nice to meet you, Alan Leger," Reggie said.

Reggie's face was covered in shadow now, but his eyes still gleamed. "Tell your Dad," the shadow said, "I said get well soon." Even in the shadow, the man's grin was still visible.

Alan's mouth opened as he watched the grin elongate, the corners turning up impossibly high. The overhang clicked as it slid closed.

Alan stepped back from the curb, his skin freezing despite the warm sunlight. The van shuddered. Alan saw movement behind the driver's side window. He watched as the van pulled away leaving him alone by the curb. The van's music started as soon as it turned the corner.

The Ice Cream Man. Alan shivered.

Chapter
Thirty-Eight

The sidewalk path followed in the Ice Cream Van's wake. He had thought about taking the back way home, but as loud as the music was, he'd have heard it no matter which direction he went. Besides, the normal route would be fastest and if Jimmy Keel was waiting for him, there would be other people around to stop a fight.

As he rounded the corner and headed down the sidewalk, he saw the van in the distance, a few kids beside it. As he approached, the side door closed back down and the truck moved on another block or two until adults or children stopped it again. The cycle repeated itself. Alan never got closer than a block away before the van began moving again.

As the road wound and snaked, the bells became more and more distant and he completely lost sight of the van. The roiling in his stomach quieted. The Ice Cream Man hadn't really been what he expected. Until the end.

Alan shivered. The voice had dropped. The grin had changed. The man had become... He didn't have a word for it.

"Is that what Daddy saw?" he wondered. Alan continued putting one foot in front of the other. This part of the road was lined with pine trees snaking toward the sky, their needles bright green with the recent winter rain. As he walked, he heard the shuffling of something in the trees. Squirrels. Possum, maybe. Or perhaps a stray dog. The feeling of being watched made him walk a little faster.

The road finally began to straighten again and around the bend, he saw the back of the Ice Cream Van. The vehicle was parked on the shoulder, hazard lights on. Alan halted. The tingling in his spine was electric. The birds chirping in the trees stopped. Alan let loose a long breath. He turned and saw only the empty road behind him.

Alan looked both ways and then ran to the other side of the road, as far from the ice cream van as he could get. As he made it to the other side, he heard the sound of a car behind him. He looked and watched a blue sedan drive past. A dark haired teenager behind the wheel was singing to a song Alan couldn't hear. The sedan disappeared up the road and around the next bend.

Alan let out another long breath. "Being stupid," he thought.

Something rustled on the other side of the road. Alan turned his head. Behind the white van, something was moving through the thick pines. Alan took a step backwards and the movement stopped. He squinted, trying to make out exactly what it was. White. No, cream-colored. He took a step forwards and it matched him. Alan's heart beat rose in his chest like a thrash drum beat, loud enough to block out any other sound. Alan ran.

He could hear it running through the brush, crunching dead leaves, snapping through dead falls, and breaking branches to keep up the pursuit. His pack smashed into his middle back again and again, flapping in time to his pounding heart. Alan was afraid to look across the road, afraid he'd see his pursuer break through the tree line and fly toward him.

Alan was barely aware he was nearing the end of the road's dead space. A car honked as its brakes squealed. Alan was halfway through the intersection, stumbling to a stop. He skidded on his

Nike's and fell to the concrete, rolling in front of the car. He ended up facing the sky, the car's engine growling in his ears.

"Hey, kid! You okay?" a woman's voice said from above him.

"Yeah," Alan muttered, rolling over on his chest. He tried to lift himself from the road on lacerated and bleeding hands. Arms snaked beneath his own. A slight moan of effort from the person behind him and he was on his feet. "Thanks," Alan said.

"Jesus, kid," the woman said as he turned around, "you need to be more careful." Alan stared up into her kind, pale face. "What the hell were you running from?"

He turned to look back from where he'd come.

The Ice Cream Van's music had started up again. Loud. Coming closer.

He looked back at the woman. "Nothing," Alan said. "Just got spooked," he said.

"Where do you live?" she asked. Alan pointed down the T. She nodded. "You want a ride?"

The Ice Cream Van's engine downshifted as it passed the T. Through the dark, tinted window, Alan could just make out the driver's silhouette, eyes forward, head straight.

Alan shivered. "I can walk," he said.

"God I hate those bells," the woman said from behind him.

Alan nodded. "So do I."

Chapter
Thirty-Nine

As Trey slid into the car, Carolyn smiled at him. "Kinkaid said you're sane," she said as he closed the door. Trey turned to her, leaned in, and kissed her. "

No, she didn't," Trey grinned. "She just told you I was ready to come home."

Carolyn sighed. "Are you?" she asked.

"Yeah," Trey said. He turned and looked out the windshield. "Are you ready to take me home?"

She reached out and patted his shoulder. "Yes, Trey, I am."

Trey turned back to her. "Let's go, baby."

Carolyn put the car in drive and headed out from beneath the hospital awning. "Before you ask," she said as she wheeled the car through the turn, "Alan's doing fine."

Trey nodded. "Okay. Glad to hear that." He tapped his fingers on the console "Question is, are you okay?"

She smiled. "Will be. Missed my man," she said, placing her right hand on his knee.

"He missed you too."

The two drove in silence as they headed out on the freeway. Carolyn skirted through the traffic, heading for the toll road. "The Ice Cream Man came by the house."

Trey turned to her, a frantic look in his eyes. "What?"

She nodded. "He came by to see how you were doing."

"Jesus, he didn't come into the house, did he?"

"Hell no. Dick and I met him outside." The car merged onto the relatively clear toll road. Carolyn accelerated to 70 mph. She glanced at Trey. "Kind of spooked me, though."

Trey sighed. "What did he say?"

She shrugged. "Just... He was sorry he didn't stick around after I came to pick you up." She forced a giggle. "Said you spooked him."

Trey said nothing. An uncomfortable, palpable silence filled the car.

"I don't like him."

Trey nodded. "What did he call himself?"

"Reggie," she said in a flat tone.

"Hmph," Trey said, but a smile appeared on his face. "Reggie. Christ."

"Yeah."

"Has Alan met him?" Trey asked, a quiver in his voice.

"No," Carolyn said, glancing at him. "I don't think so. He hasn't said anything at least."

Trey nodded. "Good." He glanced at the clock in the dash. "Alan will be out of school now."

"He's fine."

"I know," Trey said. He leaned back in the seat and closed his eyes. She glanced at him again. He was already asleep.

Chapter
Forty

The house was quiet. His heart rate had finally managed to leave the race track and settle into its slow, steady rhythm. Even the walk across the T intersection to his house had been heart palpitatingly brutal.

The Ice Cream Man. The ice cream van. The woman in her car. Too much. Just too much.

Alan sat on the couch, his scratched and ripped backpack on the floor beside him. His trip to the concrete had worn a hole in his sweatshirt as well as one through his jeans. Mommy was going to ask questions. Alan looked at the bandage on his arm. The wound wasn't all that bad. Just friction burn, what Daddy called road rash. Small price to pay to get away from the thing in the woods.

Alan surveyed the darkened living room. The white blur of a figure moving through the deadfalls, breaking branches, matching him stride for stride.

It had to be the Ice Cream Man.

The memory of the word "YUMMY" glaring from the back of the parked truck in those bright, happy, crimson letters. Alan shuddered.

Daddy had seen something when he looked at the ice cream man. Something strange. Now Alan had seen something too.

A car rumbled outside. He cocked an ear and furrowed his brow. Mommy was home. Why was she home this early? Alan stood from the couch and walked toward the kitchen. He heard the garage door closing and smiled. The laundry room door opened. "Mommy, you're—" He froze and then smiled. "Daddy?"

Daddy stood in the kitchen, the corners of his lips rising upwards. Alan ran to his father, hugging him around the waist. "Here, champ," Daddy whispered.

"You're back?" His father nodded. "You're not going away again?"

"Not if I can help it," his father said. Daddy stared down at the boy. "You okay? Did you have an accident?"

"Fell down."

"Hey, you're blocking the road, guys," Mommy said from behind them. Alan peeked around Daddy's waist and saw Mommy, one hand clutching her valise, the other holding a fat manilla envelope.

"Okay, Mommy," Alan giggled.

He let go his father's waist and walked to the breakfast table. Daddy followed him, sitting down in one of the black wooden chairs. Alan cocked his head, his own smile disappearing.

"You okay, Daddy?"

Daddy looked up at him from the table. His face was a little pale and his eyes were scrunched. "Arm hurts, kiddo." Daddy nodded to him and smiled. "But I'm glad to be home." He pointed his index finger at Alan's arm. "Must have been a bad fall."

Alan bit his lower lip.

"Want to talk about it?"

"I'm going upstairs to change clothes," Mommy called as she made her way into the living room.

Daddy's eyes continued staring into Alan's. "Can you talk about it, Alan?"

Alan sat down in the chair opposite his father. "I don't know what happened."

"Okay, can you tell me what you think happened?"

The Ice Cream Man chased me, Daddy. It was what he wanted to say, but— "I got spooked and I ran," Alan said, "and I fell."

Leaning forward, Daddy's good hand reached across the table and grasped Alan's. "What scared you, son?"

Alan said nothing.

Daddy face was gentle and reassuring. "We have to make a deal, boy." Daddy cleared his throat, his eyes dropping back down to the table. "You know about the Closet Man."

"Yes, Daddy," Alan whispered.

"The Closet Man's not real, Alan. Never was." He raised his eyes back to Alan's. "You know that, right?"

Alan nodded.

"But I saw him anyway. It's something the mind does. It scares me, but it can't hurt me, right?" Alan opened his mouth to speak, and then closed it. "Hey," Daddy said, "we have to make a deal, kiddo. You tell me everything, and I tell you everything."

"No matter how crazy it sounds?" Alan asked.

"No matter how crazy it sounds. I," Daddy laughed, "am the master of crazy." He stuck his tongue out and crossed his eyes.

Alan smiled in spite of himself. His father leaned back in his chair, his lips a flat, expressionless line. "Okay, Daddy." Alan took a deep breath. "I met the Ice Cream Man."

Daddy's brows furrowed. "You met him?"

"Yes," Alan whispered.

Daddy leaned forward a little, placing his good hand on the table. "What happened?"

Alan shrugged. "I don't like him, Daddy. Something's wrong about him." Daddy said nothing. "He—" Alan swallowed hard. "He changed somehow."

"What do you mean?" Daddy asked.

"His face, his voice. He stopped looking...friendly."

"What did you see?" Daddy asked, his face growing stern.

"I don't know," Alan said. He tried to find the words, but they wouldn't come. The face growing longer, the nose jutting forward, and the teeth. The teeth. "He just changed."

Daddy leaned all the way forward in his chair, his face filled with excitement. "What about the eyes?" he asked in a rush of air.

"What are you guys talking about?" Mommy asked from the kitchen entrance.

"Nothing much," Daddy said without breaking Alan's stare. "Nothing we can't finish talking about later. Right, kiddo?" He nodded at Alan. Alan nodded back to him. Daddy grabbed Alan's hand and squeezed.

"Yeah, Mommy," Alan said to his mother.

"Okay," Mommy said.

"I'm going for a smoke," Daddy said. He stood up from the table, slid open the glass door and walked out into the sunroom.

Alan watched him go. He felt better, but something in the way his father had reacted when he told him about the Ice Cream Man brought goose pimples to his skin.

Chapter

Forty-One

The sun had dropped very low in the sky, threatening to
disappear altogether. Trey stared up at the thin, herring-bone
cirrus clouds, one hand on the wooden deck rail. The backyard
was where he loved to come when he needed to think. The
massive deck. The inviting furniture shaded by large oak and
gum tree branches. But not this time of year. The leaves had long
been shed and it would be at least another month before the trees
began sprouting new ones.

"Trey?" Carolyn's voice called from the backdoor.

"Yes?" he said without turning around.

"Alan and I are going to get us something for dinner. You want
to come?"

Trey thought for a moment and finally turned to her. "No," he said.
"I'm going to enjoy the last of the sun. You know where you guys are
going?"

She rolled her eyes. "Hell no. We'll figure it out at the last second
like we always do."

He laughed. "Okay, fine. You know what I like."

She walked from the backdoor to him, her nose close to his. "Yes, baby, I do." She kissed him quickly on the lips and then turned to walk back.

He grabbed her with his free hand, drew her close and kissed her hard. When he was done, he drew back.

She was flushed. "And that'll get you everywhere later," she whispered.

As she walked away, she turned to smile at him over her shoulder. The gesture made everything seem so normal, as though he hadn't spent the last couple of days in the nut-hatch.

Trey sighed and turned back to watch the sun. It was completely below the houses, nothing left but a fading glow.

"He changed," Alan had said.

The boy hadn't been able to explain it in any detail, but he had been close to saying something important. Trey was sure of it.

Bells. Distant. Trey swung his head toward the sound. It was getting closer, louder. Trey stepped toward the house and then stopped. The grubby man's lined, wrinkled, and angry face jumped into his mind. He shook it aside, clenching a fist.

"Not, now," he whispered.

The image left him, the world snapping back into reality. Heart thrashing in his chest, he went into the house and headed to the front door.

He peered through the tempered and warped glass. The world beyond seemed jagged and out of focus. The bells grew louder. Trey reached for the door knob and stopped.

"The Ice Cream Man. Traveling the blocks again? This late?" His skin tingled with electricity, heart still slam-dancing away.

"If you go out there," a voice inside said, "you're going to panic again." Trey's fingers began to loosen from the metal knob. "You're going to pass out in another fit. Or worse."

"Face. Your. Fears," Tony Downs' voice said in his mind.

Before Trey could stop himself, his fingers swiveled the knob and the door creaked open. That inside voice, the child within, screamed in fear. Trey stepped through the open door, closing it behind him. The bells were deafening. Across the street, Dick was already on his front porch, glaring at the oncoming van. Trey continued walking down the front deck and onto the driveway. He didn't bother looking up the street. Instead, he focused on Dick, watching as the man turned to follow the van's approach.

The bells. Trey closed his eyes for a second, and then opened them. In his peripheral vision, the cream-colored van came into view. Trey felt blood pounding in his ears, his electrified skin, and the buzz of fear. But he stood his ground.

The van was in full view. Ice Cream Treats. Sandwiches. Yummy! Trey smiled. The blood red words and images of children being tortured were gone. He blew out a long hiss through his teeth and watched the van head to the cul-de-sac.

"Nothing, nothing, nothing," he thought.

The van rounded the cul-de-sac, the bells blasting loud enough to hurt his ears. But he didn't care. The van. It was nothing more than an ice cream van. Plain and simple. Trey watched as it passed him again. The passenger side window was dark. Trey's smile faded. Glowing yellow eyes stared at him from the van's cab. He felt dizzy, but managed to stay on his feet.

"Hey!" Dick's voice said above the din. Trey turned his eyes to the front of the driveway. The big man strode toward him, a warm smile on his face. "You're back!"

"Yeah," Trey said, extending his hand. Dick's grin was infectious. "They let the cuckoo out of the nest."

"Uh-huh," Dick said. His smile faded a little as he pointed to Trey's arm. "How's the arm?"

Trey looked down at it. The pain from hitting Tony had subsided quite a bit, but it still ached. "Doing okay, I guess." He raised his eyes to Dick's and smirked. "You just want to know if I can still play disc golf, don't you?"

Dick laughed. "That obvious?"

"Hell, yes." Trey put his good arm on Dick's broad shoulder.

"And this time I'll have an excuse for sucking."

"No you won't," Dick said. "Not like it's your throwing arm." He turned toward the sound of the ice cream van's bells. The van had moved off the T and was heading deeper into the neighborhood. "Fucking. Hate. That. Thing."

"Yeah," Trey agreed.

Without turning, Dick asked "You feel okay? You looked a little wobbly."

Trey shrugged. "No, I'm all right. I just—" Trey dropped his eyes. "I just need time."

Dick nodded and turned back to Trey. The smile on his face had returned. "All you need, bro. I'm here, okay?"

One corner of Trey's lips raised in a smirk. "Yeah, you fat fuck. You're always there."

"Ha," Dick said. "Juvenile. Very, very puerile." His grin grew wider. "I'm proud of you. Never thought you'd descend to my level."

"Well," Trey chuckled, "was bound to happen sooner or later."

The sun's glow had finally disappeared from the sky leaving the street shrouded in deep shadow. Headlights broke through the gloom.

"Guess dinner's here," Trey said as Carolyn's car pulled into the driveway.

"Yeah," Dick said. He clapped Trey on the shoulder. "Let me know about disc golf."

He walked back down the driveway, saluting Carolyn as she pulled the car into the garage. Trey watched him go, the smile still on his face.

The morning walk to school, the return to routine, was somewhat cathartic. He'd managed to keep from passing out after seeing the Ice Cream Man the previous night, but he'd still seen something that wasn't there. When Carolyn and Alan came home with a bucket of fried chicken and all the fixings, Trey had put it out of his mind.

He'd listened with interest, catching up on Alan's days at school and Carolyn's stories about her pain in the ass client, or "The Jackass" as she referred to him.

Alan had laughed at that. When the boy started braying like a donkey at dinner, Trey had nearly spat a piece of chicken across the dining room table.

Even Carolyn had been laughing when she told Alan to stop it, all three of them giggling at the dinner table like nothing had happened the last few days. None of them mentioned his time away and Trey had been glad of it.

That night, he'd dreamed of the grubby man. But he hadn't screamed. He'd been back in the dank, pitch black, shit smelling closet, his hands rummaging through turds and puddles of piss to find anything with which he might cover himself.

Trey had awakened with a start, but was surprised to find he wasn't sweating or screaming. Instead, he felt drained.

In the bedroom's darkness, the monotonous sound of the heater broken only by Carolyn's soft snores, Trey flexed his fingers, playing the chromatic scale.

The grubby man had let him go. The grubby man had gotten what he wanted— complete submission.

Trey wondered what had caused the man to fracture into that beast. Parental? Something later in life than childhood?

Trey knew if he saw the man, he'd remember to ask him before he killed him with his bare hands.

"That could have been Alan," he thought, "instead of me.

Fast forward all these years, and that sonofabitch could still be out there, another child trapped in a closet, sitting in its own feces, hungry, terrified, and cowering in the darkness. Another child.

He had shivered then, rolled onto his side, and pressed his naked body against Carolyn's. Within moments, he was on the verge of drifting off.

Tony Downs' voice spoke in his mind: "Face. Your. Fears."

As he closed his eyes and headed toward deep, dreamless sleep, he'd smiled.

It was the best sleep he'd had in a long time. He was almost late in getting Alan up for school and out the door. The two of them walked fast through the dark, brisk morning to the school.

Alan was bundled up against the morning chill, but Trey's teeth chattered as the air bit through his light jacket.

There were more parents that morning than he had seen in quite a while. He meant to ask Alan what was going on, but figured he just hadn't gotten Alan to school this late in a long time.

Rather than walking back the same old way, and to warm up from the chill wind, Trey wound around the school toward the wood-lined path that snaked through the neighborhood. The subdivision, a little more forward-thinking than most, had actually left most of the forest intact around it, as well as through it.

People could walk for miles around the perimeter of the subdivision, hidden by tall pines and oaks. Although they kept the edges and the path itself neat and tidy, the rest of the green belt was unmaintained and as wild as they could keep it. It was one of the reasons he and Carolyn had moved there.

Although the oaks had long since shed their leaves to the forest floor, the pine tree branches still obscured the path; it was difficult to see through the tangle of green and brown to the road just beyond. Hearing the cars, however, was easy enough. Sometimes, late at night, he'd walked the path in the dark, marveling at the silence and stillness of the forest when no cars prowled the streets.

But at that time of the morning, the road was filled with commuters heading to work. The hum and growl of engines made the forest buzz. Trey wanted to take a deep breath of morning air, but knew it would taste like the end of a tailpipe. He had to wait until the path deviated further away from the road.

Eyes. Were those really eyes he kept seeing in the ice cream van? Yellow? Crimson flames within them?

Trey stopped in the middle of the path and closed his eyes. He calmed himself, willing his heart to slow, breathing deep despite the horrid tang of the car exhaust.

Eyes. The eyes.

He pictured the Grubby Man. His eyes had stared down from behind a long nose, wrinkled in one place and slightly off center. It had been broken before. The eyes had been wild and crazed, but they were green. Normal.

The Closet Man, was not a boogeyman, nor was the fucker in the ice cream van.

Trey shivered again as the wind rushed through the path, the bare branches clacking together like skeletal applause. He opened his eyes, staring down the concrete path.

Eyes. Bright yellow eyes with crimson—

"What the fuck is it about the eyes?"

He continued walking. Up ahead, the path hit a T intersection. The neighborhood was filled with the damned things. He'd have to cross the street before continuing down the trail.

A rather stout woman stood at the curb ahead, fiddling with something on the stop sign. Trey slowed. She was dressed in very heavy clothes and shivered despite them. Stray strands of blond hair darted out from beneath a blue, woolen cap.

A pile of poster-board squares sat at her feet, gently lifting and collapsing in the wind. He stopped, watching as she picked up two of the squares and stapled them together below the red octagon.

"Good morning," Trey said, still some feet away from her. She turned toward him with a start. Her eyes were red as though she'd been crying. From the streaked make-up that looked at least a day old, he thought that was a pretty good guess. He raised his hands. "Sorry, ma'am. Didn't mean to scare you."

She nodded. "Have you seen my son?" she asked, picking up one of the poster-board squares and handing it to him.

Trey looked at it and frowned. The sign had a black and white picture of a large boy wearing an angelic grin. Below the picture were his age, one year older than Alan, his height, 3 inches taller than Alan, and his weight, at least 30 pounds heavier than Alan.

Trey stared at the picture. "I think I may have seen him at the school."

Her face brightened, the weariness disappearing in a look of desperate hope. "When did you see him? Today? Yesterday?"

Trey paused. Fuck. Should have thought about that before I said it. The poster-board in front of him said the kid, James Keel, had been missing since Wednesday evening. He shook his head.

"I'm sorry. I meant I think I've seen him in the past. When I pick up my son."

Her face fell. With a slow nod, the look of despair returning, she cast her eyes downward. "Yeah, okay," she said. "Can you do me a favor?"

Unsure what to say, Trey nodded back to her.

"Will you keep an eye out for him?"

"Yeah," Trey said. An uncomfortable silence fell between the two of them. "Um, when did he go missing?"

She looked at the poster-board, and then looked back up at him. "Just like the sign says."

It was difficult, but he somehow managed not to roll his eyes. "I mean when exactly. Was he at school?"

The woman nodded. "He was at school all that day. And then—" She swallowed hard and wiped a tear from her cheek. "He never came home." She raised an eyebrow at Trey. "Do you walk your boy to school?"

He nodded. "To and from, nearly every day."

"Were you there that day?"

He opened his mouth and then closed it. *No, lady,* he thought, *I was in the booby hatch getting my shit together.* "No. I was, um, on business for a couple of days."

"Okay," she said in a whisper. "Just wondered."

"I'll talk to my son, though," he said. "I mean someone must have seen something."

She nodded. "The principal's going to talk to the kids today, ask them if they know anything."

"Good," Trey said. "Look, I'm sure we'll find him, Mrs. Keel."

"Helen," she said.

"Helen. I'm Trey Leger," he said, offering his hand. She shook, but still didn't meet his eyes. "Helen," he said, waiting until her eyes met his. "We'll find him."

"Sure," she said. "I have to post more signs."

"Do you need help?" he asked.

She shook her head. "No. This keeps me busy." She wiped another tear away with her chapped fingers. "I want to be home, waiting for his call, but I know I'll go crazy there."

"You forwarded it to your cell?" he asked.

"Yeah. If he calls, I'll get it."

The silence between them stretched out. Trey wanted to hug the woman, tell her it would be okay.

"I have to get back to work now," she said. She reached down, picking up the remaining poster-board squares. "Nice to meet you, Trey." She walked down the road's sidewalk, heading toward the neighborhood entrance.

Trey watched her go, wondering just how many street lamps and stop signs she'd already visited that morning.

He picked up his feet and continued down the path. Did his parents go through something similar when the Grubby Man had kidnapped him? Did they cover the neighborhood with posters? He couldn't remember. With both of them dead now, he'd never know what happened.

He crossed the street and headed deeper into the forest area. The wind still managed to bite him through the heavy growth, but he'd stopped shivering. Another twenty minutes and he'd be home. He hoped James Keel would be home soon too.

Chapter
Forty-Three

The morning led to afternoon. According to the thermometer hanging from the pine nearest the house, the temperature was 52 degrees.

Trey sighed. The damned thing always lied. It was in the shade all year round so it never managed to be accurate during daytime. The bright sun had been unfettered all day, free to cast its rays upon the world.

Remembering just how cold he'd been that morning, Trey bundled himself in a fleece and shrugged into his leather jacket. Once he started walking, he was sure it would get too warm.

He stretched his back. He'd spent the day in his chair pouring through dozens and dozens of emails. Responding back to his client regarding a work stoppage was always tricky. Also, the folks in Bangalore were pissed he hadn't explained why he'd dumped their code. It never ended.

Another file of code cleaned up. Another round of passed tests. Getting back into the routine was good, but every time he stopped running the code through his head, Helen Keel popped into his mind.

James. That baby-fat, angelic face staring back at him from white paper. Was Helen done posting all those signs in the neighborhood? Had she moved on to other neighborhoods?

He walked out the door and into the sunlight. As soon as he started walking down the road and toward the school, he knew he'd been right about dressing too warmly. He sighed to himself, putting one foot in front of the other. A few cars passed him on the road, stay-at-home Moms and Dads heading to pick up their kids. He didn't understand why more of them didn't just walk.

The school became visible through the trees. Trey looked toward the far end. The ice cream van, its bells silent and panel door closed, was parked just beyond the trees. In a few minutes, it would open and the Ice Cream Man would wait for the children to come streaming out of the school.

Although Trey had a difficult time imagining anyone buying ice cream on a day like today, there was always the candy.

He walked up through the parking lot. Cars lined the street at the side of the school, crowding the turnabout beneath the awning, engines running. There were no other adults standing at the curb near the playground. Trey frowned. Had he missed something? Or...

Trey nodded to himself. As he had walked to the school, every stop sign, yield sign, and "Slow Children At Play" sign had been plastered with the Keel poster. The Boogeyman was among them. Everyone was certain of it. Kids would walk in large groups, be forbidden from playing outside without adult supervision. They would be carted everywhere when possible.

He turned to look at the ice cream van. He saw nothing behind the tinted driver side window. But that wasn't surprising. The Grubby Man would— Trey shook his head. "He's not the Grubby Man," Trey whispered. "He's not."

The school buzzer sounded, the insect-like drone drowning out the low collective rumble of idling engines. Trey watched the van's side panel rise. The Ice Cream Man locked the hinges into place. As before, the shadowy darkness of the van's interior made the man appear spectral.

"Not," he told himself, "the grubby man."

He heard the sound of swinging doors and the sudden cacophony of conversation.

"And here come the kids," he said aloud. The smile on his face felt awkward. The children weren't running. They weren't streaming toward the ice cream van the way they did last time he was there.

His brow furrowed.

Through the crowd of children, he spied Alan. While the rest of the kids walked fast, either toward the parking lot to meet their parents or toward the playground, Alan walked with a slow, deliberate pace. Trey smiled. His son looked less than happy, but at least he was there, safe and sound. "Hey, kiddo," Trey said as Alan approached. "How was your day?"

Alan's lips curved up just the slightest bit. "Hi, Daddy." He stopped in front of his father, holding his pack by one strap. "It was okay, I guess."

Trey nodded. "Then why so glum?"

Dropping his pack to the ground, Alan rummaged and brought out a slip of paper. He handed it to his father, holding it between thumb and forefinger. Alan looked as though the paper might bite him.

Trey took it from his son and opened it. He scanned it and then looked back at Alan. "Do you know this boy?"

Alan nodded.

Trey folded the piece of paper and slipped it into the back pocket of his jeans. "I saw his mother this morning."

Alan looked up at him. "He's still not home, is he?"

Trey shook his head. "No, kiddo. He's not." Trey placed his hand on his son's shoulder. "When did you last see him?"

Alan said nothing for a moment.

"Come on, give."

"We had a fight the other day."

"Um, fight?" Trey asked. "What kind of fight?"

Alan stared down at the ground. "Jimmy's a bully, Dad."

"Ah," Trey said. "So what happened?"

Alan shrugged again. "He said some mean things, so I kicked him in the balls."

Struggling to keep from laughing, Trey managed to keep his face serious. "That, um, that's not good, Alan."

"No," he said. "It's not."

Trey sighed. "Come on, let's walk." Alan looked up at Trey, his expression confused. "Oh, you're in trouble, all right. But," he said, kissing the top of Alan's forehead, "I can tell you're being punished already." Alan blinked his eyes and then dropped them again. "Let's walk."

Alan lifted the pack back up, making sure to loop both arms through the straps. They walked toward the road, Trey's eyes locked on the ice cream van. There were only two kids getting treats.

"Did you see Jimmy again after that?"

Alan nodded. "He met me here the day Mommy picked me up." Alan followed Trey's gaze to the Ice Cream Man. "He said he was going to get me."

"Sounds about normal," Trey said. "What happened then?"

With a shrug, Alan pointed toward the ice cream van. "He went that way. I think he went to buy something from the Ice Cream Man." Alan wrinkled his nose. "I don't like him."

"No one likes bullies, Alan. Except for other bullies."

Alan shook his head. "No, Daddy. I don't like Jimmy, but I don't like the Ice Cream Man even more."

The Grubby Man, Trey thought. No, it's not the grubby man. "I understand that, too," Trey whispered. They walked in front of the van, still far enough away he could barely make out the man's hands as he exchanged money with the two young customers. "So what did you and Jimmy fight about?"

Alan said nothing.

"Alan?"

"Yes, Daddy," Alan said, refusing to look up at his father.

"What did you fight about?"

"You," Alan whispered.

"Me?"

"Yes, Daddy," Alan said. "He heard about... your accident."

"Ah," Trey said with a nod. "So. What did he say?"

"That you were crazy. That you were afraid of the Ice Cream Man."

"And that bothered you?"

"Yes," Alan agreed.

"Why?"

Alan looked up at him. They had made it past the ice cream van without Trey seeing anything. Alan swung a quick look back toward it and then stared up at his father. "Because you're not crazy," Alan said. "You're my Daddy and you're not crazy."

The two continued walking in silence for a moment, watching the cars make their way up the street. "Do you think you're crazy because I am?" Trey asked.

"You're not crazy," Alan snarled.

"I am, you know." He pinched his thumb and forefinger nearly together and smiled wide. "But just a little bit."

Alan giggled. "Okay, Daddy. Maybe a little."

"But," Trey said, his voice losing all trace of humor, "that doesn't mean you are. Okay?"

"Okay," Alan said in return, his voice flat. "I don't like the Ice Cream Man."

Trey nodded. "I don't either."

"He—" Alan broke off and cleared his throat. "I saw—" He stopped speaking again. What had he seen? Something moving through the woods. Something near the ice cream van. But he had no idea what it was.

"What's that, Alan? What'd you see?"

"Nothing," Alan said. "I saw nothing."

They walked in silence the rest of the way home. Alan watched the tree line, looking to see if anything followed them, but there was nothing there. A part of him wished there was, so he could show Daddy. So he could prove neither of them was crazy. But nothing happened. They didn't see the ice cream van on the way home.

Chapter

Forty-Four

The winter wind rose and fell. Behind closed eyes, Trey imagined the pines and the naked oaks swaying to the beat. A branch outside the windows scratched at the Hardie Plank. Meant to trim that one, Trey thought.

The bathroom door opened and he heard Carolyn's soft footsteps across the carpet. The bed barely moved as she lay down next to him, pulling the covers up over her body. He felt her cool flesh rub up against him, her breasts pressing against his back.

He purred. "Ready to go to sleep?"

She kissed the side of his neck and wrapped an arm around him. "How you doing, baby?" she asked.

He smiled in the darkness. "I'm doing okay."

"Did you—" She paused for a moment. He listened to her breathing, the feel of her heart beating in her chest. "Did you see anything today?"

"No," Trey said. "Nothing to speak of."

"Good," she whispered. For a moment, neither said a word. Trey felt the gentle tug of sleep and began to fall into its void when she said "Alan was pretty quiet tonight."

As much as he wanted to let go and disappear into sleep, he fought to stay awake. "We didn't talk about James Keel tonight," Trey whispered.

"I read the slip of paper he brought home."

"Yes," Trey said. "Alan knows the Keel kid." He paused. "I met his mother this morning." He listened as Carolyn took in a deep breath. "I watched her putting up those signs. Poor woman was freezing."

"Jesus, Trey," she whispered.

"Yeah." Trey rolled onto his back. Carolyn sidled over a bit to allow him more room, and then lay her head on his shoulder, her legs entwining with his. "I told her we'd find the kid."

"Where do you think he is?"

Trey shrugged. "I don't know, baby. But Alan had a fight with him the day he disappeared. Think he's feeling pretty guilty."

"What did they fight about?"

"Me," Trey said with a sigh. Carolyn was silent. "Guess James said some unflattering things about me." He chuckled. "Alan took exception and nutted him."

"Oh, boy," Carolyn said. She squeezed him close to her. "Is Alan okay?"

"I told him that wasn't the right thing to do. I handled it."

"Okay," she said and kissed his neck once more. "Should I talk to him about it?"

Trey yawned. "Let him come to you, baby. He's pretty embarrassed about it."

She curled her fingers in his chest hair. "Okay," she said again, kissing him again on the neck, her lips lingering longer than before.

"Better stop that," he said with a sigh.

"Just glad you're home, baby," she whispered in his ear. Her hand moved lower, grasping him. He let out a soft growl.

"Getting up early to play disc golf with Dick," he mumbled as she caressed him.

She chuckled. "Then I better get started," she said, nibbling his ear.

Chapter Forty-Five

Wind, driving rain, and the apocalypse were the only natural conditions that would ever keep Dick from playing disc golf. At least that's what he always told Trey. Saturday morning, Trey dressed in his sweat pants, a thick pair of socks, and a Houston Aeros sweatshirt.

Carolyn and Alan had already left the house, on some mission of errands he guessed. That meant there might be breakfast when he got home. The thought made him smile.

He filled a travel mug with coffee, grabbed his disc bag, and headed out the front door. Dick was already in his driveway, disc gear in hand, and leaning against the Regretta.

Trey smiled. "We ready to rock?" he yelled across the street.

Dick looked at him and then the sky. It had clouded up over night, sealing in the chill. "Yeah, I think it's just about cold enough to whip your ass but good," he drawled.

"I bet," Trey said with a laugh.

Dick waved him over, opened the trunk, and Trey tossed in his bag of discs. Dick followed suit with his own and closed the trunk with a bang. The car shuddered. Trey laughed. "You sure you didn't break it this time?"

"Shit, you kidding?" Dick stepped in and put the key in the ignition. The car chuffed and spat as he tried to start it. "Fuck," he said.

Trey laughed, opening the passenger door. "You want me to push?" Dick turned his head, eyes glaring at Trey. "Okay, forget I asked." Trey sipped his coffee.

Dick stomped on the gas pedal and turned the key at the same time. The engine roared to life and then settled into a constant purr. "There we go," Dick said. He gave Trey the finger, took the car out of park and they rolled down the driveway.

At nine in the morning with the temperature hovering at just over 43 degrees, the usual joggers and dog walkers were conspicuously absent from the sidewalks. Even the morning breakfast traffic seemed sparse. Trey looked over at Dick as he kicked on the Regretta's heat.

"We're going to freeze to death on the first hill," Trey chuckled.

Dick turned to him and smiled. "Wuss," he said. "You been here in Texas your whole damned life. You're lucky. Try living in the Great White North."

"Whatever," Trey said. "I bet you weren't crazy enough to play disc golf in the freakin' winter up there."

The older man shook his head. "Hell, no. Just crazy enough," he said, "to go sledding in zero degree weather with snow blowing sideways."

"And let me guess," Trey grinned, "it was uphill both ways?"

"Something like that, young'n," Dick said.

They were both quiet for a moment as the Regretta wound through the twists and turns heading for the disc golf course. As they pulled in, Dick pointed at the parking lot. "See? We're not the only ones." A number of cars were parked. Trey watched as a stray disc flew high into the air, stalled and then swerved off into the ground. "And it looks like the wind might make things interesting."

Trey groaned. "I haven't played in a week and you get me out here in the frozen tundra and shrieking wind?"

"Oh for fuck sake, Trey. It's a 2 mile an hour wind and it's the mid forties." He parked the car and pulled the keys. Dick turned to Trey and slapped him playfully on the shoulder. "Stop being a pussy."

"And here I thought you Canadians didn't curse."

"Shit," Dick said laughing, "I've been down here too long, hanging out with Texas scum like you."

They stepped out of the warmth, retrieved their bags from the trunk, and headed toward the practice tee. As Dick pulled out a disc to throw through the trees at the first basket, he looked at Trey. "Everything okay, man?"

"Yeah," Trey said. "I'm, um, better."

"Good," Dick said. He turned back to the brush choked, wood-lined path. He pulled in a deep breath and then forehanded the disc into the air at chest level. The disc flew between the trees, pinging the metal basket stand, bouncing off the post, and landing a yard shy of the basket. "Fuck."

"Yeah," Trey said. "Shitty throw. You should practice more."

"Asshole," Dick breathed and stepped back.

Trey stepped up to the starting line painted on the concrete path. He took a deep breath and backhanded his disc with a tight snap at the end of the arc. The disc wobbled from the spin, veering the slightest bit to the right, far enough for it to slam into a thin pine. The disc bounced off the trunk and flew at a diagonal. It landed about fifteen feet shy of the basket in heavy brush.

"Wow," Dick said. "That was a stellar throw. Just like last week." He winked at Trey. "Championship worthy."

Saying nothing, Trey reached down, picked up his bag, and began walking. The recent rains had left the ground pliable and sticky. He just knew his sneakers were going to be covered in mud by the ninth basket. Dick walked with him, pointing to the disc trapped in a pile of dead branches and leaves. Trey walked over to it, picked it up from the brush and held it. "How much you bet I can get it into the basket from right here?"

Dick shrugged. "Using that disc, or another one?"

"This one."

"I will bet you breakfast," Dick said with a grin. "An expensive La Madeleine breakfast."

"Oh, fuck," Trey said. "No bet, man. I've seen you eat." With Dick's laughter as a soundtrack, Trey tossed the disc softly toward the basket where it landed just in front. "Not bad, though."

"You know," Dick said, "you can talk to me about anything you need to."

Trey walked out of the brush and glanced at Dick. "Yeah, I know." He walked and retrieved his disc, not bothering to throw it in the basket. Dick nodded and got his own. "First tee?"

"You're brave today," Dick said.

"I'm out here with you, aren't I?" Trey stopped and turned toward Dick. He raised his eyebrows. "Aren't you going to—"

Dick shook his head. "Not today, bro."

Trey laughed. "You run out already?"

"Shit no!" Dick said. "Just don't feel like it." Trey shrugged and turned back to the first tee.

The course, once a giant landfill, had been molded into contoured hills. They were steep and inevitably channeled the wind. As the two men struggled up to the first tee, a cold blast hit them both. Trey looked at Dick, smiling as the older man shivered. "Pussy," he said.

Puffing from the exertion, Dick smiled. "Uh-huh. Keep talking like that, boy, while I kick your ass with my par shots."

"Right," Trey agreed. "Because I never get those."

"Damned right you don't." They reached the top of the hill. Dick laid his bag down on the ground with care while Trey dropped his next to the tee marks. "Mugs go first," Dick said.

Trey sighed. "One day I'm going to get to say that to you, you damned Canuck."

"One day," Dick agreed. "When Texas becomes part of Canada, maybe."

The metal basket gleamed in the channel between the tree branches. Trey started to throw and then stopped. The pines, oaks, and sweet gums were all mixed together, their branches snaking in and out, creating a face made of wood. It grinned at him. It was the Grubby Man. No, he thought, not the grubby man. The fiend. The Ice Cream Man. Trey shook his head.

"What's wrong, man?" Dick asked. Trey turned to him and shook his head again. Dick walked forward, placing a hand on Trey's shoulder. "Hey, man. You got that look in your eyes again."

"Just give me a sec," Trey said. He closed his eyes, but the shape was still there. "Fuck," he said.

Dick tapped him again on the shoulder. "Take as long as you need, kid." Trey opened his eyes and looked back into the brush. He couldn't see the shape anymore. He blew out a long sigh.

"That guy creeps me out too, you know," Dick said.

"Who?" Trey asked. He turned back toward Dick, ignoring the tee.

"The guy. The Ice Cream Man. Think he said his name was Reggie."

Trey nodded. "Carolyn said he'd come by the house."

"Yeah," Dick said, "and he freaked her the hell out." Trey said nothing. Dick leaned against the course post, his disc dangling from his fingers. "I don't like him."

"Glad you're not the only one," Trey muttered.

"No, man. You don't get it," Dick said. "I like everybody. And I don't like this guy. Anyone who hides their eyes like that—"

Trey frowned. "What do you mean he hides his eyes?"

"When he showed up at your house," Dick said, "he was wearing that hat. That porky thing. Anyway, he had it slung way down. Never got a really good look at his face, other than that damned nose. And his teeth? Christ."

Dropping his disc to the ground, Trey rubbed his hands together to keep them warm. "Teeth? Dick, tell me what you saw, man."

He shrugged. "They were, I don't know, abnormal or something. Guy could use a trip to the dentist. Fucking things were curved bad. And they were stained. And his breath," he shuddered. "Smelled like he'd been eating turds."

Trey laughed. "Turds, eh?"

"You know what I mean. Like he hadn't brushed his teeth in forever. Guy belongs in a Listerine commercial."

Trey's expression flatlined. "What do you think?"

"That depends," Dick said. "What do you see when you look at him, Trey?" Dick's mouth was set in a thin line, his eyes glittering in anticipation.

Shifting to lean on one foot, Trey looked down at the ground. He tried to find the words, and then gave up. "I'll sound crazy, man."

"Fuck that, Trey," Dick spat. The sound was enough to make Trey look at him. "Tell me what you see."

Dick didn't look like he wanted to know. Dick looked as though he had to know. "I see a ghoul."

"A what?" Dick asked.

Trey sighed. "Told you, you wouldn't—"

"Shut up and describe it."

It. Trey blinked at him and frowned. "I see eyes. Glowing yellow eyes with crimson fire for pupils." Trey took in a deep breath. "I see an impossibly long nose, canines dripping with saliva and hunger. I see talons for fingers."

Dick shuddered. "You have one fuck of an imagination," he said. Trey opened his mouth to say something and Dick put a hand out to silence him. "You have psychosis." Trey nodded. "You see things that aren't there." Trey nodded again. "But," Dick said, licking his lips, "how do you know they're not there?"

Trey blinked at him. "I— Well, um, people don't see—"

"I see," Dick whispered. "I don't see the— the thing the way you do, but Reggie's not, well, normal."

"Dick," Trey said, "what do you know?" Dick dropped his eyes and rolled the disc between his fingers. "Dick? I know I'm crazy. What about you?"

Dick shook his head. "I'm not crazy, Trey." He stared into Trey's eyes. "I'm not." Dick let out a sigh. "I've been watching that fucking van go around the cul-de-sac for days." He brushed his free hand against his beard. "I hear those damned bells in my sleep." Dick was silent for a moment, looking up at the sky as if to gather his thoughts. "So, I thought I'd call the Yummy Company to complain."

Trey blinked at him. "Why didn't you just tell the guy to turn down the volume?"

Silence fell between them. Dick looked down at the ground. "I don't- -" He cleared his throat. "I don't want to be that close to him again."

Trey nodded. "Okay, man. Go on."

"Two days after your...incident, that fucker came strolling down the street again. I looked out my window and took down the license number. You know, so I could tell the company what vehicle was causing the problem." He looked at Trey. "I searched for the Yummy company, Trey. It doesn't exist."

For a moment neither of them moved, or spoke. Trey realized he'd been holding his breath and then let it out in a long hiss between his teeth. "What do you mean it doesn't exist?"

"It. Doesn't. Exist," Dick said. "The closest thing I found was the Yum-Yum Corporation in Michigan. And they don't sell ice cream. They make toys."

"Okay," Trey said, "so the guy is running around claiming he's the Yummy Company. So what?"

Dick shook his head. "I don't know. It just gave me the shivers."

"So." Trey took a long look at Dick, then furrowed his brow. "There's something else, isn't there?"

With a sigh, Dick nodded. "Yeah, there is."

"Well?"

"I looked up the license plate number."

"You what?"

Dick smiled. "Remember, I'm a geek too, you know. I, um, visited a reverse lookup site." Trey looked confused. "Jesus, Trey. Think about it. They have services out there that will take your cash and a license number and get back to you with all the information."

"Fuck, is that even legal?" Trey asked.

"Yeah," Dick said with a nod. "Great way to make $24.95 a shot, don'tcha think? Someone sends you a license plate number, you buzz your cop buddy or your friend at the DMV, and have 'em fax you the report. Then you split some of the cash with them."

"So you got the report?"

Dick nodded. "Sure did."

"And?"

"That's the fucked up part. The owner's name ain't Reggie."

"So what is his name?"

Dick's face spread into a smile. "Archibald Simmons."

Trey laughed. "Archibald? You have to be fucking kidding me."

"No." Dick sighed. "Imagine the kind of shit that kid got in school." Dick's smile faded. "But that's not the strange thing."

"Oh, yeah?" Trey asked.

"Then what is?"

"I googled the address. It's in the warehouse district."

"Really?"

"Yeah," Dick said. "Like in an actual warehouse."

"So you know where it is?" Trey asked. Dick nodded. "So what do you want to do?"

"I want to play disc golf," Dick muttered. "I don't know, man." Dick looked up at him. "That boy is missing."

Trey nodded. Dick was shivering, but Trey couldn't tell if it was from the cold. "Okay. So—"

"Fuck this. Throw your goddamned disc before we hold someone else up."

Trey looked down the hill and saw another group of intrepid disc golfers heading toward them. "Okay," Trey said. He picked up his disc from the ground and looked down the hill. He flung it toward the basket. It flew through the clear space between the branches and landed in the tall grass a few yards away from the metal post.

They managed to play through nine holes. As they were walking toward the tenth tee, Dick turned to Trey and said his fingers were frozen. Trey seconded that. Disc golf was difficult enough without gloves; Trey couldn't imagine trying to throw a frisbee while wearing them.

As promised, Dick had kicked his ass anyway, finishing one over par while Trey managed a meager 9 over. As they walked in silence toward the car, Trey stopped. "Do you hear that?"

Dick cocked his head and then frowned. "You have to be fucking kidding me." The sound grew louder as the two men stood side by side in the cold. The cream colored Yummy! truck pulled into the parking lot, its bells pummeling the morning's winter birdsong. It paused for a moment, not far from the Regretta. The squealing brakes were barely audible over the sound of the bells.

"Get in the car," Dick growled.

Trey blinked at him, opened the passenger door, and stepped in. Dick continued standing by the driver-side door, glaring at the van. The ice cream van, receiving no interest from the few people in the park, turned out and exited, its bells dwindling in the distance.

The door clicked open and Dick ducked inside with effort. The Regretta bounced as he wedged himself into his seat. He stared through the windshield for a moment. Trey cleared his throat, but Dick didn't respond to him.

"You know," Trey said, "that kind of anger—"

"You want some breakfast?" Dick asked without turning his head. Trey cocked an eyebrow.

"Breakfast?"

"Yeah," Dick said, finally turning his eyes to meet Trey's. "You know, stuff you eat in the morning?"

"Um, we never—"

"Well, we're going to today, dammit," Dick growled. He inserted the key into the Regretta's ignition and started the car despite its protests.

Chapter
Forty-Seven

IHOP was the last bastion of breakfast dives left in the neighborhood. At ten in the morning, the crowds had finally started to dwindle, but they still had to wait twenty minutes for a table. Trey spent the time smoking cigarettes outside while Dick waited.

Trey wasn't sure what Dick had in mind. The trip from the disc golf course had been made with Pink Floyd blaring from the speakers and Dick refusing to talk. Each time Trey opened his mouth to say something, Dick held up a finger and sang along with Gilmour.

The Ice Cream Man. The ice cream van. The bells ringing out across the park as the van slowly made the circle, pausing just long enough to gauge interest. Trey hadn't really looked at the passenger side window. He'd been afraid he'd see those yellow eyes staring back at him. But Dick had looked. Dick had stared, his face growing angrier by the second. What the hell had he seen to set him off like that?

Archibald Simmons. A warehouse. The man had said his name was Reggie. The missing boy. The eyes. Trey sucked down the last bit of smoke from the cigarette, flicked the cherry and watched it jump into the wind and skitter across the concrete. He rolled the butt between his thumb and forefinger. And now breakfast? He looked up into the crowded waiting room and saw Dick gesturing toward him.

Trey tossed the butt into the ashcan and headed inside. It was ridiculously warm, as though someone had decided using the heater in Houston was an opportunity not to be squandered. He and Dick were the only two people in the place dressed in sweats. Nearly everyone else wore expensive winter coats or sweaters. Just as with the heat, the chance to dig out the winter clothes and wear them was an opportunity.

Dick grinned at him and then followed the waitress back to a booth. Trey followed suit.

Dick ordered two coffees and stared down at the menu. "You might want to get something pretty hearty. May not be home for a while," Dick said. "We got some planning to do."

Trey cocked his head, one brow raised. The coffee cups arrived and Dick immediately filled them both. "Dick, what the hell are you talking about?" Trey asked.

"Cream?" Dick asked as he slid the tub toward Trey.

"Dick?" Trey said, holding the tub with his finger-tips. The large man finished pouring the contents of a small plastic tub into his coffee and looked up. "What. The fuck?"

The big man opened his mouth in a grin. "I have an idea."

"Is it another crazy whack-a-doodle idea, or is it something that serves reality?"

Dick grunted and stirred his coffee. "We go to the warehouse tomorrow." Dick gestured toward the menu. "Figure out what you're gonna eat. We got shit to do."

"Why do you—"

"Look," Dick said, rolling the coffee cup between his gnarled fingers, "we think we know something."

"We do?"

"Shut up and listen to me, Trey." Dick cleared his throat and took a sip of coffee. "Needs more sugar," he muttered and grabbed a white packet. "We think there's something not right. Right?" Dick shook the packet and then tore it open, emptying it into the cup. "This Archibald, Reggie, or whatever the fuck he calls himself, he shows up. Less than a week later, a kid goes missing. Right?"

Trey nodded. "Yeah, that could be just—"

"Stop it, Trey," Dick said, glaring at him. "Just stop it." Dick took a deep breath and then pointed at him. "You're not afraid to say you're crazy. But you are afraid to think you're sane."

"I—"

"No," Dick said, "you are, man." He sat back on the booth cushion. "You see something when you look at that guy."

It was a statement, not a question, but Trey found himself nodding anyway. "Yeah, but I don't see what I used to see."

"What do you see now?"

"Just eyes," Trey said. "Not the same thing."

"But still you see something."

Yeah, Trey thought, but it's not the Closet Man or the Grubby Man. It's something else. "What do you see, Dick?"

"Just a guy," Dick said, taking another sip of coffee. "I told you that. But I know people. I don't trust him. And I don't think it's a coincidence that all this is happening at the same time. A missing kid, Trey." Dick rolled the cup between his hands and stared at the table top. "What if he's got something to do with that?"

Trey felt his stomach plummet. The image of Jimmy Keel's frozen, bloodless body in the bottom of a refrigerator, the face locked in a scream of terror, filled his mind. He shook his head. "Okay," Trey whispered. "So you want to go check out his digs?" Dick nodded. "How are we going to know if he's even going to be there? Not like he has a phone number, does he?"

"Shit no," Dick laughed. "We'll just show up at his warehouse. He came to your house without an invitation. I think we should return the favor."

"You really are asking for trouble. If he's not there, what are we going to do?"

Dick's lips twitched upward into a maniacal grin. Trey felt his stomach drop. "We take a look anyway."

Trey opened his mouth and then closed it. He'd been on the verge of yelling in the IHOP. Instead, he leaned forward, his face close to Dick's. "We break in?"

Dick nodded. "Fuck yes. We take a look around. We see anything hinky, we call the cops. If not," Dick said, taking a sip of coffee, "I'll join you in the rubber room."

"You are fucking crazy." Trey leaned back. An old couple in the next booth looked over at him as he said this. Trey didn't return their stare. He cleared his throat. "The cops aren't going to like this. We should go see McCausland."

Dick's smile faded into exasperation. "Trey, who's going to listen to a retired software developer and an insane one?" Trey said nothing. "Besides, McCausland's got no jurisdiction there."

"Dick, this is nuts. What if we're right? What if—" He cleared his throat again, shaking off the image of the ghoul, the flesh that moved like a snakeskin, the talons jutting from its misshapen hands, and the drooling maw. "What if he's there? What if—"

The older man's fingers thrummed against the tabletop as Trey's voice broke off. The smile returned to his face. "I'm going to do it," Dick said. "You can either come, or not. But I'm going."

Trey shook his head. "I still think you're the one that's crazy."

Dick nodded. "I've been called worse." He took another sip of coffee. "You in, or what?"

James Keel. Poster board affixed to stop signs, yield signs, "slow children at play" signs. A mother walking through freezing cold to tape, staple, and graffiti the neighborhood with pleas for information. The Ice Cream Man with all his young customers. The screaming bells. Trey shivered. "Okay," he said. "I'm in." The roiling in his guts stopped. He gave Dick a grim smile. "A rebel to the end, eh?"

"Well," Dick said as the waitress approached, "us old dope smoking hippies just have to keep fighting the system, bro."

"You aren't a hippie," Trey said with a smile. The waitress pulled out her pad to take their order. "You're just another dumb ass who got lost in the seventies."

Dick opened his mouth and then closed it as the waitress laughed.

"Your tip," he growled at her, "just got bigger, darlin."

Chapter
Forty-Eight

The drive was silent. Neither of them spoke the entire trip into Houston. From time to time, Dick looked at him, but Trey didn't make eye contact. He was afraid that if they started talking, one or both would lose their nerve. But that wasn't the only reason.

The clock on the radio had changed rapidly twice. He knew what that meant—the freezes were happening again— silent, absent seizures. He wondered if Dick had even noticed. If they started talking and he just froze, what would Dick do? Turn the car around? Panic? Trey was terrified enough already.

After their breakfast on Saturday, Trey and Dick had outlined a plan. Not much of a plan, but enough to get started. He went home and told Carolyn he and Dick were going disc shopping on Sunday.

He didn't like lying to her, but he knew she'd try and talk him out of it. Or worse, she'd march across the street and tear Dick a new asshole for even suggesting it. Besides, Dick just wanted to talk to the man and see his warehouse— no harm in that.

Still, he was nervous.

The Closet Man hadn't been real, but both the Grubby Man and the Ice Cream Man were real. The Ice Cream Man wasn't the ghoulish, fiend-thing that Trey's brain presented. But he was something. Something bad.

Dick's phone called out a street direction and he exited from 59 onto Jackson Street. They passed Minute-Maid Park, the Toyota Center, and the architectural horror known as the George R. Brown Convention Center. One quick turn beneath the high, concrete river of the 59 freeway and they were in the warehouse district.

The warehouse district had once been the heart of manufacturing in Houston. Instead, it was now filled with old buildings that had been converted into lofts, clubs, or artist collectives. Vietnamese restaurants and shops had popped up, filling damned near every remaining strip mall in the area. Most of the buildings were dank, old, and distressed. Even the refurbished buildings held to that look. Despite their age, he knew that some of the lofts went for upwards of 900k.

There were still some actual warehouses left in the area, places where small companies still produced, or distributed. Dick wound through the streets, turning in time with the phone's female voice. Trey felt his heartbeat rise. He tried to calm himself by tapping out the chromatic scale on the car door, but it didn't help. It was zero hour. The most terrifying thing about finding this place, about investigating, was the possibility that he wasn't crazy.

Dick pulled the Regretta into a well-weathered business park. The car bumped up the uneven, pothole-ridden driveway. Three story metal buildings sat on either side in long rows. Each building had a faded number written in orange on its side. "23-B," Dick whispered to himself. "Ah," he said, pointing with his free hand, "there it is." He downshifted the car and slowed. Unlike the other buildings that had a sign on them, like CFC Distribution or FM Manufacturing, building 23-B had no markings other than the orange address stamp.

Car still running, Dick turned and looked at Trey. His eyes were wild. "We're here," he said in a hoarse voice.

Trey nodded. "Yeah," he replied. Trey cleared his throat. "You scared?"

"Scared?" Dick chuckled. "About to piss my pants." Trey nodded again and Dick winked at him. "You okay, man?"

"I don't know," Trey said. "Just keep an eye on me, okay?"

Dick laughed. "You keep an eye on me, buddy. You're the crazy one. You should be just fine." He slapped Trey on the shoulder. "Ready?"

Trey shrugged and pointed. "There's a door right there. If he's here, let's just talk, okay?"

Dick shook his head. "He won't be here, Trey. I know it."

"But if he is—"

"Yeah, I know," Dick said with a nod, "if he is, we'll talk. We'll knock. We'll give him plenty of time." Dick stroked his beard. "And if he's not in, we'll go in."

"Okay." Trey shivered. "I'm ready."

Dick harrumphed. "Glad someone is," he said and turned off the car. He paused for a moment, the door handle in hand, staring at the building. The huge metal overhead door was locked in place by a padlock. Next to it was a normal sized door to the building with a knob jutting from its rusted surface. "Okay," Dick whispered and stepped out of the car.

Following suit, Trey slid out of the warm car and into the cold winter air. Forties. Trey had on a light jacket, something that would allow him to move, but did little to keep the chill from his bones. Trey closed his car door as quietly as he could. Dick did the same. Trey walked around his side of the car and stood next to Dick.

"Let's do this," Trey whispered.

The two of them walked up onto the door's landing, Dick in front. Trey felt every nerve in his body humming with energy like an electrical wire. Dick rapped his knuckles on the door. Each hollow boom echoed like a distant thunderclap. Dick paused, turned his head, and looked at Trey. He frowned at him and banged again, this time with his fist. They waited; the only sound was their breath and the distant roar of cars on the freeway. "Fuck this," Dick whispered.

He turned the knob on the door. It didn't budge. "Okay," Dick said. He brushed past Trey and to the Regretta's trunk. He opened it, rummaged in the back, and brought out a duffel bag. He unzipped it, and pulled out a crowbar.

"Hardly subtle," Trey said in a low voice.

"Uh-huh," Dick agreed. "Stand beside me and watch the alley."

Trey moved aside and did so. The road between the warehouses was empty and devoid of movement. Dick slipped the crowbar in between the jamb and the door and pushed, putting his weight behind it. The crowbar's sharp edge resisted the attempt as it tried to widen the slim gap. The metal sheet crumpled and groaned against the pressure. Dick cursed and put more force against it, grunting with the effort. He was rewarded with the sharp, crackling sounds of metal tearing. Trey watched the door cave inward as the metal gave. The dead-bolt slide screeched as it ripped free from the metal. The door fell open the slightest bit. Dick pulled back on the crowbar.

"Ready?"

Trey shrugged. Dick turned back to the door, raised his foot, and kicked hard. The door swung wide with a final screech of protest exposing a perfect rectangle of darkness. Dick bent down and put the crowbar back in the duffel, rummaged again, and came out with two flashlights. He handed one to Trey.

"Let's get inside fast," he whispered.

Trey nodded, and followed him into the warehouse, flashlight on.

Chapter
Forty-Nine

The winter sky cast the world in twilight shades and even the wan light did little to penetrate the warehouse interior through the open door. Dick walked forward into the gloom with caution. Trey stumbled behind him, trying to match his steps.

"I'm going to look for a light switch," he whispered.

"Why are you whispering?" Trey asked.

"Because this place is spooky as fuck," Dick hissed.

Trey watched as Dick's flashlight beam stabbed through the darkness, lingering over the walls and reflecting off the metal sheeting. Holding his breath, Trey turned around and closed the door. It protested, but closed, and with it, the last of the ambient light disappeared. Trey heard the hitch in Dick's breath. "You closed it, right?" he asked in a shaky voice.

"Yeah," Trey said. "Didn't want anyone coming by and seeing it open.

Dick didn't reply, but took a few steps forward. His flashlight beam swerved to the right and he halted.

"Hey, Reggie? Where you at?" Dick yelled. There was no response.

Dick took a deep breath and yelled louder "Archibald Simmons! Come out here, you sick fuck!"

Trey held his breath, feeling as though his heart would burst through his chest.

Dick chuckled. "Told you he wasn't here."

He swung the flashlight toward the far wall. The narrow beam illuminated the cream colored van. It was parked on the right side of the building, its top barely visible over crates and boxes. He turned toward Trey, his flashlight pointed beneath his chin. His face was lit in a manic grin. "We got some time, I think."

"Have to find a light switch, man," Trey said.

Turning the flashlight away from himself, Dick pointed it toward the wall. "Ah," he whispered and walked a few feet away. "Let there be light," he whispered.

Trey heard the click of a switch. The single overhead fluorescent buzzed to life.

"Jesus," Dick said. "Fucker likes it dark in here, doesn't he?"

Trey clicked off his flashlight. The glow from the high ceiling was barely enough to drive away the shadows from the building's interior. Boxes were stacked everywhere, stamped with the names of candy companies.

"He's got enough supply in here to feed schools for months."

"Yeah," Dick agreed. "Guess he buys everything in bulk."

Trey split off from Dick, stepping through the maze of boxes toward the ice cream van. The large vehicle was cloaked in shadow, parked with its nose toward the roll up door. He tried to look through the tinted windows, but saw nothing but impenetrable darkness. With a sigh, Trey tried the door handle on the passenger side. Nothing. It moved up and down with liquid ease, but the door didn't pop open.

"Door's locked."

"Not surprised. Hey," Dick said, "come over here, man."

Trey walked away from the van and wound back through the maze. As Dick came into view, Trey saw the impish smile on his face.

"What?" Trey asked.

Dick pointed toward a row of dark rectangles standing against the back wall.

He looked back at Dick. "What are they?"

"Don't you hear the hum?" Dick started walking toward them. Trey realized he'd been hearing the hum for a long time.

"Refrigerators?"

"Yeah," Dick said as he reached the long row. "I count seven of them. Freezers," Dick's face was manic, his eyes wild, smile wide. Trey walked forward to stand next to him and stared. "Pretty ridiculous for ice cream, eh?" Dick asked.

The freezers were hardly industrial models. Most of them looked as though they'd been picked up at Sears on the cheap. Their faded and chipped surfaces were grimy with dust. Trey turned on his flashlight and swept the beam over the freezer in front of him. He took a deep breath. "This guy has an unhealthy fascination with cream colored things, doesn't he?"

"Who the fuck padlocks a freezer door?" Dick asked, pointing at the keyed square hanging off the side of the door handles.

"Someone who doesn't want people peeking?"

Dick nodded. "Wanna peek anyway?"

"How you going to get through the lock?"

The smile on Dick's face was no longer giddy, but grim. He turned on his own flashlight and swept it over the side of the freezer door. He smiled. "Hinges, baby. Hinges." His light illuminated the hinge holding the left door shut. Three hinges evenly spaced. He clicked off his light and bent toward his bag. "Just need the proper tool," he said. He pulled out a hammer and screwdriver.

"Um, were you ever a thief?" Trey chuckled.

Dick looked back at him. "Well, in Calgary there was precious little to do in the summer. So," he said with a grin, "we improvised. I kind of stopped when my folks moved back to Texas."

"Uh-huh," Trey said, returning the infectious grin. The giddiness in his body was thrumming again. He didn't want to see what was in the freezer. But at the same time, he knew he had to. "Do it. I'll watch the master at work."

Placing the screwdriver beneath the hinge, Dick slammed the hammer into its bottom. The ancient bolt holding the hinge together popped up and out. Dick repeated the action on the middle hinge, having to hit twice before the bolt screeched and came loose. The bottom bolt was much more difficult since Dick had to go from the top. When he couldn't get it to move, he shrugged, put the screwdriver sideways against the hinge, and pounded with enormous force. He completely missed the top of the screwdriver, the hammer smashed into the concrete with a loud thud.

Dick cursed. "Put your light down here," he said.

Trey bent and shined the beam over the hinge.

"There ya go," Dick whispered. He took aim and slammed the hammer home against the hinge. It popped off the side of the door with a screech as the metal gave way under the pressure. The door shuddered and squealed. "Hand me the crowbar," Dick said.

Trey clicked off the flashlight, picked up the wrecking bar and placed it in Dick's raised open palm. Dick stood on his toes, placed the fork end under the top bolt and pulled. The bolt shot up and out and disappeared into the gloom, jangling against the concrete.

"There we are. Hold the door," he said softly and placed the wrecking bar's fork beneath the middle bolt. Trey reached forward and lifted on the handle. Dick pulled and the last bolt popped. "Now pull," Dick whispered.

The door popped free. The sudden weight was heavy enough to send Trey backwards, but he managed to keep his balance. He felt the edge of a box against his heels and cursed. "Okay," Dick said turning toward him, lean it against the edge here." Trey stepped forward and put the door up against the edge of the freezer. Dick moved around and repeated the exercise with the other door. Once the hinges were popped, Trey lifted the door off and dropped it to the ground, the sound of metal against the concrete booming and echoing around the warehouse.

The freezer didn't have a light of any kind. Frosty air flowed out in a cloud of mist. Dick turned on his flashlight and poured over the interior. Boxes and boxes of ice cream sandwiches, popsicles and creamsicles stared back at them.

"Huh. Guess I was expecting," he said through a sigh, "something else."

Trey nodded. "That was anticlimactic."

Dick gestured toward the other six freezers. "We ain't done yet."

Trey cursed. "Fuck. I was afraid to look in this one."

"Yeah," Dick agreed. "So, let's play roulette. I don't want to do all these fuckers unless we have to." Trey nodded. "So choose."

Carrying his flashlight in his hands like a baton, Trey moved down the line of freezers. They all looked the same at first. Each a humming cream colored rectangle. At the fourth in the row, he stopped. He panned the flashlight over the freezer's front. Trey nodded to himself. "Bigger," he said aloud.

"What?" Dick said.

"This one," Trey said, pointing his beam in front of him. "This one. The lock is bigger. I think the freezer is too." He shined the light over the hinges. "Different type of hinge."

Dick harrumphed. "That's contestant number two in 'who wants to vandalize a freezer.'" He dragged the duffel bag behind him as he approached Trey. Dick dropped the bag and stepped close to the hinge. "Hmm. This might suck," he said. The hinge itself was a circular fitting covered with an assembly. "But," he said, "everything must bend to force."

"So," Trey said, turning toward him. "No finesse job?"

The wrecking bar appeared in Dick's hands along with the large, steel hammer. "Fuck no," Dick breathed. "This is a job for massive destruction."

Trey felt a sinking in the pit of his stomach as Dick lined up the end of the crowbar on the door's back edge. "Coming in from the side," he whispered, "and going to knock this fucking door off."

The sound of each blow hurt Trey's ears. Dick was sweating,

despite the warehouse chill. His right hand continued its punishing blows against the freezer door. Trey watched the metal splinter and the door's finish pucker and strip with each strike. The top hinge assembly popped up holding the door together with nothing more than a narrow strip of metal. The last blow severed it. Although the door didn't hang open, it did seem to lean a bit.

"Fuck," Dick breathed, wiping his forehead with a sleeve. "You just had to pick this one, didn't you?" Dick asked.

Trey said nothing, but shined his light on the bottom hinge assembly.

Dick groaned and knelt down, his knees popping. "Fucker," he whispered. On his knees, Dick lined up the crowbar and once again began banging the hammer. It took many hits, but eventually the assembly gave.

Trey was smart enough to have one hand against the door to keep it from falling atop Dick. "Fucker's heavy," Trey said aloud, struggling to keep the door in place. Dick dropped his tools into the duffel bag, stood, and placed his hands on the door's ruined edge. "Okay?" Trey asked.

"Okay," Dick said. The two of them sidestepped, bringing the door off the freezer. The freezer seemed to bellow smoke in the dim light, the frigid air pouring out in a wall of mist. They lay the door down and stared inside.

Trey paused for a second and then played the beam of his flashlight into the darkness.

Chapter Fifty

"Goddammit, Trey," Dick was saying. Trey blinked, and then winced. Dick's fingers were clenched in a death grip on the meat of his shoulder.

"What are—"

"You okay, man?" Dick's eyes glittered with fear, his pale face holding barely concealed revulsion. "You kind of, well, just stopped."

Trey shook his head from side to side, trying to clear it. "Yeah, that happens."

"Don't look in there, okay?" Dick removed his hands from Trey's shoulder. "Don't want you...doing whatever it was you just did."

Trey turned back to the freezer, his flashlight beam still pointed into its interior. Trey gulped and felt bile rise in his throat. "Holy, Jesus," he whispered, stepping back.

A pile of Ziplock bags were neatly stacked. Labels in a strange, blood red script were affixed to each bag. Transparent buckets that perhaps once contained ice cream were filled with a frozen crimson liquid.

At first, all he'd seen were coils of meat inside the Ziplocks, link sausages or brats perhaps. But the all too familiar shape atop the pile brought it home.

"Jesus," he whispered again. He looked closer, seeing the textured bumps and bends in the grey sausage looking meat. Intestines, Trey thought. His shaking flashlight moved sideways. The beam illuminated delicate fingers clenched in a fist, the skin white as bone.

"Is that a fucking hand?" He gulped back vomit, turning toward Dick. Dick had already puked on the floor next to the freezer.

"We have to call the fucking cops," Dick whispered. "We have to." Bags and bags piled atop one another, all labeled in that strange script. "Whatever you do," Dick said, "don't look in the bottom drawer."

"Why?" Trey asked in a shaking voice. "What— What's in there."

Dick shook his head. "I'm not saying. Just— Just don't look in there."

"Okay." Trey backed into a stack of boxes and turned off the flashlight.

"We have to call the cops, Trey. We have to."

"How many—" Trey gulped and then cleared his throat. "How many children do you think are in there?"

Dick shook his head again. "I don't know, but from what's in the bottom drawer, I'd say at least two."

Trey turned and looked at him. "I don't want to know, do I?"

"No, man. You don't. You—" Dick broke off, looking back toward the warehouse door. "Trey," he whispered. "Do you hear something?" The two men froze, Trey's head cocked to one side.

A shuffling, sliding sound came from somewhere behind the labyrinth of boxes. Dick turned and pointed in that direction and then pointed down toward the duffel bag. Confused, Trey just blinked at him. Dick bent, his body shivering, and pulled the wrecking bar from the duffel bag. He handed it to Trey who took it with numb hands. Dick reached in again and pulled out the hammer.

Dick took two steps toward the entry to the box labyrinth, Trey following behind. The sound stopped, leaving the warehouse silent. The two men froze, each holding their makeshift weapons before them.

Trey's heart trip-hammered in his chest, blood pounding in his ears. He opened his mouth to speak, and then closed it again. The shuffling sound started once more. It was closer now. Trey looked around. They were barely inside the maze of boxes. If someone came at them from the front of the maze, they'd have nowhere to go.

He reached out a hand and placed it gently on Dick's shoulder. Dick stiffened and then turned to face Trey, his face pale and terrified.

"Go back," Trey mouthed and began stepping backwards.

An inhuman scream rattled the warehouse. Trey panicked, falling backward to the concrete. Dick whirled around, once again facing the maze of boxes ahead of him. He clicked on his flashlight and screamed. Trey shuffled backwards on his hands, his feet scrabbling for purchase against the concrete. Dick backpedaled, his flashlight falling and crashing to the floor. Between the V of Dick's legs, Trey saw something moving and moving fast. A shadowy form slid toward them with liquid grace and speed. Trey opened his mouth to scream and then something loomed over Dick.

From the floor, he made out a misshapen head rising over Dick's shoulder, fierce, yellow eyes burning through the shadows. Large canines appeared from behind wide grey, lips.

Dick screamed again.

"No!" Trey yelled.

The thing's eyes blinked, and leered over Dick's shoulder at Trey. It snarled at him and lifted a taloned hand high in the air. The claw descended in a blur. The sound of ripping fabric cut off Dick's scream. Dick fell backwards to the concrete, the thing standing over him. Its taut, sinewy body pulsed with rapid intakes of air, blood dripping from one of its taloned hands.

"Go the fuck away!" Trey yelled again, his voice cracking but still lifting above the sound of Dick's own bellow. The thing grinned at him and took a step backwards. "I see you!"

It said something in a guttural, liquid string of syllables and leaped back into the shadows. Trey heard the click and clack of taloned feet on concrete. The door at the front of the warehouse opened and then slammed shut with a bone-crushing bang. He still held the wrecking bar in his clenched hands. Dick's screams had turned into whimpers. Trey shuffled forward. "Dick?" The older man was holding his chest with his hands. "Dick?"

"Can't breathe," he whispered. "Can't breathe."

Trey fumbled in his pocket for his cellphone. He managed to pull it out and it fell to the floor from his shaking fingers.

"Calling the cops," he said aloud. His clumsy fingers scrabbled over the plastic casing and finally managed to hold it. He tried to type in his code one handed. The phone vibrated and presented a "Wrong Code" message. "Fuck!" he screamed. He forced himself to slow down. Dick was taking in shallow breaths, his chest barely rising with the effort. Trey closed his eyes, let out a deep breath and he typed out the numbers slowly and carefully. The phone unlocked. He dialed 9-1-1.

The interview room was much like the room he'd met Tony
Downs in at the hospital. He sat in an uncomfortable plastic
chair facing a metal table. The mirror that covered one of the walls
showed his frazzled reflection. Trey stared up at it occasionally
with a bone-tired weariness. The massive adrenaline rush at the
warehouse had left him feeling drained and empty.

And on top of it all, he'd been there for more than an hour. A cold
cup of coffee sat on the metal table. He glowered at it, wondering
when they were going to bring someone else in the room to ask him
if he needed anything. The last officer that had come in had only
given him a blank stare when he asked how Dick was doing.

Trey laid his head down atop the table, but found it too uncomfortable
to sleep. He was slumped in the plastic chair, fighting the urge to nod
off.

Waiting. Waiting. Waiting.

The door clicked and he turned his head to stare as the knob
swiveled. A man in a crisp suit entered the room carrying a large
folder. "Mr. Leger," he drawled. "My name is Detective Dewhurst."

Trey blinked at the man and said nothing.

Dewhurst shook his head a little. "I'm very sorry you've been in this room for so long."

"Please don't ask me if I need anything," Trey whispered, "and then leave."

"Oh, I'm not leaving," Dewhurst said. He nodded toward Trey's coffee. "Do you need some more coffee?" Trey shook his head. Dewhurst sighed and sat down in the chair across from Trey. He placed the folder near the table's edge and folded his hands atop it. "Do you have any questions for me?"

Trey nodded. "How's Dick?"

Dewhurst sucked in a breath. "Mr. Dickerson's in ICU. He had a mild heart attack," he said in a toneless voice. "He lost quite a bit of blood to boot."

"Fuck," Trey breathed, raising a hand to his face. He rubbed his eyes. "Is he going—"

"My understanding, Mr. Leger—"

"Trey, please."

Dewhurst's smile returned. "My understanding, Trey, is that he's going to be okay."

Trey blew out a sigh. "Thank, God," he whispered.

"Yes," Dewhurst agreed. "Now, do you have any other questions?"

Trey nodded. "Do I need a lawyer?"

Dewhurst blinked at him, his expression flat. "Not at this time, Trey. Not at this time." The detective pulled a sheaf of paper from the folder and held it up. "I want to read something to you. And you might find it a trifle upsetting." Trey opened his mouth to say something, but Dewhurst held up a single finger to shush him. "If I may, Trey." Trey closed his mouth and leaned back in his chair. Dewhurst nodded to himself. "We looked in the busted open refrigerator. We found, uh, the remains of at least three people. Children," Dewhurst said, peering over the paper at him. "All frozen. All wrapped in plastic. And buckets that appear to be filled with frozen blood."

Trey swallowed. The color had drained from his face and the weariness threatened to crush him. "I—"

"What I want to know, Trey," Dewhurst said, dropping the piece of paper, "is what you were doing there."

"You wouldn't believe—"

"Try me," Dewhurst said, his eyes glaring into Trey's. "I don't believe you have anything to do with this, sir, but I want to know how you and your friend ended up in that warehouse."

Trey took in a deep breath, and began to explain. He told Dewhurst about the ice cream van, how he and Dick hadn't liked the man. About Dick's research into the dummy company and about the missing boy. He left out his time at the hospital as well as his visions. As he talked, Dewhurst pulled a small notebook from his suit coat pocket and began taking notes. When he was finished, the detective had scrawled several pages worth.

"Is that everything, Trey?" he asked without looking up at him.

"Yes," Trey said.

Dewhurst nodded. He looked up from the notebook, a shark's grin on his face. "How many times have you been institutionalized, Mr. Leger?"

Trey's mouth opened and then he closed it again. "I— How do you—"

"Police report, sir. From four years ago." The cop opened the manilla folder and pulled out another sheet of paper. "Although your wife chose not to file a complaint, the officer still logged it."

"But—"

"Wonderful thing, computers," Dewhurst said. "Makes it easy to search across the neighboring jurisdictions." He tapped his pen on the metal table. "I'm going to find out everything, Trey. So if there's anything you left out, I suggest you tell me now."

Eyes cast down at his reflection in the table, Trey found his right hand performing the chromatic scale. The three fingers danced in the fast repetition. He stopped them and looked up at Dewhurst. "I'm not crazy," he said softly. "I'm not."

The grin on the cop's face faded into a gentle smile. "No one says you are, Trey."

"Bullshit," Trey whispered. "You look at me. You call in some favors, maybe squeeze a little information from one of the nurses at the hospital, or you talk to someone in Montgomery County. They pull a few files for you. Let you peek at something. You'll find out all that crap. And then you'll come back here and call me crazy. Just like most other people would."

"Assuming," Dewhurst said as he leaned forward, "that I had time to do all that, Trey, and that I had that many friends, what would I find out?"

"I have not been read my rights, Detective. Is that correct?"

"That is correct," Dewhurst said in a loud, clear voice, "you have not been read your rights, sir."

"So you can't use any of this?" Dewhurst nodded. "Say it," Trey snarled.

Dewhurst leaned back in his chair, his brows furrowed. He turned to look at the mirrored wall and mimicked slashing his throat with his hand. "The department," he said as he turned back to Trey, "may not use any of this interview against you, Mr. Leger."

Trey nodded. "I suffer from psychosis, Detective," Trey whispered. "Do you know what that means?"

Dewhurst nodded. "It means you are delusional. Prone to hallucinations, perhaps."

"Yes," Trey said. "I'm amazed you know the meaning of the word."

The detective chuckled. "Afraid I have friends in the field who've corrected me more than once, Mr. Leger." He tapped his pen again against the metal table. "So, Trey, did you see something?"

Trey sighed. "Yeah." He cleared his throat. "I saw a thing." Dewhurst's eyebrow raised. "A thing dressed like a man."

Pursing his lips, Dewhurst looked down again at his notebook. "What did this *thing* look like, Trey?"

"Fuck," Trey whispered, "it looked like a thing, okay? Tall. Skin all fucked up. Jaw filled with large teeth, fingers that ended in long talons. Shit like that."

"Is that what attacked your friend?" Trey nodded. "You realize I can't put out an APB on that," Dewhurst said.

Trey shrugged. "He always wears a cream-colored jumpsuit."

"Wears? But what was he wearing today?"

"I—" Trey dropped his eyes to the table. "I don't know. I couldn't see— He just looked like a shadow."

Dewhurst sighed. "So I'm putting out an APB on a tall, walking crocodile that looks like a shadow. Oh, and he might be wearing a white jumpsuit."

"I know," Trey said. "I told you it would all sound crazy." Trey raised his eyes. "Until today, he always wore a hat too."

"Is that important?"

"He—" Trey swallowed. "It always hid its eyes. Always wore a hat pulled low so you couldn't really see them."

Dewhurst nodded and scribbled something down on the paper. "That's something I can use," he drawled. He closed the notebook and placed the pen beside it. He tented his hands and locked eyes with Trey. "You think there's a monster out there." Trey nodded. "I believe in human monsters," Dewhurst said softly. "And I believe you saw something, Mr. Leger. And we're going to catch him."

Trey swallowed again. "Thank you," he whispered.

"Don't mention it. I'm going to call your wife, Trey. I'll have her come pick you up."

Chapter
Fifty-Two

The cold wind bit through his jacket. Trey shivered, but refused to go back inside. Although the station was actually off to the side of downtown, the tall Houston buildings made the city into a wind tunnel turning a stiff breeze into a strong wind, and a strong wind into a hurricane. Every few minutes, an officer or two walked past, coming from or going to their patrol cars. Occasionally, they led in a person in cuffs.

Evening was fast approaching. The clouds had thickened, all but hiding the sun save for a gentle glow toward the west. He'd been standing in the cold for at least ten minutes, waiting for Carolyn to pick him up. He wrapped his arms around himself. It was damned cold and getting colder. He fought the urge to walk back into the station. It was warm inside, but he didn't want to see Dewhurst. And he sure as hell didn't want all those cops staring at him; he felt creeped out enough.

Dewhurst. The guy said he believed in human monsters, but Trey didn't know what that meant. At first he thought perhaps the detective was making fun of him, dismissing the story as delusion, but Trey wondered.

The detective seemed sympathetic. *No,* Trey thought, *that's the wrong word.* Was it possible he'd seen something like that in his life?

Dewhurst had left him in the interrogation room for a while after their conversation. When he returned, he wore a grim smile and put a hot cup of coffee in front of Trey.

"Do me a favor," the man drawled, "drink this, will you?"

Trey had smirked. "Any particular reason why?"

Dewhurst nodded. "You're pale, Mr.— Trey. Very pale." Dewhurst sat down across from him again. "Think perhaps you need something hot to drink."

"Okay." He took the coffee cup and sipped. The black liquid scorched his tongue, causing him to grunt. "Shit."

"Yeah," Dewhurst said. "Freshly made just for you." Trey said nothing and placed the coffee cup back down. Dewhurst stared at him. "Called your wife," he said in his soft drawl.

"I'll bet that was fun."

The detective chuckled. "I only told her you were here and needed a ride. Nothing more."

"Oh, thanks," Trey said with mock gratitude. He blew on the styrofoam cup, steam blowing back into his eyes and face, making him feel more awake.

"Can I ask you a question?"

Trey said nothing, only nodded.

"You didn't tell your wife you were coming down here, did you?"

Trey shook his head. "No. She thinks Dick and I came down to Houston to go disc shopping."

Dewhurst's eyebrows raised. "Disc shopping?"

Another sip of the hot coffee. It didn't burn him this time. The black liquid warmed his throat before exploding in his belly.

"Frisbees. We play frisbee golf." Trey placed the cup back down on the table. "Guess we won't be doing that again anytime soon," he muttered.

"You," Dewhurst said softly, "look a little less peaked." Trey looked into the man's gaunt smile and felt like hitting him. "Glad to see that."

"What's your game, Detective?" Trey asked in a growl.

Dewhurst's smile flat-lined. "My game is trying to figure out who slaughtered at least three children and wrapped them up like they were going to be sold at Hubble and Hudson's premium meat counter."

Trey blanched.

"You haven't helped me out all that much, Trey."

The meat. Flesh enclosed in Ziplock bags. Coils of grey intestines wound together like sausage for sale. The strange crimson scrawl of symbols on each bag. Buckets filled with a dark, frozen liquid.

Dewhurst's worried grimace was inches from Trey's face. "Trey?" the man said, loud enough to hurt Trey's ears.

Trey leaned back in the chair, causing the legs to tip. Dewhurst quickly placed a hand on his shoulder, steadying him back to the floor.

"Easy, sir," Dewhurst whispered.

"I—" Trey tried to speak, but his voice came out in a croak.

Dewhurst patted his shoulder and retreated a little, giving Trey some space.

"Thank you," Trey said.

Dewhurst nodded. "You okay?"

Trey nodded. "I, um, have a type of epilepsy."

"Absent seizures," Dewhurst nodded. "Yeah, I know." Dewhurst pointed to the cup. "Go ahead, drink your coffee." He walked back around the table and sat in his chair.

The coffee was much cooler now. He swallowed a mouthful and placed the nearly empty cup back on the table. "Jesus," he whispered, "how long?"

Dewhurst shrugged. "Couple of minutes." Trey cursed. "Happens when you get stressed?"

Trey said nothing, but nodded.

Dewhurst's phone dinged. The man sighed, pulled his cell from the inside pocket of his jacket and checked the screen. He grimaced and then placed it back in the pocket. "Okay," Dewhurst whispered. "Your wife said she'd be here in about forty minutes." He looked down at his watch. "You shouldn't have to wait much longer." He rose from his chair. "I have to go now, Trey. You can wait in here if you like."

"Need some air, Detective."

"Okay, Trey. I'll escort you outside." The man's smile grew wide and genuine. "Let's get you another cup of coffee."

35 miles to the north, Trey's house waited for him, Carolyn, and Alan to walk through the door and make it a home again. How long would Dick's house wait in silence for its owner to come home?

Dewhurst had told him which hospital Dick was in. The cops were waiting for him to wake up so they could talk to him, but Trey was certain the doctor would keep them at bay even if Dick woke up and wanted to talk.

Trey sighed. What the fuck had they been thinking?

No one would believe them. No one would take the psychotic and his pot-smoking neighbor seriously. The Ice Cream Man.

Fuck. The kids all loved him. "Except for Alan," Trey whispered aloud. What did Alan see when he looked at the...the thing? *Does he see what I see?* Trey shivered again.

The face. The thing in the shadows peering at him over Dick's shoulder, all teeth and scarred flesh. The stench of rot and offal. But the worst part had been that maniacal, malevolent grin. When it had spoken and pointed at him, Trey had nearly wet his pants. That sound was the most terrifying thing he'd ever heard in his life.

But where had it gone? Its lair was covered. Dewhurst said the warehouse was a cornucopia of forensic evidence and the techs would be there well into the evening. Although Dewhurst didn't say it, Trey was certain the cops would be staking it out as well. They had its van and its food.

What would happen when it got hungry again?

Trey looked up as a car pulled in. Carolyn smiled and waved at him. Trey returned the smile and walked to the car. Something past the car caught his eye and he looked up as he opened the door. Standing near a street lamp across from the police station, something glowed in the day's soft light. A tall bum wrapped in a trench coat, a baseball cap pulled low over its face so that just a pair of eyes shone from beneath. They looked as yellow as the arc-sodium street lights.

Trey shook his head and looked back. The bum was gone.

He opened the door and got in. He turned to Carolyn as he fastened his seat-belt. "Thanks for—"

She slapped his cheek. The brilliant pain lit up the side of his face. Trey blinked at her, mouth open. She reached across and hugged him. "Scared the shit out of me," she whispered. When she pulled back from him, he saw redness in her eyes.

"I—" Trey swallowed. "I'm sorry."

"Trey," she said, "how the fuck did you think I was going to react to a call from the police?"

He dropped his head to his chest. "I'm sorry, baby," he whispered.

"Where is Dick?"

Trey looked up at her, fighting back his own tears. "Dick had a heart attack."

She blinked at him, her lip quivering. "What—"

Trey nodded. "He's in the hospital."

"Oh, Jesus," she whispered. "Is he—"

"I don't know. The cops told me he's stable."

"Oh, fuck," she said. "Where is he?"

"ICU at Ben Taub," Trey said.

"We need to go—" She frowned at Trey. "Jesus. You have blood all over your shirt." Trey looked down at the dark streaks on his sweater and nodded. "Did you get hurt?"

Trey shook his head. "It's— It's not my blood," he breathed.

She wiped away a tear and put the car in gear. "I'm taking you home," she said. "We'll get Alan and then figure out what to do."

The car moved slowly out into the intersection. Carolyn wiped at her face again and got up to speed. Trey watched her hands gripping the steering wheel, her knuckles turning white.

"Dick didn't just have a heart attack, did he?" Carolyn asked after a few minutes.

Trey shook his head. His whisper was barely audible above the sound of the wind raking across the car. "No."

"What did you do, Trey?" she asked, her words an accusation.

He hadn't dragged Dick down there. Dick had dragged him. It had been Dick's idea to go see the Ice Cream Man. Dick had wanted—

"Trey!" she yelled. Her hand grasped his left, her fingers tight against his own.

"I—" Trey said. They were on the tollway now, the freeways long behind them. "How long?"

"Too long. Too damned long." She exhaled through her teeth. "Taking you home, baby. You can tell me later."

Trey closed his eyes. "Just don't leave me alone," he whispered.

Chapter

Fifty-Three

The world was sleeping, except for Trey. He had finally admitted to himself that dreamland was a forbidden place, and stepped out of bed. The day's clouds had finally moved off, leaving a crystal chipped clear night and plummeting temperature. Even with his robe wrapped about him and his feet enclosed in the fuzzy, monster slippers, the cold seeped into his bones.

Trey stood in Alan's bedroom doorway watching his son sleep. The boy's hair was already a mess, tufts springing out in all directions against his white pillow. The grey bedspread was wrapped around him along with the blanket and sheet. Trey smiled. It didn't matter how tucked in the sheets were, Alan would have them wrapped around himself before the night was done. Especially if it was cold.

His wife was another world-class cover stealer. Sometimes he would wake to find his feet hanging out from beneath the twisted sheets and blankets. He'd have to fight her for the covers, twisting them back from beneath her just so he could keep from freezing to death. She never stole the covers after they made love, though. That night, she hadn't twitched.

All the adrenaline of the day, the stress, terror, all felt very distant, as though it had happened to someone else in another lifetime. Then he closed his eyes, and before sleep could take him, he remembered that Dick was still in the hospital. Still in ICU for observation. That's what kept him awake.

That and the face of the thing.

When they had reached home, Carolyn had made him wait in the garage until she ushered Alan to his bathroom for a quick soak—she didn't want the boy to see all the blood on Trey's sweater. Trey had stripped in the laundry room, rubbing cleaning solution on the blood stains. He'd pulled a fresh shirt from the dryer and quickly dressed himself.

Once Alan was through with his bath, Carolyn ordered Chinese. The three of them ate, both Carolyn and Trey pretending that Dick had only had an accident. Trey didn't think Alan believed them. The boy was too smart for that, but to Trey's amazement, he didn't push it either.

It wasn't until after Alan was finally in bed that Carolyn sat next to him on the couch and held his good hand.

"All right, baby," she whispered, "what happened?"

Her voice was soft, her face expressionless. Trey had wanted to melt under her stare. He'd opened his mouth to speak and then closed it with a sharp click. What could he tell her? That he and Dick had wandered into a serial killer's lair? That he'd seen the zip-locked body parts of at least three children stacked like steaks in a meat market?

What he'd told her wasn't a lie, it just wasn't everything. The break-in, the discovery of murder victims, and the attack were all he managed. While he spoke of the attack, he'd had a seizure. A short one, but it was enough for Carolyn to let him off the hook.

When he finished, she sat silent for a moment, her eyes glued to the far wall. "You didn't tell me you were going."

"No," he agreed.

She swung her eyes to stare into his. Her expressionless face flushed red, the corners of her mouth turned down. "So you lied to me." It wasn't a question, but a statement of fact. "Why?"

"I didn't want you to worry."

"Worry?" she asked, her eyebrows raised. "Why the fuck would I worry, Trey?" she spat. "Why would I worry about you two assholes playing vigilante? Why wouldn't you want me to know you were going out there to get yourself fucking killed?" A tear dripped off the end of her nose. "You didn't want me to know," she said in a vicious whisper, "because you knew I'd talk you out of it."

For a moment, Trey said nothing. Finally, he nodded. "And I didn't want you to worry that I'd finally gone insane."

She barked an unhappy laugh. "Finally?" She shook her head. "Jesus, Trey. I can't believe you dragged Dick—"

"No," he said, "you are not going to make this my fault, Carolyn." He clenched his fist, the knuckles cracking. "Dick was going to go with or without me. Period."

"What?"

Trey nodded. "We both needed to know." He drew in a deep shuddering breath. "We both needed to see."

"Why, Trey? Why couldn't you—"

"Because it could have been Alan!" Trey shouted. His voice broke as his son's name crossed his lips. He shook his head at the shocked expression on Carolyn's face. "Because, it could have been my boy," he whispered. "It could have been our boy, Carolyn."

Trey broke down and held his head in his hands, unable to stop sobbing.

Carolyn let it go, helping to calm him down. After a tandem shower, they'd fallen into bed and into one another's arms. Carolyn had fallen asleep soon after. But not Trey.

He left Alan's bedroom, quietly closing the door behind him. He walked down the carpeted stairs and into the foyer. He looked out the windows toward Dick's house. Dark. Cold. Empty. He brushed a hand against his face, wiping away a stray tear. That thing could have killed them both. Could have.

Why hadn't it? Trey glanced at his study door. His machines

would be waiting for him, sleeping quietly like the rest of the house. He thought about Googling monsters. Who the fuck knew what the thing was? There was no name for it. No hint as to where it had come from.

What had Dick seen, he wondered. Had he seen the same thing Trey had? What if it was still just his brain sliding into that delusional state, seeing something that wasn't really there?

The thing...what if it was just a man? Just a man holding a knife, and snarling in a foreign language? Could be just a man. The guy who cut the tattoos off those people, he was just a man. Not some monster from a horror movie. Just a man. Yet...

Trey shivered. The Grubby Man was just a man too, although it had taken him decades to realize that. Not a monster, just a man. A mentally ill man.

"Like me," Trey whispered. His own voice made him shiver. The sound of it, so weak and raspy, seemed to echo in the foyer.

I believe in human monsters, Dewhurst had said. Trey nodded to himself in the darkness. The Grubby Man. The Ice Cream Man. Human beings who did monstrous things.

Trey yawned and looked at the stairs. His wife would be snoring. His son would be curled up in the blankets still, perhaps rolling in his sleep to a new position. Trey took one last look out the window and then made his way to the second floor.

He walked to the linen closet and paused with his hand on the knob. He took a deep breath and opened it, half expecting a pair of green eyes to stare back at him, and opened the door. Nothing but bed linen. He exhaled and tried to ignore the pounding of his heart.

He pulled a heavy blanket and a spare pillow out as quietly as he could. He didn't bother closing the door. Walking heel to toe, he once again entered Alan's room. He put the pillow down next to Alan's bed and slowly lay down on the carpet. Once he was covered in the blanket, he closed his eyes, listening to Alan's breathing. In no time at all, he was finally asleep.

Chapter Fifty-Four

Trey felt pressure on his chest and opened his eyes. A face was nose to nose with him. He choked back a scream before he realized it was Alan. "Hello, Daddy," Alan chuckled. "You're not supposed to sleep in my room." The boy was crouched atop him, each leg to the side with his rump on Trey's bladder. Alan kissed his father's nose and then giggled.

"You," Trey groaned as the boy slowly bucked up and down, "better get off me if you don't want me to pee all over you!" Each word exploded with a puff of air.

Alan squealed and then leaped off his father.

Trey moaned and rolled on to his side. "Now I really have to pee!" he whined.

"Daddy has to pee-ee! Daddy has to pee-ee!" Alan sang, dancing from one foot to the other. He stopped as Trey stood up. His smile dropped. "You know what, Daddy?" Trey blinked at him. Alan leaned forward. "Now I have to pee!" Alan ran giggling from the room.

Trey sat up. His bladder really did feel like it was going to explode. He headed out Alan's door, not bothering to pick up his blanket or pillow, and stumbled into the hallway. He walked into the bedroom. Carolyn was already gone and it was nearly 730.

Trey cursed as he made his way to the master bathroom. He flipped up the lid, held himself, and paused, waiting for the stream to start. His bladder burned, the pressure more uncomfortable every second until the plumbing started to work.

"Daddy?" Alan's voice called from the hallway. "Are we walking to school?"

Brow furrowed, Trey turned his head slightly toward the open door. "Why wouldn't we?"

"It's cold, Daddy. Very cold."

Trey grinned. "Tough. Put on some warm clothes, kid. And deal."

"Okay!" Alan yelled back.

As soon as he finished and tucked himself back into his pajama shorts, Trey turned to the closet. The closet. Since the hospital, he hadn't felt nervous about entering it. He knew there was nothing there but clothes. Trey smiled. "Wonder if there's room in there for my stuff?" he said aloud.

Without turning on the light, Trey walked into the large closet. The walk-in was at least three times larger than the space the Grubby Man had kept him in. Trey sighed. "Fucker," he said softly and walked back out.

No time to take a shower. He'd have to get dressed quickly and get Alan some breakfast. Trey stripped off his pajama bottoms and walked naked to the chest of drawers. He pulled out a t-shirt, a pair of socks, thought about underwear and decided against it. He was going to wear jeans anyway. Dressing in silence, Trey wondered how Dick was doing. That was a call he'd have to make once he got Alan to school.

"Alan?" Trey called as he pulled on his socks. "Are you dressed?"

"Yes, Daddy!"

As he stepped out of the bedroom, he pulled on a sweater and made his way to the stairs. "Come on, kid, let's get you some breakfast."

They sat at the table. Alan wolfed down his mini-wheats while

Trey drank coffee. Alan put down his spoon, crunching the last of the cereal between his teeth.

"Daddy? Is Dick going to be okay?"

Trey took another sip of the coffee. "Yeah. I'm going to go see him today, kiddo."

"Will you tell him I said hello?"

"Sure will," Trey said. "You about ready to get to school?"

Alan's brow furrowed. "Why were you sleeping in my room?"

"Because," Trey said, putting down his cup, "Mommy kept stealing the covers."

The boy giggled. "That's not why."

"Yes it is."

"No, it's not," Alan said, still laughing.

Trey leaned forward, his face inches from his son's. "Because I wanted to be in the same room as you. That's all."

"Why?"

"Just wanted to," Trey said. "You got a hat?" Alan pulled a snow cap from his jacket pocket and waved it in his father's face. "Good. Let's do it."

They walked out the door and into the cold. Trey shivered. Alan donned his gloves in silence as they made their way down the driveway. Trey cursed himself for not bringing gloves and a hat himself. Alan stopped in the driveway staring at Dick's house.

"What's wrong, kiddo?" Trey asked.

"Dick's not home," the boy said. "Does that mean his house is lonely?"

Trey laughed. "Yeah, something like that." A black SUV passed by the driveway, heading to the T. Trey never could remember the neighbor's name. "Come on, kid. We gotta get moving."

They walked in silence. Many cars and SUVs passed them on the way out of the neighborhood or on the way to the schools. Although most of the children on their block were much older than Alan, the high school and middle school weren't far from the elementary school. It made every school morning complete bedlam for traffic, and always reminded Trey how happy he was not to drive.

Trey slowed his pace as they came upon a stop sign. The James Keel notice was still up, but a new one had joined it. Another picture of another boy below it with the word "MISSING" in large type. "Bryan Greely," Trey said aloud. He looked down at Alan. "Do you know him?"

Alan looked up at Trey and shook his head. "No, Daddy. But I think he goes to my school."

Three bodies. At least three bodies in the warehouse.

"Okay," he said as he took Alan's hand, "let's get moving." They crossed the street in silence and continued down the path. The cold began biting into Trey's ears and hands with reckless hunger. He kept one hand in his pocket, the other still clasped around Alan's. "I'm cold," Trey said aloud. "See, this is what happens when Daddy doesn't take his own advice."

"So why didn't you?"

"Because I'm dumb," Trey laughed.

"No, you're not," Alan said. "You just forget things sometimes."

"Sometimes," Trey agreed.

"Daddy?" Alan asked, looking up at him.

"Yes, son?"

"You seem better." Trey said nothing.

The image of the thing from the warehouse, saliva dripping from its exposed canines, flesh pulsating in fevered breaths, filled his mind. Trey shook it off. "I am better," he said.

As they entered the school-yard, Alan stopped and turned to his father. "You going to be here to walk me home?"

Trey smiled. "I will, kiddo. I'll be here."

Alan readjusted his pack. "Okay, Daddy," he said. Trey bent down and Alan kissed his cheek. "See you later."

"Okay, Alan." He watched as his son walked quickly toward the school entrance and joined the horde of students heading in. The school buzzer went off in two sharp bursts. Ten minutes to class. Trey grinned. He'd still managed to get Alan to school early. With a shivering sigh, Trey turned and started back to the house. As he passed more traffic signs, he realized the Greely missing notices were on every one of them.

Three bodies.

The cold bit, but he wasn't certain it was why he was still shivering.

Just as Trey walked in out of the cold, his phone rang. He pulled it from his jeans pocket, teeth still chattering, and looked at the number. It wasn't one he recognized. Bracing himself for another telemarketer, he pressed the phone and held it to his ear. "Hello?"

"Mr. Leger?"

"Yes?"

"This is Detective Dewhurst," the caller drawled. "May I have a moment of your time?"

Trey took in a deep breath. "Good morning, sir. Sure."

"Are you going to be available today to answer some more questions? This afternoon, perhaps?"

"I'm going to go see Dick," Trey said. "If he's awake."

"Ah," Dewhurst said. "That's actually a good thing. Last I checked, they moved him out of ICU and into a regular room." Dewhurst paused. In the background, Trey heard the sounds of a truck backing up and voices. "What time do you think you'll be there?"

How the fuck was he going to get to the medical center? "I, um, I don't drive, Detective. I'll have to find a way to get there."

"You don't drive?" Dewhurst asked, shock in his voice.

"Um, no. I'd rather not—"

"How do you get around Houston and not drive? That's gotta be a pain."

Trey nodded. "It is, sir. It is. I'll try and be there around 11:30 or so."

"Okay," Dewhurst said. "I'll be there around 12:30. I have to wrap up a few things here first. I have questions I can ask, but I'd rather they be in person."

Trey didn't like the sinking feeling in his gut. Dewhurst sounded anxious and excited at the same time. "Sure," he said. "Sure."

"Mr. Leger?" Dewhurst asked. "You okay?"

With a sigh, Trey clucked his tongue. "Yeah. No. Maybe. Look, I'll see you at the hospital."

"Thank you, sir," Dewhurst said. The line went dead.

Trey pocketed the phone and tapped his foot. He had to get downtown. Fuck. There were only two ways to do it. Take a cab or take the bus. Trey picked up his wallet and looked inside. Five crisp twenties. It would be enough for one way. But he'd have to take the bus to get back. He sighed and went to his computer.

Cab companies in The Woodlands were few and far between, but they did exist—they just cost an arm and a leg. Plus, 30 miles just to get downtown was not a small distance for the meter. Trey pulled up the number for a cab company and started dialing.

He'd called Carolyn while in the cab and told her where he was going. She asked if he thought he would be home in time to walk Alan from school. He assured her he would. When the cab reached the Medical Center, Trey gave up four twenties to pay the fare. The driver grumbled about the small tip. He felt bad not giving the driver more, but Trey knew he'd have to hang on to the last twenty to pay for the train and the buses to get back home.

The Medical Center was bustling. Nurses and doctors wearing jackets over their scrubs walked along the wide sidewalks beside the light rail. They held coffee or sodas in their cold hands, looking dazed as they stepped off the train and onto the platforms. Others departed from the medical buildings, heading to the train. Shift change. Trey watched the shivering mass of people as they passed one another.

People on canes, walkers, and crutches wandered the sidewalks, heading to or from their doctors' offices. Tests. Medication. Every one seemed to come here to see a specialist at some point or another. Trey walked through them, heading toward the tall white building jutting from the street.

He thought about entering through the emergency entrance, but one look inside told him that was a bad idea. The waiting room was stuffed with Latinos wearing denim and holding their coughing children as well as street people of various colors hiding in the building's warmth. During the winter months, when the temperature might actually drop below 50, the emergency rooms were filled to the brim with uninsured people.

Trey headed toward the hospital's main entrance around the corner.

The cold air retreated as he walked through the revolving door. The wide foyer was strangely empty save for the counter staffed by two women dressed in white. Trey shivered off the last of the cold, enjoying the relatively warm air. He walked to the counter. One of the two staffers looked up at him with casual boredom. "May I help you?" she asked in a husky voice.

"Hi," Trey stuttered. "I'm here to see a patient." She stared at him and pursed her lips. The pause lingered. "Oh," Trey said and blushed, "his name is Dick Dickerson."

Her lips curved up in a smile, but her eyes were stern. Trey wanted to ask how a stick had gotten shoved up her ass, but said nothing.

"He's in room 334," she said. "Visiting time ends in an hour."

"Thank you," he said.

"Elevator's over there." She pointed toward the bank to the left.

Trey walked toward them and made his way into an open elevator. He stabbed the button for floor three. The door closed and Trey felt the pressure on his feet as the elevator rose. Trey felt a little claustrophobic, but it wasn't the usual weight that threatened to crush his brain into jelly. He wondered for the second time if those days were finally over.

The elevator dinged and the doors opened to a scene of busy people doing busy things. The nurse's station was alive with conversation and clacking keys. Families waited in a row of cushioned seats, all looking as though they hadn't slept in days. Trey stepped out, nervous to see so many people. A cart made its way down one of the halls.

Trey looked up at the signs. Rooms 300-350 were on the far hallway. With a deep breath, Trey walked in that direction.

He passed open doors with people coughing, quiet conversation, and the occasional moan of pain. All the rooms on that side were private, but that didn't change the fact it was a hospital. The sounds of oxygen machines, the beeps of monitors, were all wrapped up in a quiet, but ever pervasive drone.

As Trey reached room 334, he stopped next to the entry. How would Dick react when he saw him?

"Shit," Trey thought, "I should have called." He steeled himself, forced a smile, and walked into the room.

He stopped dead in his tracks. Dick's body was stretched out on the bed, his face pale and haggard. Clear, plastic oxygen tubes snaked up his nostrils. Although he was covered in blankets, he shivered.

"Dick? You awake?" Trey asked from the doorway.

Dick's eyes slowly opened. He turned his head, blinking into the light. A wan smile lit his face. "Yeah," he said in a raspy whisper. "I'm awake." Dick raised his right hand a little, waving Trey in.

"You look like shit." Trey said it with the best smile he could manage, forcing a chuckle as he finished the sentence.

"Fuck you," Dick said back.

"So," Trey said, grabbing a chair and pulling it to the bed, "want to go play some disc golf?"

Dick held up his middle finger. "Suck it," he said between breaths, smiling.

"That's better. You already look more alive." Trey shook his head, his smile fading. Dick looked bad. Very bad. "What they say?"

"Had a heart attack," he said in a breathy whisper. "You know, that thing where your heart fucks up."

Trey nodded. "Yeah, I heard that, but what else did they say?"

Beads of sweat dotted Dick's forehead as well as his face. He shivered once more. "Have a fever," Dick said. "They're not sure what caused it." Dick idly scratched at his chest. "Guess the fucker cut me with something that wasn't sterilized."

Trey sat up. "Dick? Can you tell me what you saw?"

Dick closed his eyes, his face turned down in a frown. "Don't— Don't know. Doesn't make sense."

"Dick? I need to know, man. What did you see?"

"You're the crazy one," Dick breathed. "You tell me."

Trey blew out a hiss between his teeth. "I— I saw it. The thing."

"The thing," Dick repeated.

"Yeah," Trey agreed. "The thing."

"You remember those aisles of boxes?" he asked. Trey nodded. "I— I had my flashlight pointed down there. Saw something move." Dick turned his head and coughed. It sounded like broken glass being shaken in a jar. "It came up from the floor, Trey." He stared into Trey's eyes with a haunted look. "Like it had been there all along, scuttling, or slithering there."

Trey felt a shiver creep up his spine. Dick pointed toward the water bottle sitting on a metal tray. Trey picked it up and placed the straw between Dick's chapped lips. Dick managed a few sips from it before letting the plastic straw pop from his mouth. He nodded.

"You're welcome."

"Bastard rose up from the floor," Dick said. "Stood there. I—" Dick swallowed a sob. "I just froze, man. The flashlight beam lit up those, those teeth. The lips. Saliva dripping..." Dick shook his head, tears leaking from his tired eyes. "I just froze."

"Shh," Trey said. He reached out and held Dick's hand. The skin was hot and clammy. "It's okay, Dick. No more, man. Just let—"

"It said something to me. Said something. And then those claws..." Dick let the words drift off, his eyes closing tight. "It attacked me. One swipe."

"Yes," Trey agreed. A tear tried to escape his eyes, but he fought it. "It's over now."

"The cops," Dick said, swallowing hard, "they get him yet?"

Trey shook his head. "No, Dick. But they will."

Dick opened his eyes, struggled to sit up, and clenched Trey's hand. "Did you tell them?" he asked, his voice practically a yell.

Trey flinched. "I told them—"

"Did you tell them he's—he's not human?"

Trey opened his mouth to speak, and then closed it.

"They wouldn't believe us anyway," Dick whispered. He closed his eyes. Dick's grip went limp. Trey tucked his friend's hand back under the sheets, but refused to let go. He sat, watching Dick's chest rise and fall in an uneven, ill rhythm.

Chapter
Fifty-Seven

"Mr. Leger?" a quiet voice asked.

Trey's eyes fluttered open. For a moment, he didn't know where he was. He felt something warm and clammy in his left hand and turned to look. He was still holding Dick's hand. "Shit," he whispered.

"Trey?" the quiet voice said.

Trey turned and looked at the room's door. Dressed in a crisp suit, not a hair out of place, Detective Dewhurst stood in the doorway with a calm, almost disinterested expression on his face.

He looked back at Dick. His friend was still asleep, his breathing uneven and shallow. Trey let go Dick's hand. It dropped without resistance. He tucked Dick's hand back under the sheet. "Get better," he whispered.

As quietly as possible, Trey stood from the chair and walked to the door. He fought the urge to turn and look back at his friend. Dewhurst nodded toward the hallway. Trey returned the nod and the two men left the open doorway. They walked in silence toward the bank of elevators, Dewhurst in the lead. Trey's back twinged. He wondered how long he'd been asleep in that chair, listening to his friend struggle to breathe.

Dewhurst turned around. "Cafeteria?" he drawled.

Trey shook his head. "I need a smoke." Dewhurst smiled and then nodded. The elevator took its time in coming, but it gave Trey a moment to shake off the sleep. He stood as straight as he could and then leaned back from the waist. His back popped like bubble wrap. Even with the din of the nurse's station, it was loud enough for Dewhurst to raise an eyebrow at him. They rode the elevator in uncomfortable silence.

When the doors opened on the lobby, Trey walked out, Dewhurst following, and headed toward the revolving glass doors. The cold bit into him immediately. After the hospital's warmth, the air seemed colder than ever. Shivering, Trey pulled out his pack of smokes, slotted one between his lips and lit up, his teeth chattering.

"Nasty habit," Dewhurst said with a smile. "Mind passing one over?"

Trey blinked at him and then silently handed over the pack and his lighter.

"Used to smoke these all the time. Afraid the department frowns on it, but every once in a while, I just have to have one." Trey nodded, looking at the sky. "How is Mr. Dickerson?"

Trey shrugged. "Bad fever. I talked with the nurse a little after I convinced her to let me stay." Trey took a long drag. "She said the heart attack was minor. The infection that's causing the fever may require them to send him back to ICU." Trey exhaled smoke from his nostrils and turned to regard Dewhurst. "Guess he didn't get off so light after all."

"I'm sorry to hear that."

"What did you want to talk about, Detective?" Trey asked.

"Are you, um," Dewhurst coughed into a hand, "sure you're up to talking about yesterday?" Trey nodded. Dewhurst cleared his throat. "After he attacked Mr. Dickerson, why didn't he attack you?"

Trey shrugged. "I don't know, Detective. He could have." Trey turned from the slate sky to regard Dewhurst. "I was on the floor, behind Dick. All I had was the damned flashlight in my hands. I'd sort of dropped the wrecking bar." Trey blushed against the cold. "Afraid I didn't make much of a stand."

Dewhurst nodded. "Doesn't make sense, though, does it? I mean after he attacked Mr. Dickerson, sounds like he could have killed both of you. Or at least attacked you without any interference from Mr. Dickerson."

"Yeah," Trey said. The taste of the cigarette grew sour, and the sudden surge of acid in his stomach didn't make it any better. Trey ignored both and took another long drag. "Maybe he thought we'd already called you guys," Trey said. "Fuck, I don't know, Detective."

"There was another freezer," Dewhurst said quietly.

Trey dropped his cigarette to the concrete sidewalk. The breeze rolled it away into the street. "Another freezer?"

Dewhurst nodded. "Yes, sir."

"Do I want to know?" The sudden pained expression on Dewhurst's face gave him the answer. "Fuck."

"We figure six children. Altogether. Six, Mr. Leger. Six."

Trey shook his head. "How is that... You identified them, yet?"

Dewhurst shook his head. "It'll be days before we manage that. Going to have to go against missing persons and then against dental records. By the looks of things, I will bet that the other four children were from the poorer side of town. Maybe from one of the wards."

"But how could he have done this for so long without getting caught?" Trey asked.

"Oh, I know the answer to that one." The Detective snapped his cigarette between his index finger and thumb. The burning tip fell off and fluttered in the wind. He pocketed the butt. "Kids go missing all the time, Mr. Leger. They go missing in the wards more often than I'd like to admit. It's normal, I guess. And I'll be frank for a moment." The Detective cleared his throat. "Some of the poorer members of the city don't exactly trust the police. And I guarantee you some of these kids belonged to illegal aliens. And they definitely don't trust us. So they use the gangs to go looking for their kids."

Trey shook his head and then furrowed his brow. "Do you think that's why it—I mean, he, moved on?"

Dewhurst shrugged. "Maybe. Maybe one of them tracked him down, figured out what he was doing. Maybe they started asking questions. Either way, he moved his hunting grounds up north."

Trey nodded. "Where no one would believe it could be him."

"Maybe," Dewhurst said. "Just maybe."

"So now what?"

"Well," Dewhurst said, "we have an APB out on him, although we really don't have much of a description." Dewhurst coughed into his hand. "The, um, description you gave is not exactly one we can use."

"I thought I saw something on the way out of the station last night."

Dewhurst cocked an eyebrow. "Really? And what might that be?"

"I thought I saw, well, I saw a tall homeless man. He stood on the street opposite the station. And he, well— he looked like the guy."

The detective nodded. "It would be a good disguise," he said to himself. "I'll add that to the APB, sir. That's good information to have." Dewhurst shivered. "I think it's time for us to get out of the cold, Mr. Leger." Trey nodded. "Would you like a ride home, Trey, or you going to stay a while longer?"

"I think," Trey said with a smile, "I should stay. I have the buses to get home." He offered his hand to the detective. "But thanks for the offer."

"My pleasure," Dewhurst said with a grin. The man ran his hand through his thinning hair. "You have a good day, Mr. Leger, and please let me know if you think of anything else."

"You'll let me know if you find anything?"

"As much as I can," the detective said.

"Thank you."

Dewhurst tipped an imaginary hat and walked toward the parking garage across the street. Trey watched him go. He shivered again in the cold as the breeze bit into him once more. He turned toward the revolving glass door and walked back into the warmth.

Chapter
Fifty-Eight

After Dewhurst left, Trey started for the elevator. He looked at the clock on the wall. It was already 1300. Trey cursed and pulled out his phone. He'd turned it off while he was in Dick's room, remembering the dictates from the hospital. They claimed the cellular signal interfered with their machines. Trey wasn't sure he believed them, but he'd turned it off anyway.

He turned it on and waited for it to power up. The hospital lobby was busier, people wandering in and out of the elevators. Although most were dressed in street clothes, he saw quite a few sets of scrubs and wondered if it was lunch-time for the second shift. The phone finished powering up and immediately buzzed. Trey looked at the text messages and saw one from Carolyn.

Clucking his tongue, he selected her name from the contacts list and pressed her phone number. The phone rang in his ear. "Carolyn Leger."

"Hi, honey. It's Trey."

The voice no longer sounded tired and bored. "Hi, T. You still at the hospital?"

Trey nodded in reflex. "Yeah, I'm still here."

"How's Dick?" she asked.

"Not good," Trey said. He took in a sharp breath. "The heart attack was minor, but he's got a high fever."

"What's the doctor say?"

"Didn't get a chance to talk to anyone except the nurse."

Carolyn paused on the other end of the phone. "Trey? Go up there and ask the doctor what's going on. Dick doesn't exactly have anyone but us."

Trey nodded to himself. "Yeah, okay. Look, I'll go up and figure out what's going on. I don't know if I'm going to be home in time to pick up Alan, though. Can you leave early and meet him?"

"Does he know not to wait for you?" she asked. Her voice sounded strained now. Near panic.

Trey paused. Had he told Alan that? Had he? "I, um, think I told him that, yeah."

"Okay," Carolyn replied. "I'll leave a message at the school for him. Just in case you, um, forgot. Or he does."

Trey smiled. "Yeah, okay. Love you, C."

"Give Dick my best, T. Call me and let me know, okay?"

"Sure will."

"Love you."

The line went dead. Trey turned the phone back off and headed to the elevator. He waited with a large group of people crowding around the bank. He had to wait for the 2nd elevator to get on. Packed. He felt the claustrophobia trying to blanket and strangle him but he pushed it away. Just people, he told himself, just people. Nothing to worry about with all the people.

When the doors finally opened to the third floor, Trey breathed out a long sigh and stepped off. The nurse's station was empty save for a single woman. An alarm was going off at the desk. The nurse behind the counter typed frantically on a computer. He walked toward Dick's hallway and stopped. The alarm was louder. He watched as three people ran into Dick's room. Trey blinked. "Fuck," he whispered and then he was running too.

He made it to the doorway of room 334 and peered inside. The three people in the room, two in red scrubs, and a young man in blue scrubs, were chattering to one another in frantic voices. The blue scrubbed young man grabbed a pair of paddles and had them on Dick's chest. "Clear!" he called out and then pressed the paddle buttons. Dick's ashen skinned body jumped in the bed. Trey began to cry. The steady, annoying tone continued.

"Sir?" a voice said from beside him. "Sir?"

A stabbing pain in his head. His eyes burned, feeling scratched and too dry. "What?" He was still staring into the room. A white sheet covered Dick's body. No one else was in the room with the body. "Where's—"

"Sir?" the voice said again and Trey felt a hand on his shoulder.

He turned slightly. The young man in scrubs was beside him, eyes frantic and concerned. "What's going on? Why is—"

"Sir? Do you have epilepsy?"

"I—" Trey coughed into his hand. "What happened to Dick?"

The young man nodded to him. "Let's walk over here, okay?" The man led him by the elbow to an empty room down the hall. Trey wanted to shrug the man off, but he felt strangely weak. He allowed the man to sit him in one of the visitor's chairs. He stared up into the man's blue eyes. "Sir? What's your name?" the man asked as he pulled a penlight from his scrub pocket.

"Trey Leger," Trey said in a broken, scratchy voice.

The man flashed the light into Trey's right eye, then his left. Frowning, the man put the penlight back in the pocket and reached for Trey's wrist. Trey said nothing. "I'm a doctor. You've had an absent seizure."

Trey blinked at the doctor as he took Trey's pulse. "Yeah," Trey said in a flat voice, "I guess I did."

"So you've had them before?"

A tear fell from Trey's eye. "Dick's dead," he whispered.

The doctor looked up from his watch. "Mr. Dickerson?" Trey nodded. "I'm sorry, sir. Yes. He is." Trey tried to shrug off the man's hand, but the young doctor just tightened his grip. "Sir? Please let me do my job. I want to make sure you're okay."

"How long was the seizure?" Trey asked.

"Too long," the doctor said.

"How fucking long?" Trey growled.

The doctor looked up from his watch and took a step backwards. "Five or six minutes, I think. That's how long it took for us to notice you," the doctor said.

"Fuck," Trey whispered. He held his head in his hands.

"You need to see someone about this immediately," the doctor said.

"No," Trey said, "I need my friend." The doctor said nothing. Trey sobbed once, wiped away another errant tear, and then stared up at the doctor. "Why? What did he die from?"

"I don't know," the doctor said. "His fever spiked. I don't know why."

"Will there be an autopsy?" Trey asked. The world felt unreal now, as if it were made of fog and he was somehow trying to walk through it. The doctor's face grimaced.

"Mr. Leger?" the doctor asked. "Do you see lights?"

Trey cocked his head and stared at the man. He smiled. "No. I don't. I never have," Trey said. "Will there be—"

The doctor nodded. "Yeah, there will be. If the family allows it."

"There is no family," Trey said, standing from the chair. The doctor came forward to try and lower him back down, but Trey shrugged off his hands. "I'm the only family he has," Trey said.

The doctor blinked. "Are you on his—" The doctor swallowed hard. "I need you to wait here, Mr. Leger. I'll— I'll get someone. But I want to make sure you're okay before we let you leave."

Trey nodded and watched the man go.

Chapter
Fifty-nine

The last meeting of the day. Thank God, Carolyn thought. She wondered if another two hours of meetings would have caused an aneurysm. Her head already pounded from the constant questions. The client, a French company, had sent her one of the dumbest women on the planet. Each time Carolyn answered a question with a negative response, the woman rephrased the question, somehow believing that would change the answer.

Just when Carolyn was on the verge of saying "The law is the law," the woman would move on to a new topic and the cycle would repeat.

Carolyn opened her desk drawer and pulled out a bottle of Excedrin. She popped off the childproof cap, shook three of the tablets into her palm, and dry swallowed.

"Great," she thought, "an hour from now and I'll get her idiot stink off my brain." She stared down at the cell phone on the desk. It had rumbled twice while she was in the meeting.

She reached for it and checked the screen. Two missed calls from Trey. She sighed and clicked the "messages" button. One message from Trey. She frowned at the phone. Two missed calls, but only a single message. Carolyn pressed the "play" button and listened to the message.

"He's dead, Carolyn. Dick's dead," Trey said in a broken voice. "I'm trying to find out what happened and I may be here a while longer." Trey paused. She could tell he was trying to get control of himself. He cleared his throat. "I'll call you when I know something. I love you."

Carolyn stared down at the desk. "Dick," she whispered, the phone still held to her ear. She slowly placed it on the wooden surface, fighting the urge to throw it against the wall. Dick was dead. Trey sounded... broken. She shook her head.

3:15. Alan would be leaving school soon. He'd be heading home to an empty house and he would have no idea the neighbor would never be coming home. Carolyn choked back a sob.

She stared out the window, looking into the darkened sky. It would rain soon, or, God forbid, sleet. The temperature was already hovering just above freezing. If any moisture came down, it would turn the streets into a skating rink.

"I have to get home," she whispered.

She quickly packed her valise and placed her laptop inside. Donning her coat, she grabbed both her purse and the valise and headed toward the office door. Traffic was going to be murder. If she left that minute, she might be home in an hour. That was, of course, if everyone else in Houston hadn't noticed the weather and decided to leave at the same time.

Chapter
Sixty

The buzzer droned. Instead of a crowd of crazed children heading toward the exit, his classmates moved with slow, trudging steps. Alan knew it was the weather. Too cold outside for recess, they'd played in the gym. Bored and listless, most of the kids headed toward the school parking lot through the front doors.

Alan headed toward the playground.

As soon as the glass doors swung open, the cold bit into him like a wild, rabid animal. The sky was dark enough to have tripped the street-lights in the parking lot. Alan walked to the curb and shivered. One of the admins had brought him a note during class, letting him know that Daddy wouldn't be there to pick him up. But he waited anyway.

He watched the large line of cars that stretched all the way through the next block. Everyone, it seemed, wanted to pick their kids up from school today. Headlights glowed in the street and parking lot. Children silhouetted against the light clambered into cars or, like him, shivered in the cold. Waiting.

Without thinking he looked toward the group of pines near

the schoolyard's edge. No Ice Cream Man. No piercing bells. Alan smiled against the wind. At least he was gone.

A woman walked toward him from the parking lot. She wore a heavy woolen coat, her hair wound tight in a ponytail. The woman looked tired and a little lost. She looked at Alan and stopped about five feet away from him. "Hi," she said.

"Hello," Alan said. He knew he shouldn't talk to strangers. But she looked so... "Are you okay?" he asked.

The woman managed a grim smile. "Do you know my son?" she asked and handed him a small piece of paper.

He looked at it. Bryan Greely's smiling face stared back at him. Alan shivered. "I know who he is," he said. "Are you Mrs. Greely?"

"Yes, I am," she whispered. "Have you seen Bryan?"

The woman looked at him with desperate hope. With a pang of sadness, he shook his head. "No, ma'am, I haven't." The way her expression collapsed into misery hurt some part of him.

She nodded. He handed the paper back to her, but she shook her head. "Give it to your parents," she said. "Make sure they know he's missing. Okay?"

"Yes, ma'am," Alan replied. The woman nodded again and turned around, heading toward the dwindling line of cars. Alan watched her trudge forward, head cast down to the concrete.

When Daddy was in...that place...Alan had felt like that. Like some part of him was missing. Mrs. Greely didn't know where her boy was. Alan had a feeling she never would.

He turned away and stared again at the copse of trees. Before the Ice Cream man had turned up, he and Daddy had often walked through those tall pines. Especially during early fall and late spring when the heat was so intense. The cold wind bit through his jacket, causing him to shiver once more.

Daddy wasn't coming. Mommy wasn't coming. He was going to have to walk. So he better get moving.

One foot in front of the other, Alan headed toward the trees. So many happy children had sprinted that way, heading toward the

Ice Cream Man's van, money held out in front of them. In a way, Alan wished he'd been one of them. Wished Daddy hadn't seen what Daddy had seen.

Alan made his way beneath the tall pine limbs and out into the street. He looked both ways before crossing. That was something Daddy had made sure he knew to do.

The cold air was getting more biting by the second. Alan walked fast, trying to make it to the tree-lined main road where he would at least have some protection from it. Cars passed by him, each carrying at least one child. A boy his age, tucked into the back seat of a black sedan, stuck his tongue out at Alan as the car passed by. Alan shook his head and wrapped his arms tighter around himself.

Usually if Mommy and Daddy couldn't pick him up, Dick would have, but he was in the hospital. The real one. Not the place Daddy had been.

Alan walked a little faster. Daddy wouldn't tell him what happened, only that Dick had been hurt and he wouldn't be home for a while.

Alan reached the main road at last. He walked as far to the right as possible, hugging the tree-lined path. More cars passed, heading toward the newer parts of the subdivision. Above him, the wind rushed through the green pines and bare-branched oaks. It was still cold, but at least the wind no longer chomped his skin.

As Alan walked down the path, still shivering in the cold, he became aware of a different kind of rustling. He turned his head toward the trees. The wind rushed through the tree tops, the bare oak branches clacking together and the pine trees swishing against one another in the breeze. But there was something else. The sound of something walking through dead leaves, its weight cracking against dead limbs and the forest floor.

But he saw nothing. He heard it, or thought he heard it, but there was nothing to see. That part of the path was thick with pine trees, the branches wide and low before sprouting straight toward the sky. Tall bushes covering the forest floor still held onto their leaves in defiance of the cold weather.

Alan turned back to the path. The crowd of cars passing by on the road had thinned. The sound in the brush continued as he walked. Alan stopped. The rustling did too. He shivered again and turned his head back toward the trees. Nothing. Still nothing but brush.

He started walking again as fast as he could without running. Despite the cold, he felt sweaty beneath his jacket. His breathing was rapid, the cold air hurting his lungs. He knew that if he started running, he risked falling down. The idea of crashing to the concrete, flat on his back with the thing in the woods bearing down on him chilled him to the bone.

Whatever followed him in the woods paused each time he stopped to catch his breath. He was so intent on trying to see what was in the woods that he failed to hear the car's approach until it was already past him. As he watched its tail lights progress into the gathering gloom, a numbness crept into his mind.

He was alone, out on the road, with whatever was in the trees. Alan started walking again, quickening his pace as much as he dared.

Quarter mile. Each step brought him closer to the distant, shining street lamp, its acetylene glow spooky and foreboding in the darkening day. The crashing in the brush stopped as he continued to walk. Alan was afraid to turn around, afraid to look into the woods. Had it gotten ahead of him somehow? Or had it stepped out of the brush and onto the concrete so it could pursue him with reckless speed?

Alan started running. His pack bounced between his shoulder blades, thumping in time as each of his small feet connected with the concrete. The crunch of gravel beneath his feet was a grinding symphony keeping time with his pumping legs. He passed the street lamp. The T was up ahead. He could make it. He could—

The world flipped on him as his foot slipped on stray, wet leaves. He looked up into the slate sky as his body went parallel to the concrete and then fell to the ground. The pack pressed into his back, the hard edge of a 3-ring binder pressing into his skin. Alan struggled to regain his breath. His head had connected with the ground hard enough to blanket his vision with pinpricks of starlight. Trying to ignore the shrieking pain in his back and the pounding in his skull, Alan rose, pushed himself to his hands and stood.

He managed a low lope, stumbling to get up to speed. The thing could be right behind him, closing in fast. Alan reached the T and trotted past the mailboxes. He saw a neighbor getting the mail. He saw three kids outside, throwing a ball in the cold. He slowed, ignoring the puzzled look of the old lady at the mail box. She called out to him, but he didn't understand her and didn't care. Breathless, he made it to the front door.

It seemed to take forever to pull the keys from his pocket. He juggled them, struggling to find the right key and push it into the brass deadbolt's keyhole. He finally managed it, turned the key, and heard the blessed click of the bolt striking back.

"Young man?" a voice croaked from the driveway.

Alan turned, a scream locked in his throat.

The old lady stood on the edge of the driveway frowning at him. He tried to speak, but nothing came out. "You almost—" She stopped in mid-sentence, her face turning from a frown into a look of shock. "Young man, are you all right? You look—"

Alan held up a hand and caught his breath. "Yes, ma'am," he managed. "I'm okay. I—"

She pointed toward him. "You have a rip in your jeans. Did you fall down?"

"Yes, ma'am. I—"

"Are you okay, son?" She had taken several steps up the driveway, squinting at him.

Alan forced a smile. "Yes, ma'am. I'm okay."

She nodded to him. "Were you running from something?"

"Just spooked myself," he said.

The old lady shook her head. "Be more careful, son. Don't kill yourself out there." She turned from him and walked up the street toward her house on the cul-de-sac.

Alan blew out a hiss of air and turned back to the door. His key was still in it. Alan turned the door knob and entered the warm house.

The run had left sweat beneath his sweater, but it wasn't until the warmth of the house blasted against him that he realized just how cold he'd been. His feet hurt, his back ached and twinged and his head pounded.

Mommy was going to be mad. He'd torn his jeans, all right. The slip on the concrete had made a jagged hole in the back of the left leg. He unshouldered the pack and took three steps toward the living room before he stopped and turned to look at the front door. The dead-bolt was in the vertical position—open. He leaped to the door, grasped the lock and swiveled it shut in one smooth motion. The bolt slid into place and he let out a long sigh.

Through the smoked glass, he watched another car pass on the street. Normalcy. The world was normal; he was the crazy one.

Alan bent and stepped out of his shoes. He stripped off his heavy jacket, tossed it on the coat rack, and went into the living room.

The pain in his back forced him to lean forward. He sat on the couch, listening to the sound of his back pop as he straightened. The pain was exquisite and for a moment it offset the pounding in his head.

The thing in the woods. The thing that had kept pace with him. He closed his eyes. Nothing. It was nothing. He laughed in the living room's twilight. He hadn't turned on any of the lights, and the fading day barely illuminated the room through the window blinds.

God, his head hurt.

He stared at the cordless phone on the end table. He picked it up, getting ready to dial his mother's number. His finger paused near the keypad, his head swiveling toward the kitchen. A scratching sound came from the sliding glass door that led to the deck. Alan's hand began to shake and goose flesh broke out across his body. From the living room, he couldn't see what was behind the door. He didn't want to either. He slowly raised himself from the couch, his back protesting the movement. With the adrenaline dumping into his bloodstream, he barely noticed.

Phone still in his hands, he took two steps toward the foyer, away from the kitchen. "Daddy?" he called out to the empty house. The scratching at the sliding glass door became louder. Alan paused, his body leaning toward the foyer hallway. Three steps to the stairs. If it wasn't Mommy or Daddy at the back door, he could make it to the second floor before whoever it was came in.

The hammering in his chest, the pounding in his ears, was not enough to drown out the insistent scratching at the door. There was a metal click and the sound of the glass door sliding across its tracks. Alan's mouth opened to call out, to ask who it was. A cream colored leg thrust through the vertical blinds. Feeling as though someone had punched the air from his chest, a scream trapped in his throat, Alan stumbled toward the stairs, his eyes still focused as the vertical blinds parted. A cream colored sleeve, soiled and ripped in places, reached through. The hand was taloned in long, black nails.

Alan turned and ran for the stairs. His feet pounded on the carpet. He tripped halfway up, falling to his knees on one of the steps. The phone bounced from his hand and fell down the stairs. Screaming, he managed to make his way up the steps in a fast crawl, running for his bedroom.

He managed a quick look over the balcony and saw the cream-colored figure staring back at him from the foyer. Bright yellow eyes, crimson waves of fury burning in their center.

Alan screamed again and ran into his room.

He slammed the door, his ears ringing with the gunshot sound, and fumbled with the pushbutton lock. He ran to his desk and pulled out the wooden chair, quickly placing it beneath the knob.

Footsteps. Heavy. Loud. Deliberate.

Alan stepped backward toward his bed and whimpered as he listened to the breathy gasps on the other side of the door.

Chapter

Sixty-One

Her nerves were shot. Accidents cluttered the interstate. What should have been a forty-minute commute had turned into an hour and a half of watching the speedometer crawl between 0 and 10 mph. Although she'd used the traffic map to try and plot a speed course, a new wreck had appeared at every turn.

Stomach rumbling from hunger, eyes irritated from looking at taillights, foot cramped and tired from flipping between brake and accelerator, Carolyn wondered if she'd be able to stay awake more than five minutes once she hit the couch.

Entering the neighborhood, the nervous tension in her body began to unwind. She let out a long sigh. Her jaw relaxed and she finally realized she had been grinding her teeth. Great, she thought, her dentist was going to give her more shit.

The darkness was complete. She wound through the main street, the trees swaying in the wind. The occasional car passed her. Someone else heading for dinner or shopping. Heading out into the night to do the normal things people do.

Another sigh. She wondered if Trey would be home yet.

Trey hadn't answered his phone. Alan hadn't answered the phone. Carolyn had felt a bit nervous about not being able to get in touch with Alan, but he usually didn't check the messages. Besides, he was probably sitting on the couch, working on his homework, or playing the Wii.

But Trey...

When she'd called him, it had immediately gone to voice mail. Maybe his phone was dead or maybe he had it turned off since he was still in the hospital. She'd left him a message, to make sure he was okay, but he hadn't called her back.

While fighting the traffic to get home, she'd tried to think about Dick as little as possible.

The T-intersection that led to the house was before her. She stopped at the stop sign and felt a hitch in her chest. She turned onto the street. A tear welled up in her eye and she wiped it away as she pulled into the driveway. She saw Dick's dark, lifeless house in the rearview mirror.

Dick wasn't coming home. Dick would never come home.

Carolyn sniffed back another tear and brushed at her eyes again. God, what was she going to tell Alan about Dick?

She shook the thought away and then frowned. The porch light was off. The house was dark. The other houses along the street were lit, but not hers. Did Alan fall asleep? she wondered. In a way, she thought, that would be a good thing. If Trey were there when she had to talk about Dick, it would be easier. She killed the engine, pocketed the keys, unfastened the seat belt, and stepped out into the biting air.

Removing the laptop bag from the backseat, Carolyn closed the doors, locked up the car, and headed onto the dark front porch deck. This wasn't the first time Alan had forgotten to turn on the light. She'd been after Trey to install a timer on the damned thing, so they wouldn't have to try and unlock the door in the dark. With the pine tree canopies overhead and the roof overhang, the front porch always turned into a murky abyss at night. Carolyn fumbled for the house key and then attempted repeatedly to find the keyhole.

At last, the key found the slot and slid in. She turned the key, letting out a deep breath as the lock clicked and the door opened. She walked into the foyer, closing the door behind her and placing her laptop bag out of the way. She reached for the foyer light and then stopped.

Something wasn't right. There was a sound coming from the second floor. She furrowed her brow and walked to the edge of the stairs. Carolyn flipped on the stairway light. She blinked at the muddy and soiled Berber carpeted steps. "Alan? What the hell—"

Alan's voice yelled something from his bedroom, but the words were indistinct.

"Dammit, Alan," she muttered and began trudging up the steps.

She was furious. Alan knew to wipe his feet. And the footprints were so large. What the hell had he done? Twisted his feet on each step? "Alan? You're in big trouble!" she yelled.

"DON'T COME UP HERE!" Alan screamed.

The sound was muffled, almost distant. "Why? Alan," she said as she reached the top landing and stared down the darkened hallway toward his bedroom. "What's—"

"The Ice Cream Man is here! He's here!" Alan shrieked.

The confused and angry expression on her face faded. A cold chill touched her spine. She looked down at the floor. As the light faded down the hallway, she saw the muddy footprints stop at Alan's door. And then they became indistinct, as though they had turned.

She swallowed. "Alan?" she said in a shaking voice. "Where is he?"

"Mommy, go away! Get help!" Alan screamed.

She took a step backwards toward the landing and then froze. A shadow moved at the end of the hallway, something emerging from the guest bathroom door.

Carolyn's heart slam danced in her chest as a pair of bright yellow eyes opened in the darkness, furious crimson embers burning in their centers.

She tried to scream as the thing advanced.

Chapter
Sixty-Two

The walk from the bus stop to the house was fucking cold. Trey was shocked he hadn't frozen to death before getting close to home. A fifteen minute wait for the warm train to whisk him away to the center of downtown so he could catch the commuter bus was followed by a twenty minute wait in the downtown wind tunnel before the bus finally appeared.

Both times, he'd had to fight to find space. The lines were stuffed with people trying to leave early. Gulf moisture had struck the cold front and the air was heavy with moisture.

When the commuter bus landed in The Woodlands, Trey pulled out his phone. He clicked the button. Nothing happened. Right, he thought. Turned it off at the hospital. He cursed and turned it back on. The screen lit up. The phone vibrated. He unlocked it. Voicemail.

Carolyn's voice came through the speakers. "Hi, honey. Just wanted to check in on you. I'll be leaving here soon and heading home. I'm so sorry about Dick, baby. Please call me. Worried about you." Her voice paused for a moment as though she was choking back a sob. "I love you." The message ended.

Trey deleted the message and tried her phone. Got her voicemail. Then he called home. Same. She wasn't answering her mobile and no one was answering the home phone. He'd heaved a heavy sigh and walked down to the nearest bus stop that would take him near the neighborhood.

It was a long walk from the neighborhood's mouth to the house. As he made his way down the concrete path and wound through the trees, all he'd thought about was Dick.

Dick had listed him as the closest family and Trey had had to sign dozens of forms, including approval for the autopsy. They would take him to the morgue, perform an autopsy, and figure out what happened. The doctor asked Trey for a better description of what had occurred in the warehouse, but Trey refused to say anything. Instead, he'd stepped out into the cold and made his way home.

Even in the dark, he recognized the well-worn path leading from the concrete sidewalk to his backyard fence. Surrounded by the forest, many of the residents had installed back gates allowing them access to the main sidewalk via their backyards. Trey's house was no different. He often enjoyed walking through the trails and ending up at his own back gate. It also gave him a chance to wash off his shoes on the deck to remove any mud and dirt.

Trey reached the back gate and frowned. It was partially open. He wondered if Alan had entered and neglected to fully close the door. Trey mentally shrugged and stepped through, closing the door and latching it behind him. As he turned toward the house, he frowned again. The first floor was dark, not a single light on. He scanned the upper floor. Alan's room was the only light he could see.

Trey's stomach crawled. Something didn't feel right.

He walked up on the deck as quietly as he could, peeking through the first floor windows. The gloom was complete. He wasn't going to be able to see anything. Taking a deep breath, Trey walked to the sunroom screen door. He opened it as slowly as he could, praying the hinges wouldn't make any noise. The slight creak as the door opened set his nerves on edge. He closed it with care, making sure the latch didn't make its customary loud click.

When he turned toward the glass door, the crawling in his stomach became an anvil instead. Even in the darkness, the glass looked cracked. He walked to the door, feeling around. The metal edge was caved inward toward the glass, as though it had been pried.

The world suddenly seemed silent. The wind swishing through the skeletal oaks, the brushing of pine branches, all of it was silent save for the hammer of his heart in his ears. With a shaking hand, he reached out and slid the glass door aside.

The interior enveloped him as he stepped in. Trey let his eyes adjust. It was dark outside, but the house was positively pitch black. With the exception of the green display of the microwave and the kitchen clock radio, there was no light to be had. Trey pulled out his phone, touched the screen and used its light to find his way to the island. He stepped carefully, making sure he wouldn't stumble over any hidden obstacles. If someone was still in the house, he didn't want them knowing he was there. Not yet.

Once he was at the island, he waved the phone's dim light over the butcher block. He pulled on the handle in the center and the silver, serrated cleaver slid from the slot. He placed the phone back in his pocket and switched the knife to his left hand. It didn't make him feel any safer or stop the thrashing beat of his heart. Trey turned. The phone on the wall blinked red at him. There was a message on it, most likely the one he'd left.

He stepped toward it and heard something upstairs. A soft thump. Trey reached his right hand to the cordless receiver and pulled it from its charger. The keys lit up in white, the light blanketing his face. He pressed the button for emergency, then held the receiver as close to his ear as possible.

"9-1-1 emergency."

"There's an intruder in my house," Trey whispered into the phone.

"Sir, are you in the house?" the female voice asked.

Trey took in a breath to answer and then stopped. Another thump from the second floor, followed by the sound of liquid pattering onto wood. A whimpering sound from upstairs. Alan's room was right above the kitchen.

The beat in his chest grew faster, so loud he could barely think. "Just get here," he whispered and placed the phone on the counter.

As he stepped out of the kitchen and into the living room, the metallic phone voice continued asking questions, but he ignored it.

The living room was pitch black as well, save for the lights from the cable box. He stepped down into the sunken living room, making his way to the foyer.

Drip. Drip. He couldn't see it, but he knew something dripped from the balcony and onto the wooden foyer floor. Trey's body shook with a fear induced adrenaline rush. Through the front door, a sliver of light from the streetlamp cast its glow. Something sat at the edge of the light.

Trey bent down, his fingers touching something hard and wet. He felt its edges. Shoe. High heel. Trey took in a shuddering breath and placed the heel back on the floor.

Another sound from above him. Trey looked up. A drop of something hit the back of his jacket with a patter. Trey stepped into the pooling liquid on the floor. Some part of him was afraid to turn on a light. Terrified. He reached for the light switch, his eyes trained on the balcony overlooking the doorway. Nothing moved up there. Nothing. He flipped the light switch. Nothing happened.

He let out his breath as slowly as he could and swallowed. He looked from the balcony to the staircase. The edges of the lower steps were barely visible in the shadows. Too fucking dark, he thought. He moved with slow, cautious steps, wincing at the squeak of his runners on the liquid. With a shaking right hand, he flipped the switch for the staircase lights. Nothing happened. He took another deep breath. The whimpers grew louder. They were words, but he couldn't make them out.

He wanted to yell Alan's name, Carolyn's name, anything to break the gloom, but held off. Whoever was up here had to have Alan trapped in his room, and he didn't know what they would do if the cops showed up. Or if he made any noise.

Trey put his feet on the steps and slowly made his way up. The wood creaked under his weight and he winced again. He held the knife handle in his palm, the blade in front. He crouched low and turned the corner to proceed up the other side of the staircase. He was so low, knees bent, that the hallway was still out of sight. Each stair was torture as he tried to be quiet, so quiet. Final four steps. He made his way up the last few, still crouched on the balls of his feet.

The hallway was shrouded in gloom. "Please help me," Alan's voice whimpered from the end of the hall. "Mommy—" Alan's voice turned into an exhausted sob.

Rage replaced his fear; the adrenaline pumping through his system had his every nerve tingling. Something moved at the end of the hall. Trey froze, one foot slightly forward. "Come out, motherfucker," Trey said to the darkness.

The dark form at the end of the hall seemed to grow, as though it had been crouching on its haunches. The narrow band of light from beneath Alan's door barely provided enough illumination, but Trey could see it.

As the figure unfolded itself, it grew tall. A pair of eyes opened. Two ragged glowing yellow ovals in the darkness, cruel crimson embers burning in their centers. It took a step forward.

Trey gritted his teeth. "Get away from my boy," he hissed. The sobbing from Alan's room stopped, as though he were suddenly listening. Trey barely noticed.

The figure took another step forward. "You," it hissed back at him. "You took away my home," it spat in a low growl.

Trey fought the urge to flee down the stairs as it moved another step closer. Mindful his back was against the stairs, Trey took a step toward it. The thing in the hallway paused. "Took my food," it said. "I can't go back there." The thing was holding something toward him. Trey struggled to see what it was in the darkness. "My home!" it screamed at him.

"Get away from my son!" Trey yelled back at it.

"So," the shadow said in a calm, low voice, "I'm taking everything that's yours." The light in the hallway flicked on. He clenched his eyes against the sudden bright wash of light.

Something rolled across the floor in front of him. Trey looked down. His wife's face stared up at him from the carpet. Her left eye dangled by a gossamer thread of flesh, blood still curling out from the empty socket. Her mouth was frozen in a scream, crimson lines snaking out from broken lips. A ragged chunk of flesh was missing from the side of her cheek.

Trey tried to scream but nothing came out of his mouth. The world wavered, the face shimmering before him. Trey felt himself losing his balance.

"Everything," the voice growled from the end of the hallway.

Trey fell backward, his eyes still locked on the blood crusted hunk of meat that used to be his wife. Body parts were scattered throughout the hallway. Her naked torso sat at the end of the hall, huge chunks of flesh missing from the savaged corpse.

Trey tried to scream again. A shadow crept over him and he slowly looked up.

The fiend. The thing. The Ice Cream Man. The angled head, the drooling, blood-crusted canines, a forked tongue hanging from one side. It held a hand before him, the long taloned nails inches away from his eyes. Its own eyes flared and glowed even in the hallway's harsh light. It glared at him. "I. Take. Everything."

Rolling down the stairs. The steps digging into his back. He screamed from the sudden searing pain in his face and chest. He rolled to the bottom, his head smashing onto the floor, facing upward at the balcony. His left eye was blind, his face a single, sizzling nerve. The thing looked down at him from the balcony and said something in a greasy string of syllables. It cocked its head to one side and then growled at him. With a sneer, it walked back down the hallway.

Trey could hear it too: sirens. They were coming. They were coming and would be there soon.

Thump. Thump. The sound of strong fists smashing into wood echoed from the balcony. Alan screamed.

Trey rolled on his side and felt something tear away from his face. His entire body was stiff. He tried to move his right arm, but it refused to do anything more than scream back at him. He managed to get to his knees and stared at the stairs. Another scream. There was the sound of splintering wood. Trey raised himself, shrieking from the pain.

Stumbling step by step, bones grinding in his limp right arm with every jarring movement, he turned the far corner. The cleaver sat on the second to top step. He bent at the waist, trying to ignore the searing pain in every muscle. He raised himself again, grinding his teeth to keep the shriek in his throat.

The thing was clawing at Alan's door, its long nails shredding the wood. It had already made a ragged hole. Trey shambled toward it in a drunken stumble. It stuck its head into the hole, growling something at Alan.

Alan's shriek of fear drove the pain away from his mind. Trey raised the knife and plunged it as hard as he could into the thing's back. Wood shattered as the thing jumped upward.

The noise it made shook the house, an inhuman cry that rang in Trey's ears. He tried to pull the knife back out, but it wouldn't let go. The thing jerked backwards, its head shredding the remaining wood and fell back atop him. Something snapped in his chest and he couldn't breathe. The heavy, leathery body crushed down on him. His mouth filled with the copper taste of blood.

The thing rolled off him and hit the wall. Trey tried to sit up, but the excruciating pain in his ribs kept him prone. He turned his head and stared at the thing next to him. Black blood poured from beneath its back. The monster, its cream colored clothes covered in streaks of wet crimson and dark fluid, slowly rolled to its side. As it dug its talons into the wall for purchase, plaster dust and paint chips exploded into the air.

Trey coughed, his chest screaming with the pain.

It groaned and lifted itself further up the wall, its talons finally catching on a stud. Wheezing, chuffing breaths rattled from its chest. Its right hand struggled to free the knife, now buried to the hilt, in its back.

"Fucked you," Trey whispered. "Fucked you good."

The thing turned toward him as it managed to stand. Its eyes burned red, the yellow reduced to simple rings. It growled and took a step toward him. The sirens outside stopped. Trey heard the sound of voices at the front door. The thing glared down at him, heaving in pain.

Trey smiled at it. It roared and shuffled past him into the master bedroom. The front door opened with a bang just as the bedroom's picture window shattered. An inhuman howl filled the air as the cops climbed the stairs.

Trey closed his remaining eye, Alan's screams still ringing in his ears.

Chapter

Sixty-Three

The bench of seats was empty except for Alan and the deputy sheriff. Alan took a sip from the water bottle one of the nurses had given him. He didn't want it, but she'd told him to keep drinking it. He readjusted the blanket. He still felt cold. The same nurse that had given him the water had said something to him about shock, but he barely remembered the words. Everything was numb.

The Sheriff had stepped through bloody plaster and wood to get him out of the room. By the time they reached him, his voice had departed, leaving his throat raw and every breath was an experience in pain. One of the men dressed in the blue uniforms had tried to cover his eyes as they brought him downstairs, whispers of air still trying to make sound past his tortured and ripped vocal chords. But he had seen.

Alan took another sip and shivered. Deputy Sheriff Wallace turned to look at him, his dark mustache jumping at the ends in a soft smile. "You okay, son?"

It took every ounce of effort to nod. His neck hurt. His chest felt as though a huge weight had been placed atop it for hours on end.

But the drain, the exhaustion, had left him feeling dull and dazed. He took a shuddering breath and let loose a silent sob. He couldn't even make that noise anymore.

Daddy. He'd seen Daddy lying on the hallway floor, blood covering his face. Two men in white hovered over him, one whispering in his ear while the other pulled a syringe from a black bag. A red hole where Daddy's right eye used to be seeped blood down his face, joining the red rivulets streaming from his nose. Daddy's left eye had seen him, though. Daddy's left eye had blinked at him and the corners of his mouth had twitched.

"Daddy," Alan tried to whisper, but the words came out as hiss of air.

"Son?" Wallace asked.

Alan turned toward him, but looked past him. The man didn't seem to be real. The nearly empty lobby, the muted words over the intercom, the occasional nurse passing by in the hallway, none of it was real. He was back in his room while the thing outside smashed its way in, its fangs drooling blood onto the white door.

"Alan?" Wallace's voice reached through the memory and Alan jumped with a start. He focused on the man in front of him. "You gotta stay awake, buddy." The Sheriff raised himself from the bench, and moved two places over. He lowered his bulk into the seat next to Alan's. "Okay?"

"Can't sleep," Alan tried to say. His voice came out in a small, dusty croak.

"Right," the deputy said. The man leaned in toward him. "You cold, kid?"

The blanket was doing little to warm him. Alan nodded. The deputy smiled at him. "I'll get you another blanket," he said. He shook his finger at Alan. "You stay here, kid. Okay?" Alan said nothing, only nodded. Wallace sat up and left the small lobby and walked toward the nurses' station just outside.

Alan watched him go. People wandered by the opening, some staring inside to see just a lone little boy with a lost expression on his face. Alan didn't meet their eyes. He couldn't. The white hallway wall was his door. His door that crumbled against the thing's battering fists.

"Kid?" A large meaty hand snapped its fingers beneath his nose. "Hey, kid, wake up!" Wallace's voice growled. Alan looked up into the man's pale face. The deputy's eyes were frantic. Alan blinked at him. "Alan?"

He was in a bed. The room's lights were low. A woman in red scrubs stood next to the bed. She held his hand, her index finger tapping against the V between his thumb and forefinger. He blinked at her. "Alan? You back?"

"How—" Alan tried to say, but nothing came out. He coughed, his throat screaming with the pain.

"Shhh, honey," the nurse said. She was shorter than Mommy, her red hair tied up in a bun. She smiled at him. "Do you know where you are?"

Alan shook his head, and then nodded.

"Are you at home?"

Alan shook his head and felt a tear squeeze from his eye.

The smile on her face dimmed. "Are you in the hospital?"

Alan blinked at her and then nodded.

"Yes," she said, trying to recapture her smile. "Good. I'm going to get the doctor," she whispered. "Stay with me, okay?" Alan squeezed her hand twice. "I'll be right back."

She turned from him and walked out of the room. Alan's eyes hurt. They felt as though someone had filled them with dirt. He rubbed at them. He scrunched his eyes closed and then opened them.

Sheriff Wallace appeared in the doorway. The man sighed with relief and waved to Alan. Alan didn't return the gesture.

The doorway cleared again. Daddy's ruined face. The empty eye socket streaming blood, his broken and crunched nose, the awkward angle of his previously unbroken arm, the deep slashes through his clothes all up and down his chest...

A light shined in his eyes. "Alan?"

Alan blinked.

"Okay, good," a voice said. The penlight moved away from him. His eyes struggled to readjust from the bright light. A man older than Daddy hunched over his bed, salt and pepper hair shining beneath the bright fluorescents. "I'm Doctor Moody," the man said. He placed the penlight back in the front pocket of his white lab-coat. "Do you know where you are?"

"Yes," Alan said. His voice had finally returned a little, but his throat still burned with the effort. "I'm at the hospital."

"Excellent," the man said in a squeaky voice.

"Where's my Daddy?" Alan asked.

The man's smile faltered. He lowered his eyes for a moment, cleared his throat and then returned Alan's stare. "Your father is in surgery, Alan." He cleared his throat again. The gentle smile on his face had faded into a flat line. "Your father needs you to help him."

"How?" Alan asked.

"I need to know what happened, Alan."

Alan felt a shudder go through him. The Ice Cream Man. The thing. The yellow eyes with their fiery pupils.

"Stay with me, Alan," the doctor said. He snapped his eyes back to the doctor's. The doctor nodded to him. "Good. Can you tell me what happened?"

"The bad man," Alan said after a deep breath, "the Ice Cream Man got Daddy." The words came out in a breathy rush that set his throat back on fire. "The bad man—" Alan's voice drifted off.

Fingers snapped in front of his face. Alan looked up. The doctor's face peered at him. "Alan? You're having seizures."

"Just like Daddy?"

The doctor frowned. "Yes, like Daddy. Who hurt your daddy?"

"The Ice Cream Man hurt Daddy."

"Alan," Moody said, leaning in so close the end of his nose nearly touched Alan's, "your Daddy is very sick. Something poisoned him."

"The Ice Cream Man poisoned Daddy."

Moody pulled back a little. He exchanged a glance with the nurse and then stared back at Alan. The smile on his face was somewhat forced. "Did the Ice Cream Man smell bad? Did he—"

"The Ice Cream man eats little children," Alan said. A tear made its way from his eye, but he didn't know why. He didn't feel anything anymore. "He told me he eats little kids like me."

"I—" Moody shook his head, stuttering.

"He smells bad. Bad. Bad."

The room was dark. Alan had drifted off, drifted away until his mother's screams brought him awake, shivering and crying. He'd wet the bed. Outside in the hall, he heard distant conversation, shoes on tile, and the sound of squeaky wheels.

There was another sound too. A scratching.

"Hello?" Alan raised his head.

A pair of yellow eyes winked at him from the foot of the bed, their centers burning like fire.

Chapter Sixty-Four

The man, George, walked behind Alan down the hallway. The floor felt pliable, as though he were walking on a deep shag rug instead of tile. Since he started taking the pills, every footstep felt like that.

George was a nice man. Big man. George always smiled at him, always asked him how he was doing. Alan thought George was a lot like Daddy. Before—

"Here we go, Alan," George said and placed a hand on Alan's shoulder.

Alan stopped and turned as George opened the door. A table sat in the middle of the room. Alan smiled. "Tony," he whispered.

"Hey, kid," Tony said, waving.

Alan walked as fast as he dared on the flexible floor and sat in the chair across from Tony.

"We're good, George," Tony said. The door closed behind them. "And how are you today?" Tony asked, his smile wide and friendly.

"Doing good," Alan said. "I've been playing chess with George."

"Have you been beating him?"

Alan looked over his left shoulder and then his right, as if checking to see if anyone was listening. He leaned in across the table and whispered "I think he lets me win."

Tony chuckled. "Uh-huh. That's okay, Alan. One day," he whispered, "he won't need to." Alan leaned back in the plastic chair and kicked his feet beneath the table. "I'm here to ask you a couple of questions."

"Okay," Alan said.

"You still seizing?"

Alan shrugged. "Sometimes. George told me that when— George said that I should stare at the clock when I feel bad, and see if a lot of time passes."

"And does it?"

"Sometimes. I think about a minute or so is the longest."

Tony nodded. He wrote something down in his large notebook. "Good, that's real good, Alan. That means we're getting close with the drugs."

"Can I see my Daddy soon?"

Tony's pen stopped in mid-scratch. He looked up from the notebook, his smile dampened. "We're going to talk about that in a minute, okay? I need to ask you some more questions first. All right?"

Alan frowned. He knew the answer would be "no" or "not yet." It always was.

Tony had a tough time hiding his feelings from Alan. Alan didn't know why, but he could almost feel the man talking to him, as though he could sometimes hear what Tony was saying before he said it.

"Okay," Alan whispered.

"Good," Tony said. "George and the others say you're not sleeping very well." Tony tapped the pen against the notebook. "Eyes?"

Always the yellow eyes, the burning centers. Always staring into the eyes, losing himself in them like they are a whirlpool pulling him down and down and down—

"Alan?"

"What?"

Tony looked down at his watch. "20 seconds that time, Alan. Do you remember what I asked you?"

Alan nodded. "It's him."

"I'm not going to say his name, Alan. I know that upsets you. So, he still comes at night?" Alan nodded. "But all you see are the eyes?" Alan nodded again, watching Tony's smile flatten into a thin line. "Until we get seizing under control, there are lots of things we can't talk about."

"Can we talk about my Daddy now?" Alan asked.

"Sure," Tony said and dropped his pen to the notebook. He folded his hands into a tent, elbows on the table, and rested his head atop them. "Your Daddy's doing better, Alan. Much better."

"He is?"

"Yes," Tony said.

Alan frowned. "You're lying to me," he whispered.

Tony's eyes widened. "Why do you say that?"

Alan stomped his left foot. "Your feet, Tony. When you say things that make you uncomfortable, you tap your left foot."

The man laughed, shaking his head. "You are too damned bright, Alan, I'll give you that." Alan's face remained impassive. Tony's laugh disappeared. "Okay, Alan." He brought his arms back in and rested his hands on the table's edge. "Your Dad's health has improved. He's no longer sick."

"He's not? You promise?" Tony nodded. Alan frowned. Tony was telling him the truth. He knew that much. But Tony was definitely holding something back. "Then why can't I see him?"

"The doctor's fixed him up, Alan. His ribs, lungs, all that's okay. The last of the poison is gone too."

Alan knew Daddy had been very sick. The Ice Cream Man had done something to him. Blood poisoning was what Tony had called it. Alan didn't know what that was, only that Daddy had almost died.

"How long have I been here?" Alan asked.

Tony shrugged. "Three weeks, I think. About that, anyway."

"How many more before I can see Daddy?"

Sucking in a breath of air and then exhaling slowly, Tony looked down at the table. "Alan, I—" He stopped speaking and then looked up. Tony cocked his head slightly. "I haven't seen your Dad yet." Tony swallowed. "I'm going to see him today, though. Right after this. If he's better, I'll take you—"

"You just said he's better," Alan said.

Tony thrummed his fingers on the table. Alan watched them in fascination. Daddy had done something similar to that. "I said his body's better, Alan. But he's not talking to anyone."

Alan blinked. "But, he'll talk to me."

The flat expression on Tony's face turned into a soft smile. "He might, Alan. He might. But let me see him first, and then we'll know."

"I know—" Alan wiped at his eyes. "I know Mommy's gone. She's not coming back," Alan whispered. Tony said nothing. "But I want Daddy."

Alan wiped away another tear. "I want to see my Daddy."

"I know, Alan," Tony said. He reached his hand across the table and touched Alan's. "I know. And I want that too."

Alan nodded. Tony was sad. Tony was always sad when he came to see Alan. He wanted Alan to get better. He wanted Daddy to get better. He wanted Mommy to still be alive.

"I think I want to go back to my room," Alan said. "I— I feel very sleepy."

"Okay, Alan," Tony said. He patted the boy's hand. "Okay." Tony stood up and placed his notebook inside a battered leather valise. "I'll see you soon, okay?"

Alan met his eyes. "Tony?"

"Yes, Alan?"

"What is he?" Tony blinked at him, looking confused. "What is the Ice Cream Man?"

Tony swallowed hard. "I—" His voice cracked and he cleared his throat. "We don't know, Alan. But I promise, he's never going to bother you again."

"Or Daddy?"

Tony smiled. "Or Daddy." Alan frowned. "What's wrong, Alan?" Alan pointed down at Tony's left foot. It was tapping.

Epilogue

He swam in darkness for days, poison streaming through his blood. Each short period of consciousness was filled with pain and confusion, the bright lights, the constant beep of a heart monitor, followed by distant screams, and the inevitable rush of cold, liquid sleep.

He was haunted by dreams of the Closet Man, the Grubby Man, the Ice Cream Man, dreams where a severed head rolled to a stop in front of him and opened its eyes. Sometimes it was Alan's head, sometimes Carolyn's, and sometimes, it was his own.

The lips always moved in those dreams, speaking words he couldn't hear. Regardless of whose head came flying at him in the hallway and what words it tried to speak, the dream always ended with the thing, the Fiend, standing over him and groaning in pain. In those dreams, Trey always smiled—Alan was still alive and safe.

The periods of consciousness finally grew longer, the dreams fading. He knew people came to see him—Dewhurst, Kinkaid, nameless doctors and nurses. They would sit next to him in a plastic chair, ask him questions he didn't understand. Through his remaining eye, they looked out of focus, somehow not real.

Trey couldn't wait for them to leave, to stop their questions, and let him doze through the day.

When Tony Downs showed up, things were different. The questions he asked echoed in Trey's mind, bouncing around until he was finally able to grasp them firmly in his mental hands.

What did it look like?

Trey didn't speak, didn't try to form words. His only answer was an image, the thing standing above him, its long nose dripping with blood, puffed out scaly flesh, the yellow rings of its eyes barely discernible in the sea of crimson.

How did you make it go away?

The knife. The cleaver buried to the hilt in the middle of its back, black ichor washing down.

Did you hurt it?

Only a sound, the groan, an inhuman wail of pain.

Where are you?

He couldn't speak, couldn't find his voice, only think the answers. *I'm safe*, he thought. *He can't get me here.*

You're hiding, Tony's voice bounced in his head.

I'm safe here. Alan's safe here. Carolyn's safe here. Carolyn. Carolyn sat on the couch with him, her arms wrapped loosely around his neck. Alan was on the floor, racing his Koopa through the Mario Kart tracks, giggling while he did it. Trey smiled.

Tony's voice faded away. Trey didn't want to listen anymore. He didn't want to hear, didn't want to see. He was safe, and nothing else mattered.

A Parsec Award winning writer, podcaster, and software architect from Houston, Texas, Paul E Cooley produces free psychological thriller and horror podcasts, essays, and reviews available from Shadowpublications.com and iTunes.

His stories have been listened to by thousands and he has been a guest on such notable podcasts as Podioracket, John Mierau's "Podcast Teardown," Geek Out with Mainframe, Shadowcast Audio, and Vertigo Radio Live. In 2010, his short story Canvas and novella Tattoo were nominated for Parsec Awards. Tattoo became a Parsec Award finalist. He has collaborated with New York Times Bestselling author Scott Sigler on the series "The Crypt" and co-wrote the novel "The Rider" (projected release in 2016). In addition to his writing, Paul has contributed his voice talents to a number of podiofiction productions.

He is a co-host on the renowned Dead Robots' Society writing podcast and enjoys interacting with readers and other writers.

For more information about current and upcoming projects, please visit Shadowpublications.com.

Stalk Paul on social media:
- Twitter: paul_e_cooley
- Facebook: paulelardcooley
- Email: paulATshadowpublications.com
- Mailing List: http://mailinglist.shadowpublications.com

Made in the USA
Middletown, DE
10 January 2018